The Undertaker's Daughter

A Novel of Supernatural Horror

JOHN JAMES MINSTER

HELLBENDER BOOKS

an imprint of Sunbury Press, Inc.
Mechanicsburg, PA USA

an imprint of Sunbury Press, Inc.
Mechanicsburg, PA USA

For information about special discounts for bulk purchases, please contact Sunbury Press Orders Dept. at (855) 338-8359 or orders@sunburypress.com.

To request one of our authors for speaking engagements or book signings, please contact Sunbury Press Publicity Dept. at publicity@sunburypress.com.

FIRST HELLBENDER BOOKS EDITION: October 2022

Set in Adobe Garamond Pro | Interior design by Crystal Devine | Cover by Lawrence Knorr | Edited by Lawrence Knorr.

Publisher's Cataloging-in-Publication Data
Names: Minster, John James, author.
Title: The undertaker's daughter: a supernatural horror novel / John James Minster.
Description: First trade paperback edition. | Mechanicsburg, PA : Hellbender Books, 2022.
Summary: Anna and Timmy's summer of love has turned into a nightmare. In an attempt to frighten bullies into peace, Anna experiments with old Jewish magic, but the ancient Abrahamic ritual doesn't go as planned. The eldritch power takes dark and unexpected turns, endangering those she loves and forcing her to decide who she is and who she wants to be.
Identifiers: ISBN 978-1-62006-956-1 (softcover).
Subjects: FICTION / Horror | FICTION / Occult & Supernatural | FICTION / Thrillers / Supernatural.

Product of the United States of America
0 1 1 2 3 5 8 13 21 34 55

Continue the Enlightenment!

Dedicated to Means E. Smith, Jr. –
Deus solus novit quid ego ipse sine te

Dear Meigan,
Thank you for
the read and
review!

JJM

CONTENTS

CHAPTER ONE

Junior Year

"Anna, be a dear, go write a check to Crematory Repair Services for two hundred eighty-seven bucks, sign my name to it, and hand it to the service technician."

This she did, upstairs in his office warmed by a kind sun, then sped back down to the chilly embalming room because today, there stood a new crop of two apprentices on their first day. By now, at seventeen, she had heard her father's little initiation-day quick-tour at least a hundred times. One of the apprentices appeared to be only a few years older than she, maybe early twenties, with an interesting face and great hair. She hung in for one more speech. Usually content to work alone, studying for the ACT and SATs, or doing homework for her high school junior year AP class assignments, at this moment, she felt a little lonely, something she noticed happening more often lately.

Like something big and important was missing from her life.

"This mortuary table we use for the arterial embalming. We lay the guest in the supine anatomical position with the head slightly elevated in the plastic mold. We evaluate him for rigor mortis, lividity, skin condition, fecal matter, edema, tissue gas, track marks or previous injections, knife or gunshot wounds, ice pick holes, electricity burns, noose marks. Believe me, at one time or another, during your three thousand hours with me, you will see just about every way a person can die lying here. We'll give him a bath with germicidal soap. As your noses can tell, this one is long overdue. Since there are three of us, it shouldn't take us long to give him a nice flex and massage to reduce stiffness and break up blood clots.

"We'll insert the needle here." David Dingel touched his latex-gloved finger against the elderly black male's right common carotid artery. "This is called a 'single-point injection,' which seven times out of ten should get it done."

He pointed at the mechanical device on the counter. "The centrifugal pump will do all the work for us. It'll push my own pink-tinged mix of embalming chemicals with lanolin to plump up the vessels and restore his lividity. If he's one of those exceptions with stubborn clots, we'll use the femoral artery as the drain."

Anna Dingel was the only child of David Dingel, a man who answered to many titles, including funeral director, mortician, businessman, undertaker, Freemason, and proprietor of Dingel's Funeral Home in Norristown, Pennsylvania. As impressive as her father's résumé was, however, today, Anna could not peel her eyes from one of his two newest young apprentices. The other student of mortuary science appeared to hang on her dad's every word as if it were the *Gettysburg Address*. Alert, tense, posture-perfect, hands in the ready-go position before him. In contrast, the younger, cuter one hung back a little, fingers interlocked behind his white lab coat as his eyes darted about.

That's three times now. She kept a silent count of how many times he glanced over at her. She wore faded tight jeans and a modest peasant shirt. This time she caught him checking out her slim waist and hips. *Next time, I'll give him half a smile and a long look as I walk out.* She still felt self-conscious over Sue Nastro calling her 'Snaggle' as she pointed and laughed at coffee and tea stains on her tooth enamel. *Half a smile, for sure*, she decided.

"While we fill his arteries, vessels, veins, and capillaries with my magic elixir, we can start on the cavity treatment. We'll suck out his internal fluids from body cavities using these two bad boys right here," David said and held up his aspirator and trocar. "We'll make a small incision here." His finger touched two inches above the navel and two inches to the right. "Then push in the trocar to puncture the hollow organs and aspirate their contents. Then we'll fill those with cavity chemicals containing formaldehyde—a smell that I have grown to love, by the way. Wish I could make margaritas out of it, though if I did, it would be me lying here. You boys should seek a woman who dabs a little of it behind her ears before a date."

Both grinned, happy to have a mentor with a sense of humor since they would necessarily spend a great deal of time with him. "We will push the trocar into the chest cavity here, through the diaphragm."

The cute apprentice shot a glance at Anna. She read it as, 'Your dad's pretty cool!'

"Now, I know they taught you to use trocar buttons to cover the holes, but I'm old school. You guys are going to learn how to suture, which may come in handy if you ever have to close up your own guts after your jets crash in the Andes. I'll teach you the purse string and what we call the 'N' suture methods. All that is the heavy-lifting.

"Now, you get fairly adept at judging what sort of people the clients were in life. Take this old guy. What can you tell me about him?"

The boys searched each other more than they did the corpse. They shrugged.

"He lived a clean life and left us a good-looking corpse. We'll have to wait for a future guest in order for me to teach you hypodermic and surface embalming, as in a motorcycle crash. The fun part we save for last. We'll insert the eye caps, pin and glue the mouth shut, give him a shave, and then, friends, my specialty: we'll do his hair and makeup. That's the nuanced bit that separates slogs from true artists. I'll make Rembrandts out of you. You'll put Hollywood makeup artists to shame. So, Grant and Taylor," he nodded at each in turn. "You boys ready to rock 'n' roll?"

Taylor. So that's his name, Anna thought. She glued her large, wide-set, husky-blue eyes onto him. Her wavy strawberry-blonde tresses hung midway down her back; she whipped her head around and back with a snap directed at him as she exited. She felt eyes on her backside. She tried to see in her mind the view she hoped Taylor saw.

———————

"Anna?"

"Mom?"

"Come down, help me with dinner." It was nearly half past five, the first Wednesday afternoon in June, when Margie Dingel walked through the door, kicked off her shoes, flushed the toilet, then screamed up the stairs. Same as yesterday; same as the Monday before that. Volunteering at the First Baptist Church had become an unpaid full-time position for her.

Anna stood in the kitchen, peeling and chopping onions. She still wore the same clothes as earlier in the embalming room. Wisps of formaldehyde escaped creases, though all she could smell were the onions. "Mom, it's 2022. The school issued computers, and I'm the only student out of hundreds whose mother makes her do homework at the kitchen table then locks up her computer at night. Embarrass me much? I think you had me just to torture me."

Margie dried her hands on an apron embellished with colorful but well-faded Amish hex patterns. "No! I've told you before. Social media is evil. I don't want some eldritch demon pretending to be a schoolboy seducing my daughter."

"Mom." She paused her chopping. At five-foot-seven inches and one-hundred-two pounds, she looked down on her shorter, thicker mother. "A gun is a simple machine used to combust cordite inside a brass casing to fire a projectile at a target. It isn't evil until someone points it at another. It's merely an object. Same goes with cars. They aren't evil until someone drinks too much then kills others with it. Same with the social media. It's a tool to be used for evil or good. Don't you think I'm a good person? Don't you trust me?"

Margie did not stop peeling onions or look up. "I don't trust the people who lurk there. You're a young woman, Anna. The world is filled with predators. You won't even see them coming."

Anna gritted her teeth. "You're right, Mom. I'll move out, go to college, and be completely unprepared for what's out there . . . thanks to you."

"Go to your room!"

——— • ———

"Try down-tuning. Key of A, blues scale, but it needs to sound dark, ominous, gritty. Try that. Indulge me, Tim. Reverb and distortion are good, but something's missing." Keyboard fanatic Jon D'Alessio, who called himself 'Joda' in hopes that his self-assigned stage name would catch on someday, had plans to graduate high school, then set the music world on fire. He would attend Berklee College of Music next year. One day, he would be ultra-famous; of that, he had zero doubt whatsoever.

To him, this high school garage band, SpaceJunk, was merely an early primer for that. He figured that if he got accepted into the most prestigious music school, he'd show up leaps ahead of other newbies in that super-competitive environment. For SpaceJunk, he did all the composing and arranging and led the three other members. He carefully evaluated feedback from adult audiences in the local bar scene and internalized it. To him, it was all invaluable experience toward the goal of one day besting his favorite all-time keyboard tinkler, the UK's Rick Wakeman.

Jon smiled patiently as he watched Timmy Caperila make the requested changes to his vintage 1978 Gibson Les Paul Black Beauty electric guitar, a hand-me-down from his father, who was too busy working two jobs to play it anymore.

"Son," his father had said, "There's nothing else like it. Solid, deep rich tones, sturdy as an oak, will never need neck adjustments, maybe get new frets and pick-ups every so often. Trust me, kid, this will feel like an M-16 and rocket launcher in your hands. I know you love Hendrix, don't we all, but Stratocaster necks are a smidge longer, giving them a harsher edge. Once you've played both, you'll understand why I fell in love with this baby right here. Treat her right, and she'll bring you luck. Coax the sweetest sounds out of her, hard and mellow. Wishing you better luck than I ever had."

Timothy Caperila, who chose the stage name of 'Timmy C.,' had so far not experienced the luck he so dearly sought with the ladies—perhaps not the primary driver toward local rock stardom but definitely a factor high on the list. Still a virgin despite that, at six feet, he was the tallest member of the band. With thick, wavy brown hair that hung below his shoulders to frame a boyishly handsome face, he was by far the best looking, too.

Chicks only dig guys with muscles, he thought. These words often echoed in his head. He had convinced himself that girls in his class only seemed to want the brawny, loud guys. At one hundred fifty-nine pounds, brawn escaped him. No matter how much he ate, he never could seem to gain weight. *Guess I'm a terminal ectomorph, dammit.*

"How's this, Boss Joda?" he said, backward stroking a D chord, then an A minor to G chord before he shredded a blues scale key of A. He delivered bending and ripping arpeggios and hammer-string pyrotechnics, all of which filled Mr. D'Alessio's finished basement with more dark, ominous, gritty sound than it could hold.

"Yeah. Yes! I think that's it! Okay, let me work something out on the keyboard. Tim, go have one of my dad's beers. He won't even know it's missing."

———

When Naomi Silver met Abe Jacobs at her Reformed Jewish family's bat mitzvah four years prior—Abe there as an unexpected guest of a friend—fireworks had exploded inside both. A fact that soon after, they would mutually confess. "Love at first sight: it's a real thing!" they both insisted to all who would listen, and they were more convinced now than ever. Both had breezed through class schedules loaded up with AP courses. They took their college board standardized tests early in their junior year. Abe earned early acceptance into pre-med at Harvard Medical; Naomi won early acceptance into Brown's computer science program.

"Every weekend, Abe, I don't care how much work we have on our plates—and it will be daunting—we will meet every weekend halfway between Boston and Providence at the Hampton Inn in Foxborough, Massachusetts. You do have an excellent bedside manner."

He wore a mischievous smile. "Your sweat is the only food I need. I'd gladly starve in exchange for tastes of you."

When she smiled into the camera, he melted as the familiar fire spread through him. Objectively, he found her to be the prettiest female not only in the school but that he had ever seen anywhere, even in broadcast media. His attraction to her had not diminished since age thirteen. *Thank you, God,* he thought. Every meeting with her was a conscious effort to marshal all his self-discipline to hold back just a little. To not let slip the full and true depth of her hold on him. Instincts told him to play it just a little bit cool with a woman of her physical beauty and intellectual self-possession.

He sighed. "But for now, it's getting late, so I must bid you Shabbat shalom, my lady."

She blew him a kiss, then closed the web meeting software and tried to refocus on a thread of great interest. She collected her thoughts. Before the cyber date, she had glanced at something about excavations similar to those at the Qumran Caves, where some caves were natural, others clearly were dug by humans long ago, discovered around the archaeological site of Qumran in the Judaean Desert of the West Bank where the Dead Sea Scrolls were unearthed, deteriorated but restorable.

This piqued her interest: 'Archaeologists unearth stone tablets from the Timna Valley mines in southern Israel which date back to the reign of King Solomon, when copper mining activity was conducted by Solomon's Edomite subjects, in a previously unexplored offshoot of one of ten thousand mine shafts .'

A junkie for any cable TV segments about Middle East history, she was aware of speculations about the mines discovered back in 2013, assumed to once belong to the fabled King Solomon, which challenged the millenniums-old tradition that his wealth had come from gold, which made Solomon the wealthiest man in all human history. Gold was prized for jewelry but was too soft a metal for any other practical use at the time.

No, she thought. *Copper was the engine of Bronze Age warfare, worth more than gold to conquerors and their armies.* "The wise King Solomon's blood flows through my veins; I am truly lucky to live in a time for the world to see scientific evidence piling up," she muttered aloud. Excitement prickled her arm and neck hairs.

She read, 'Today, an artifact believed to date back to the time of Abraham was unearthed in the Caves of Solomon.'

What are the odds of something like this happening? Millions to one against? To find a perfectly preserved relic hidden away, unmolested by weather and geologic machinations and upheavals. Wars. Thievery by treasure hunters. My clever ancestors found a cave that somehow defied it all. An object that survived intact for three thousand years, she thought.

She read on.

———————

"Yo. Admit this is just a wee bit creepy," Tammy Goldsworth said as she slid into shotgun position inside Sue Nastro's gleaming new Grabber Blue Ford Mustang convertible, a gift from her architect father on her seventeenth birthday in January.

Sue fired the engine and stared at Tammy. "Tell me. Why is it creepy?" She peeled out in an oily cloud of fossil fumes. Only three cars separated them from the red Camaro that had just squealed tires a little while making a right out of the high school parking lot.

Tammy shook her head. "Tailing a guy? C'mon, Sue. He isn't even your boyfriend. Okay, I take it back. This is *majorly* creepy. Off-the-charts creepy."

"What? Okay, so what do you call the boy who took my virginity two years ago and still worships me every chance we get?"

"Con artist horndog comes to mind. Has he ever said anything like that you two are exclusive? No. Has he brought you flowers, ever, just once? No. Mark his territory, give you a shiny thing to wear as a symbol that you belong to him? No. Has he met your parents? No. He's only *using* you, Sue. How can't you see that? Are you fucking blind? Or just blonde?"

"Pfft," was the sound Sue made with a flick of her right hand. She swerved around a slow driver, an aggressive move to keep up with Bruce Barnette's testosterone-fueled driving. They watched him turn into the first of many big indoor shopping mall entrances two miles west of their high school. She drove past it to the second entrance, parked in the anchor department store lot, grabbed her purse, and flung open her door. "C'mon, let's go!"

The two moved fast and silent in their running shoes. They wove through the women's clothing section without glancing at all the cool new summer fashions, which Sue knew she would need for after-finals parties. At five-foot-nine and one hundred twelve pounds, with her father's northern Italian blonde hair and blue eyes and her mother's tiny waist and ample chest, she knew, as the only student in school who had earned money on Fashion Week runways in New York City modeling for BCBG, Chanel, Dolce & Gabbana, and von Fürstenberg, that she was unquestionably the number one hottest girl in the school. In the county, in the state, in the entire universe, as far as she knew.

Tammy, shorter by four inches, stockier by thirty-seven pounds, and with powerful legs from field hockey, seemed an unlikely best friend for Sue, the willowy waif. Her upper body strength was greater than that of many boys in the class; muscles developed from carrying bundles of asphalt shingles up extension ladders as she helped her dad in his contract roofing business.

Tammy was content to serve as Sue's wing-woman. Males of all ages ogled Sue, but Tammy caught enough overflow attention to make the alliance worthwhile. The few times guys had gotten pushy or rough with Sue, both on campus and in the city, Tammy kicked their crotches; as they bent over, she snapped her right knee into their jaws and noses until everyone heard the snap-crunch of damaged tissue. When asked what she is to Sue, her response of "bodyguard" was true, in part.

"Do you think he'll see me?" asked Sue.

"Tall stick-figure blondes with big boobs are hard not to see from space, girl."

"Okay, well, he came in the food court entrance, so let's walk slowly behind that family pushing the baby carriage. The dad, look at him: he's like Shaq after a few too many all-you-can-eat dessert buffets. Good cover."

They fell in behind the family, who cruised slowly along the left side of stores on the mall's two lower floors. They swivel-headed at storefronts and gawked but never stopped. They strolled past a jewelry seller, a few high-end fashion accessory places, a sporting goods store. It became obvious to Sue and Tammy that the family's ultimate destination was the food court.

Kiosks bedecked the floor area that separated the left and right rows of incumbent stores. About twenty feet away from a piercing boutique, they spotted a circular affair with mobile smartphones and accessories under glass. One little vendor cart nearby was selling T-shirts emblazoned with the latest catch phrases and coffee mugs available to personalize with a child's name and photograph. A larger kiosk next to the cart, more upscale, was filled with sunglasses.

"Sue! What did I frickin' tell you!" Tammy said a bit too loudly. The family's mother turned with a stare of disapproval.

"What?"

"Look!" Tammy pointed at the sunglasses kiosk.

A young man was bent over the glass counter with his butt stuck out at them—could be anyone's butt; however, Bruce's motorcycle boots were one of a kind, purchased from some illegal Mexican immigrant, black leather embossed with stylish hand-tooled Aztec patterns like something out of Banderas mezcal-soaked gunslinger movie. He was engaged in what appeared to be a conspiratorial discussion with the pretty retail clerk. Sue recognized what sensation animated the smile threatening to split her face.

She's trolling for underage hunky boys, she thought.

"My God, Sue. She's older. Like, *really* old. Twenty-four, maybe. Look at her. She's gorgeous."

The family had disappeared into the food court, which left the girls widely exposed. "Tammy," Sue whispered. "Let's get out of here before he turns around."

"Wait. Just one more minute. Keep looking."

Sue picked nervously at the white Chanel logo on her black quilted Cambon tote. She shifted, suddenly aware of her bladder.

She took it all in. The female sunglass seller was shorter and more petite than Tammy, with long straight black hair and skin like bone china, dark blue Spanish eyes, and highly Euro-fashionable large gold-bejeweled hoop earrings. She leaned across the glass countertop, shot glances left and right—and kissed Bruce Barnett on the mouth. She pulled back; ruby-red lips immediately curled back into a smile.

Sue had had enough. She walked so fast that Tammy found it a cardio workout to keep up. Outside, back at the Mustang, Tammy thought she saw a novel expression on Sue's face, greasy with shock and fury. Despite a blaring hot sun, Tammy felt a cold eddy slip through her. She knew something was coming and that it would not be good.

Whatever Tammy thought she'd seen, she knew only that she never wanted to see it again.

CHAPTER TWO

School's Out

"Thanks. I may be reasonably smart, but you make Abe laugh. You're so pretty he would drink your bathwater. I'm ugly. And even I don't laugh at my jokes."

Naomi glanced down at the time display on her dash: eleven-thirty. Friday night. She yawned. She loved her little strawberry-headed goy bestie, Anna; found her fascinating in ways she could not readily verbalize. But she also loved her rest periods and jealously guarded them. "Anna. You are beautiful. You know, the contrapositive of ugly?"

"LOL. Guess I owe you fifty cents for using that word."

"Didn't think I had it in me, did you? I don't only read zeroes and ones, babe." She could barely keep her eyes open.

"Ha. Except it's true. I think maybe Timmy Caperila might like me as a friend. At least he's always really nice to me. I don't turn any male heads, not even the old creepy ones. No one asked me to junior prom. Not looking forward to another two-point-five months of lonely summer nights."

"Timmy's super cute! But shy. Musicians and artists tend to be a little distant, in my observation. You might have to make the first move. Okay, tell you what—and don't answer because I'm claiming final word here. You will get out of my car. I will drive straight home and crash into bed. Next week, the last bell rings, and it's summer vacation. Friday morning, I'm taking you for a makeover. Saturday is the Sabbath, and Sunday, you have church, so it has to be then. Some of it we'll have done to us both, like mani-pedis. Other tricks of the trade I will do to you myself. I'm going to seriously up your game, girlfriend. You're naturally beautiful, Anna; truly, you are. But like a fine painter, I can work the Anna canvas into something truly special. Tricks we Jewish girls learn early.

"That Bible-banging mother of yours should have taught you, but she was too busy trying to keep you plain, holding you back, protecting you from all the evil boys out there. Well, I'm here to tell you, those evil boys will be begging to lick your toilet seat when I'm through with you. Now, bedtime. Goodnight, Anna-banana."

———

It was unheard of in the school's seventy-year history for a teacher to give detention to a student on the last day of the semester, as teachers around this time felt just as casual and rambunctious about summer recess as the students. In health class, the unpopular teacher seated all students alphabetically by last name on the first day of class. He had started with the front row, his left to right, to help him learn and remember names. Because he was so quick to assign detentions for the slightest offense, it was accepted protocol never to switch seats. To toy with him was juice not worth the squeeze. Students maintained their original seating positions to this day, the last of their junior year.

Timmy Caperila scribbled possible lyrics to his new original song while guitar chords played in his head and the boring, untalented teacher droned on.

On and on, he plans to tell her she lives in his heart to the end; like an obsession, he pulls up her number, enters the words, knowing he will never send.

Eyes on him. He felt it so acutely that it pulled him out of his lyrical reverie and caused him to look up and glance left. Anna Dingel, alphabetically next in line, seated beside him all year with not a peep out of her, stared at him. When his eyes met hers, she did not look away. Hers was the face of placid self-containment, but he recognized a curious interest in her eyes.

She broke eye contact to jot something on the lower right margin of her ruled notebook. She tore a jagged piece from the page, folded it once, then again, and pinched it tightly closed. Having checked first that Mr. McGonigle wasn't looking, head down, furtively she held out the paper pinched between her right forefinger and thumb. Timmy took the cue and snatched it from her.

The teacher, still talking, walked to Timmy's desk and stood before it. "Okay, Caperila. Let's see it."

"See what?"

"Open your hand."

Timmy glared back. "You'll have to open it."

McGonigle smirked. "Open it, or I fail you. Won't look so good on your college transcripts, now, will it?"

His face the color of pomegranate, Timmy opened his left hand; McGonigle snapped it out and made a grand show of unfolding it. Clearing his throat, he said, "Because you and Ms. Dingel disrespected me by not paying attention in my class, I shall now read to the class what could possibly be of more import than my lesson.

"It reads, 'If your band plays near here before my curfew of eleven, text me, I'll come,' and a phone number and, oh look, isn't that cute; a little smiley face.'

"You are an asshole, McGonigle."

Anna felt her face incandesce, along with a sudden and absolutely absurd desire to reach out and touch Timmy's hair. Many students giggled. The teacher smirked. "Mr. Caperila, I will see you here in detention at three o'clock. It'll be just the two of us. Think of the quality time we'll get to spend together on the lesson you missed passing notes with your little Mata Hari over here."

———

"You know what your problem is? You listen, but you don't hear; zero dots connect whatsoever. Given your mental shortcomings, do you really think I'd lay there and let you cut me open someday, Doctor Dumb-dumb?" said Naomi.

"Ouch. Harsh. Listen, I'll gladly cut you open ten years from now if you let me inside you today. We'll call it our layaway plan," Abe retorted.

"Ha-ha. Funny guy. I'm telling you—they found this relic inside of King Solomon's copper mines. This is beyond big. Bigger than anyone can possibly imagine."

"How so?"

"Because Abraham was born over four thousand years ago. In one of the oldest and first-abandoned mine shafts, they unearthed a limestone tablet engraved with Paleo-Hebrew script going all the way back to Abraham. If this is true—and my mind is still trying to get around how it could even be possible—do you have the slightest concept of what this means?"

"That some guys found a very old rock?"

"Really now: I wouldn't let you take my temperature, let alone prescribe treatment."

"I'd take your temperature with my tongue if you'll leave it completely up to me where I put it."

"Moron, think. First of all, it's more than one tablet. There are several, some in better condition than others. They're taking them to a lab in Tel Aviv to carefully clean and preserve them, then they plan on posting high-resolution images online for scholars everywhere to study and decipher. The oldest artifact from our people only goes back three thousand years; some models of ancient shrines from the Qeiyafa excavation."

"Have I mentioned that I find you captivatingly, intoxicatingly attractive today?"

"Imbecile. I'm hanging up now; bye."

"No, wait! Okay, so what is the point? In a few words, tell me what has you so excited about this ancient artifact in Israel."

"Abe, don't you see? The man after which you were named lived four thousand years ago. He's considered the father of the three main world religions, arguably the most important man in recorded history. King David, and his son, Solomon, came a thousand years after him. Imagine finding Hebrew language carved into stone by ancient Israelites from the earliest time of our people. Catching on yet? This evidence supports the case for the Bible's accuracy because it meant that four thousand years ago, Israelites could record events and transmit their history that had only begun to be compiled eight hundred years later. If the Old Testament was ever on trial for its authenticity, this new evidence just introduced the biggest reasonable doubt of its innocence ever found. It's . . . it's stunning."

"Yes. Yes, Naomi, it really is. Now consider this: if not for the passions of Abraham, genetically passed down to me by my awesome and randy forefather, neither you nor I would exist today."

"I know where this is going."

"Please let me stop by tonight, if only for an hour. I promise to unleash the passions of our forefathers upon you. C'mon, it's the last day of junior year."

She let out a sigh of exasperation. Finally, she yielded. "Okay, fine. Eight-thirty. I'll tell my parents we'll be discussing our course loads for senior year."

"She said, 'loads.'"

"Dim-wit."

———

"I don't like 'I told you so' people," Sue said, fuming in the mall parking lot. "You don't think he saw us walk out, do you?"

Tammy barely considered this response and completely ignored the question. As she climbed into the Mustang, heat blasted like an oven door opening. June sun against black upholstery made her wonder what it would feel like inside the car in August. She wiped a wisp of mousy-brown bangs from her greasy forehead.

"Hey, Sue. Would you rather hang out with somebody who shines you on? I'm the little guy on your shoulder telling you things you don't want to hear but need to. Keeping your blonde ass out of trouble is my job."

"Pfft," and with a brush-off flick of her hand, Sue Nastro flicked the switch that opened the convertible roof. Heady and sharp new-car smells released into the crisp June air. She popped the clutch to squeals from the rear tires.

"Pissed?"

She made a left out of the mall entrance and never looked right, which caused the driver of a pick-up truck to slam on his brakes and lay on his horn. Comfortable now in the traffic flow, Sue focused her attention inward. It was a valid question.

"Disappointed in myself a little."

"In yourself? My God, why? You're the best thing that ever happened to that jerk!"

Sue flipped down her visor and made a right onto Germantown Pike, headed directly into the bright late-afternoon sun. Whenever a road had two lanes, she would cruise in the left and completely avoid the right as though it did not exist. At a red light, she braked to a hard stop. To the right a car full of boys she did not recognize. *Sophomores*, she figured. They called out to her. She ignored them completely.

"I trust people too easily. My dad tells me that. He's old-school Italian: everyone's guilty until proven innocent. I need to be more like him."

Tammy nodded. "You know both my parents are shit. Dad cheated on Mom; he left us years ago. Her rotating cavalcade of boyfriends included a few who flirted with me when she stepped out for a bit. One asshole even said I was a bad girl in need of spanking and tried to pull me over his lap. I saw the big bulge in his pants. Listen, I haven't trusted any man since I was in the fifth grade."

"Wow, Tammy, that sucks. I'm so sorry."

"Tuh. Don't be. Life goes on. No rearview mirror. After next year, I am outta here, for good. Poof! Gonzo."

"Really? Where will you go?"

"California. One more shitty winter here, then color me gone. If I get into UCSD—that is, with a sports scholarship."

"Hmm. You're the best field hockey player in the entire PIAA conference. You'll get in, for sure."

"Which isn't saying much. Maybe. Fingers crossed. How about you?"

"Full-time modeling. Save up my earnings, then decide if I want to go to college. I hate school—you know that; always have. Feels like a State-mandated prison sentence to me."

"You like to design stuff, just like your dad. Maybe it's genetic. Why not try to get into a fashion institute?"

"Pfft. Go from State prison to Federal prison? Not in the cards, Tammy-Tam-Tam."

"What are you going to do about Bruce Barnette?"

Sue glanced over. "Right now, I want to rip his balls off."

"Speaking of prison . . ."

"Yeah, Tam, I know. He's not worth it. I mean, look at him. He's a techie. Ever drive past the VoTech school at closing time when they're all slithering out? He might not look like one of them, but he *is* one of them. Blue collar. Low expectations for life. Grease monkey. Yeah, he's got the face and body and does all the right things in bed, and believe it or not he's really smart—"

"No, he really isn't."

"Book smart, I mean. There's more to him than he lets on. But he bullies other kids. Got a mean streak in him a mile wide."

"Look at what he's doing to you, Sue."

"Ha. Yeah right. What he *thinks* he's doing to me."

"So, what are you going to do, dump his ass?"

She pulled up in front of Tammy's mother's little pillbox house in Plymouth Valley, stopped, and shifted the automatic transmission into park. She stared down at fidgety hands. "Not sure yet. Need to sleep on it."

"You're not actually thinking of staying with him, are you?"

Still looking down, "Maybe. I need new sunglasses. Let's pay the little kiosk lady a visit tomorrow. In the morning, I'll pick you up around nine, right before the mall opens."

———

"Mom, I'm nearly eighteen. Legal to vote, to join the military, and shoot people dead. No, I can't drink in a bar yet, not for three years, not that I have any interest in that. I only want to go see my friend play guitar."

"Nn-nn. We'll talk about it. I don't like it."

"Why, Mom? What don't you like about me innocently watching a friend play music?"

"No one is innocent inside a bar, dear. Dens of iniquity. Evil men will paw you. You're a young girl."

"Young woman, Mom."

"They will come at you. Alcohol makes them audacious; determined. They absolutely will not stop coming on to you until one of them takes from you what you do not want to give. I don't like it."

"I'll see what Dad says. Naomi is coming over tomorrow morning bright and early to pick me up."

"Oh? Still palling around with the little heathen?"

"Mom! Jesus was Jewish! Stop it!"

"Where is she taking you?"

"Out. Girl's day."

"With boys?"

"No, Mom."

Her father's voice interrupted from a distance. "Anna? Can you grab a case of Thirty-Four Special Arterial Fluid from the garage and bring it down, please?"

She rolled her eyes, then complied.

———

"Let me come too! I'll get one!"

To gauge interest, Bruce glanced at his two loyal acolytes, Carmen DeSalvo and Earl Gallo. He spotted none. "You're out, Frank. No go."

"Bruce, come *on*, man! I want a tat," Frank pleaded. He seemed on the verge of tears. This struck Bruce as pathetic and weak. Frank Watson was never part of Bruce's inner circle; no member of Bruce's crew had ever been to the apartment where he lived with his parents. They considered him a 'hanger-on' and a wannabe, a loner mostly with wildly bushy hair and aviator eyeglasses that made him appear older than seventeen.

"Bye, Frank," Bruce said. He motioned for Carmen and Earl to get in the car. The plan was to head straight to Sailor Tuck's tattoo parlor in Willow Grove. With Pennsylvania's minimum age for tattoos set at eighteen, Bruce knew that Sailor Tuck is the only one who doesn't require I.D. He, Carmen, and Earl were all seventeen. The one kid in tech school who tattooed a teardrop on his own hand using a needle and black calligraphy ink when he was fifteen had them all convinced that Tuck was the best, a true artist.

"Dude's out of it, man. Thought he was gonna cry," said Carmen, laughing. His high-pitched chortle infected Earl into the mirth. "Did you see him, Bruce? He was starting to cry."

"Yeah, I saw. Pussy. Hey, you fags aren't going to chicken out, are you?"

"No way, man, we're with you all the way," said Earl. "I've always wanted a skull and cross-bones."

"Yeah, and I've always wanted Icarus with wings flying up to Heaven. You sure about this Aztec thing?" asked Carmen.

"Damned sure. I had this girl Kathy in commercial art shop draw it for me. All it cost me was . . . well. I had to go down on her."

Laughter. "She's pretty good-looking. Where was this?"

"Handicapped bathroom near the principal's office. Only one toilet and sink in there; locks from the inside."

"How'd she taste?"

Bruce blew out air. "Exactly like the rest of them."

Carmen and Earl, virgins both, neither of whom had ever seen a real live girl naked, laughed at this as Bruce turned on to the Pennsylvania Turnpike.

Frank had walked from the tech school parking lot back to his parents' apartment and found it empty, as expected. By twelve minutes past four, he had finished composing his note to them about feeling alone, trapped, and hopeless; that there was no future. In the note, he placed all blame for his wretched life squarely upon them; on their dysfunction, yelling at each other, taking it out on him. He added a special 'thank-you' to Bruce Barnette for not saving him when he had the chance. He used adhesive tape to affix the note to the microwave oven door in the kitchen.

At twenty past the hour, he seated himself on the ratty fabric sofa and chambered a round into his father's .30-06 Springfield bolt-action deer rifle. He wedged the stock firmly against the worn area rug under his feet. At twenty-one minutes past, Frank Watson inserted the barrel in between dry lips, the muzzle pressed against the roof of his mouth. At minute twenty-two, his final thought before he pulled the trigger: *Hoppes gun cleaning fluid tastes bitter, far worse than it smells.*

CHAPTER THREE

Metamorphosis

"Your mother is staring out the window at us."

Anna grinned. "To make sure you aren't an 'evil boy,' I'm sure."

Naomi shook her head. "She hates me because I'm Jewish."

"I wouldn't say that she *hates* you because you're Jewish. Basically, she thinks all non-believers are going straight to Hell."

Naomi nodded. "How tolerant! So, a Jew spends her entire life chaste and pure, doing nothing apart from helping and serving others out of the compassion overflowing from her unselfish heart, and dies a virgin—but a serial killer who is also baptized, occasionally attends church and confesses faith in Jesus with his lips—that guy goes straight to Heaven, and the Jew goes to Hell? Got it. Thanks, Mrs. Dingel."

Anna laughed. "With God, all things are possible. She conveniently forgets that part."

"I can't go straight to Hell because Jews don't even believe in Hell. But I do. I think Hell is living in a house of corpses twenty-four-seven with a batshit crazy mom who will commit suicide the day her daughter gets laid out of wedlock."

Laughter rocked Naomi's little red Mercedes C-300.

"Thank you."

"For what, Anna-banana?"

"For being my friend." She offered Naomi her left index finger. Naomi touched her right index finger against Anna's, and they locked them together.

"Besties. So, what's the plan after graduation next year?"

Anna shook her head. "Dad wants me to follow in his footsteps, become a mortician, three-thousand hours of apprenticeship. Eventually, he'd like to die and leave me the family business."

"In that order?"

The laughter felt good. Summer felt like it had arrived. Stress, like elephants seated on their chests, had finally stood up and ambled away for a good long while. Liberty resonated handsome and free within both. "So, like, where are you taking me?"

Naomi shot her a smirk. "You'll see. About to flip your world on its edge. My treat, everything today is completely on me. Today is the day when the achromatic caterpillar trapped in its chrysalis busts out, unfolds its wings, and blossoms into a magnificently beautiful and elegant butter-fly. I'm excited."

"I can't let you do that," Anna said, reaching into her jeans pocket for cash. Naomi pressed her hand down against Anna's wrist.

"Hush! Nonsense. I most certainly can. Naomi Silver does whatever the hell she wants to do, dearie. Besides, my dad, as you know, is the senior partner in his law firm, and he just landed the biggest corporate account in the firm's history. This morning he hands me this." She held out a rolled-up wad of hundred-dollar bills. Anna's eyes appeared to swell.

"Right? So then he says, 'Naomi, I've been an absentee father lately and feel terrible about it. Go out and spend every last penny of this today. Don't come home with anything except bags of clothes.' I mean, how awesome is he?"

"Geez. You have the best dad; you really do. I love my dad, and he's cool and funny and all. Love the guy. What I still can't figure out is what the hell he ever saw in my mother."

"She's wild in bed, everybody knows that. Total kinkster. A world-class piece of ass, our Lady Dingel is. Keeps that gnarly old bait of hers nice and fresh."

"Oh yeah. Marge and her snappin' gyro." They laughed nonstop until Naomi pulled into a parking space in front of her friend Sergio's home and hair studio. Both wiped their eyes and honked into facial tissues. "You'll love this guy. He normally starts his appointments later, but he made this

8:00 a.m. slot just for me." Anna followed Naomi inside. Sergio, the hair stylist, was all smiles. He handed each a pony bottle of spring water, then ushered Anna into his vinyl barber's chair. He covered her with a black plastic styling cape. His non-judgmental chit-chat won her over. "You are such a pretty lady, Anna! Natural beauty! You just need a little help to bring out more of it."

She shook her head. "Amen, Sergio. If you only knew. My mother is so overly protective and skeptical of newer technology, styles, and such that she's basically kept me a decade or two behind my peers."

"Like the Amish!"

Anna laughed. "Exactly! The only times I ever saw my face with makeup on it was Naomi messing around at her house during sleepovers. I had to scrub it all off before they came and picked me up in the morning. I've never seen myself in a non-church dress. You do realize I'm forced to cut my own hair, don't you?"

"Oh my God! That's so . . ."

"Amish?"

"You said it! And really, Anna, we must do something about these giant blackheads in your ears. I've never seen any so large. They're like black holes, sucking in all matter and energy with their immense gravity. That sound you heard at the beach was never ocean waves; it was the event horizons of your blackheads pulling beach chairs and sand into their no-escape depths."

"Stop," she blushed. "What can I do? I can't even see them in a mirror to try and squeeze them."

He grinned and turned. "Naomi, second drawer down, pull out the thing that looks like a hypodermic syringe."

She held it up to the light for inspection. "Serge—this *is* a syringe. Just without the needle."

"Actually, you're right. Hand it over. Now watch." He pressed the open tip against the largest blackhead in Anna's left ear. He used his right to pull back on the plunger. After continued attempts, the waxy blackhead with yellowish sebum mixed with dead skin cells, accumulated over many years, suddenly filled the syringe tip. He held it up to Anna. "See? Sergio the Magico! Works better than any comedones extractor, as we see." By the time he finished with the right ear, the entire long tip of the syringe was now completely packed with pungent black, gray, brown, and yellow waxy material.

He spent thirty-five minutes with hairdresser scissors and thinning shears. "And you thought I only cut hair. Look in the mirror, darling," he said,

"Wow! Sergio! Oh my God!" she said. "He held up a racquetball paddle-sized mirror to show Anna all views of her new 'do. "Naomi said you were some kind of magic, but I don't believe in magic. You've made me a believer, seriously! Is this really me?"

He laughed. "Nope. Anna is no more. Meet Anastasia, sublime princess of the Royal House of Sergio!" Shorter now, the hair reached only to her shoulders. He had transformed her entire look. She could not stop looking at herself, her Duchenne smile permanent, Botox-frozen in place.

"C'mon, kiddo." Naomi broke the silent reverie. "We need to be at the mall when it opens. Makeup and clothes, next. This will take up the rest of the day, so c'mon, hustle-hustle, let's get a move-on."

Naomi peeled off a few crisp Ben Franklins and pushed them into Sergio's palm. Anna hugged him like someone stranded atop a flagpole. They returned to the Mercedes. The first thing Anna did after buckling her seat belt was to pull down the visor to check herself in the little lighted mirror. "Nope. I was beginning to think it was a dream, and now it's time to wake up ugly."

Naomi grinned triumphantly. "Did I tell you, or did I tell you?"

"Oh. My. *God*! I still can't believe it."

At 10:00 a.m., Naomi pulled into a space in front of Asia Nails & Spa just as they opened. Manicure, pedicure, and eyebrow threading behind them, Naomi started the car. "Anna-banana, the heavy lifting is behind us; now comes the fun part. My friend who works the makeup counter is one of the best. I mean, seriously, she could work in Hollywood; she really is that good."

"I know a little about makeup."

"Oh really? Then how come I've never seen you wear any? Not once?"

"My entire life, I've watched my father turn pallid, waxen corpses back to something more like their living selves using makeup. For sure, *he* could work in Hollywood. But the reason I don't wear any is because my mother thinks makeup on girls is 'disingenuous'—her word. Says it's a lie, a mask, a disguise, which is exactly what Satan wants—people lying to one another."

"So how then does she justify what her husband does for a living? Using her logic, his lies to the world keep her fed."

"To her, it's two totally different things. Hypocrisy is one of her strengths. Claims he is comforting the grieving, which is of God."

Naomi shook her head once. "Oookayy. Well, I'll be making a liar out of you today. Then we shop for dresses, skirts, and shoes. And a bag."

"Dresses? I own two, for church on Sundays. Otherwise, I wear jeans and trousers, that's it. They make my butt look half-decent."

"Your butt is amazing! So high and tight. Most girls would die to have your perky butt. No, you must get inside the minds of guys for this to make sense. Well, maybe not their minds, per se. Pants are boring to guys. Everybody wears them. They leave little to the male imagination. Guys like to be teased, to be worked up."

"I sort of follow."

"Okay, consider: a dress and skirt show legs and still show butt, but the male mind is climbing underneath, aching to see, sniff, taste, and touch what's so tantalizingly available up there, separated from him only by air—not by a fortified wall of denim. Dresses and skirts force his entire imagination into action. Trust me, Banana, dresses drive men wild with desire. The ultimate tease. With the right shoes giving nice angles to your calves and ankles, few men will be able to resist getting pulled into your orbit. Today," she said with a knowing grin, "we increase your gravity times a hundred. Who's the one girl in school all guys dream about the most?"

"You?"

"Ha-ha. You're very kind. Nope, try again."

"I wasn't being kind. I see how they look at you." Anna paused. "Sue Nastro?"

"Bingo! Right on. And what does Sue Nastro wear, dresses and skirts, or pants?

"Dresses and skirts. I have never once seen her wear pants."

Naomi shrugged for dramatic effect. "I rest my case," she said as she pulled into the department store entrance. "Speaking of Sue Nastro, I'd recognize that platinum blonde head of hers anywhere. And that miniature defensive tackle she travels with, Tammy Goldsworth. See?" she said. Anna followed her pointed finger to the employee parking area in the distance. "What the heck are they doing standing over by that Civic? Like, that doesn't look suspicious *at all*."

———

"Perfect timing. That's her white Honda, I'm positive," Sue pointed. She checked her Rolex. 11:21 a.m. She pulled into a space in the far corner of the mall employee parking lot.

Tammy nodded. "Yep. Guess selling sunglasses doesn't pay very well. That there is one Class F beater."

"Tiny little troll, she is. Bet her apartment smells like cat piss and cig smoke."

Tammy snickered. "So, what's the game plan, Coach?"

Sue snorted. "One thing my dad taught me. 'Money talks—bullshit walks.'"

"Um, what does that even mean?"

With a savage glance, she said, "It means threats are empty and useless. We're going to give her some for fun, but a swift kick to her wallet will drive the point home."

Sue motioned for Tammy to get out. Silently, Tammy kept pace with Sue until they arrived at the white Honda. From her purse, Sue withdrew two Benchmade Barrage drop-point spring-assist folding knives. She handed the black-handled weapon to Tammy and kept the slightly more elegant-looking black-silver knife for herself. Tammy watched as Sue gave hers a little flick. What snapped out was a very sharp and sturdy, mean-looking blade, which she pointed down at the tires.

She checked for roving security vehicles with blinking yellow lights; she spotted one far off in another parking lot. *Not a threat*, she thought. She scanned the horizon for any possible witnesses; satisfied that there were none, Tammy popped open her blade. With all of her strength, she thrust it into the right rear tire of the Civic and ripped sideward. Air exploded from the wounded tire in a hiss. Both watched the driver's side rear of the vehicle drop three inches. Sue smiled. She did the same to the front, though her attack was weaker than Tammy's; no rip, but still an effective puncture wound. Air hissed out slowly.

"That tire is repairable, weakling." Tammy bumped her aside and slashed it. The driver's side of the car plunged down. They repeated the crime on the passenger side. Sue showed Tammy how to safely fold the knife closed.

"Keep it," she said. "My gift to you."

Tammy hefted it and grinned. "Badass. Thanks, Suebeedoo!"

"Okay, let's go grab a latte across the street at the café until the mall opens in fifteen minutes. It'll be good to get my memorable car out of sight for a bit. We're sticking out here like a sore thumb. Then we'll come back, park in a regular spot with the commoners, and have a chat with the old hag."

———— • ————

"We're first in! Straight upstairs to see Wendy about some makeup tips; let's hustle!" Anna followed Naomi to the counter, shook hands with her friend, an elegantly dressed woman in her mid-twenties, and took a seat. Over the next hour, newly arrived shoppers perused summer fashions and milled about noisily nearby, which left Wendy free to focus on Anna entirely. She taught her how to make the blue of her eyes pop. She lay various cloth swatches against her shoulder and shined a lamp onto her face.

"Color analysis," said Wendy. "You, my dear, are decidedly a 'winter.'" She advised Anna on what shades of eyeliner, lipstick, powder and cream blush, even clothes to stick with for life; colors that will compliment her skin tone and hair. After applying the products, Anna looked in the mirror.

"My dear Lord. Who *is* this?

Naomi beamed. "Competition for Sue Nastro, I'd say. What do you think, Wendy?"

With a glance left and right, Wendy grabbed a generous pile of samples and slid them across the counter toward Anna. She looked at Naomi. "On the house. Shh, don't tell. When she comes back for more, I'll give her my forty-percent employee discount."

Only half aware of the exchange between Naomi and Wendy, Anna stared at herself. Wendy broke her reverie. "Anna, give me your phone. I'll snap a few selfies so that later, you can compare my work against your own application and make sure you nail everything."

Slowly, Anna returned to the present. "Um, I don't own a phone."

"You don't—" Wendy shot Naomi a puzzled glance.

"My mom thinks they're evil."

Naomi shook her head almost imperceptibly at Wendy, with 'don't push it' in her eyes.

"Naomi, help her out? Take a few pics?"

"I will, once I get her into a dress and shoes."

———

Downstairs, Sue and Tammy approached the sunglass kiosk. Right away, the woman behind the counter recognized two authentic prospects. She blessed them with her first salesperson smile of the morning. "Hey there, ladies!"

Sue picked up on a Spanish accent. She forced a smile. "Hi. Was hoping you might have the perfect pair of sunglasses for me. Something new for the summer." She omitted that she owned two pairs of Olivia Palermo Mayfair 01 and Mayfair 02 sunglasses that cost her about the same as it would cost the woman to replace four tires.

The woman extended her hand to Sue. "I'm Sofia."

Sue took her hand. "I notice the hint of an accent. Are you from Spain? If I had to guess, Madrid?"

Sofia's face changed to an authentic surprise. "My gosh, nobody has ever guessed that accurately! How did you know?"

"I get around. Did some modeling for Manolo Blahnik, met a lot of Spanish models over there, and they all sound like you."

"Wow! That's amazing! I'm sorry, I didn't get your name?"

"Bruce Barnette's girlfriend."

Her jaw unhinged. Sue and Tammy studied her face. They watched surprise morph into acceptance, sprinkled with nervousness and shame.

"Don't say a thing, Sofia. Just know this." Sue flicked open the Benchmade with a loud click. "Touch Bruce again, and I predict bad things for your future." At this, Tammy clicked open her own knife. "*Muy mala*," said Sue. "Am I pronouncing it correctly? Nod if you understand."

Mouth in a grim rictus, she chanced a brief look at Tammy. She saw a silent, self-possessed, thinly leashed pit bull, ears pricked for the German kill command from its master. Thick muscles slithered edgily like eels just under the skin. Sofia nodded.

"Great! Then we can all get along," Sue said. She folded her knife and slid it into her bag. "Have a wonderful day, Sofia. So nice meeting you. By the way, all your sunglasses are shit."

"I can't possibly let you buy me these, Naomi. They cost too much."

"Relax, we agreed this morning. My treat."

"Yes, but these Jimmy Choo shoes are six hundred dollars! That's insane!"

Naomi shot her a look. "Insane is cutting your own hair in 2022. This is a gift to my eyes. Tired of looking down at those bobo canvas sneakers with holes worn in them. Girl, this is as much for me as it is for you."

Anna stood before the mirror. In her new Adrianna Papell one-shoulder floral organza dress, Choo shoes, hair, and makeup to perfection, she felt positive that if she were to attend Sunday service like this, no one in the church would recognize her.

"You look amazing, Anna. We're going down to the water fountain; I'm going to shoot a few pics."

As she and Naomi rode the down escalator, Sue Nastro and Tammy Goldsworth were about to pass them on the up escalator. The four made eye contact. Nobody waved or said a word. At the fountain, following Naomi's instructions, Anna struck one pose after another as Naomi snapped pics. Every eye in the vicinity was drawn to Anna. Husbands beside wives stole glances, old men on benches, store managers carrying coffee cups. Little children, too, were mesmerized by unparalleled natural beauty at its young adult peak. Not yet a grown woman, yet no longer a little child.

As they reversed course and headed back outside toward Naomi's Mercedes, so caught up in their mission that both had ignored the passage of time, they realized from the sun's location that it was well past time for some food. Stomachs suddenly awakened, growling in unison like a matched pair of ravenous wolves.

"Banana, I'm taking you to brunch. Then, to the outlets. I'll teach you how not to spend six hundred on new shoes that are still decent knock-offs. We'll go to Nine West. Remember, accessorizing is key. We'll get you a decent purse. And, we'll stop by the pharmacy for whitening strips."

"At least let me buy lunch. Are my teeth that bad?"

"I've seen worse, but yes. I drink lots of green tea, and mine darken up. These work! And no! The entire day is my treat; already told you. You press these thin little plastic films on your teeth before bed every night, and like magic, in a few days, your teeth will be glowing white. You know, like when you add bleach when washing your white clothes? Except these are perfectly safe to put in your body. And then there's one last thing you'll need."

Back at the car, Naomi fobbed it open and reached into the back seat. She withdrew a paper gift bag. "Go ahead, open it."

Anna set down her multiple shopping bags on the back seat and took the gift bag from Naomi. Inside was a small flat rectangle. She ripped open the wrapping, her face a puzzle. Naomi smiled. "It's an eight-inch tablet with a lifetime data plan. At lunch, we'll set you up with an email account, and I'll mail you all the pics I just took by the fountain. You can choose the ones you like best and create an Instagram account. This way, you and Timmy Caperila, or whomever, can chat any time your horny little heart desires. Slim enough to tuck in your school notebook. No chance your snooping mother will think to check there. Slim and small enough to hide anywhere, really. Under your mattress or a carpet . . ."

Anna blinked in sheer amazement. Holding the tablet, she threw her arms around Naomi. For three minutes, she poured out her soul in tears of gratitude and relief.

Dark wet spots blossomed on the back of Naomi's turquoise top. "My love for you is more than love. How could God ever not love a heart and soul as beautiful as yours, Naomi Silver?"

"Ask your mother if Hell has a post office. I'll definitely send her a postcard."

Tears of joy turned to squawking peals of laughter.

CHAPTER FOUR

Summer Break

"The Sefer Yetzirah, meaning Book of Creation. Jews in Western Europe during the Middle Ages believed it to be an authentic guide to magical usage."

"Mm, magic, got it. So?"

"The Babylonian Talmud states that 'On the eve of every Shabbat, Judah HaNasi's pupils, Rab Hanina and Rab Hoshaiah, who devoted themselves, especially to cosmogony—the origins of the universe—used the words and process spelled out in the Sefer Yetzirah to create a delicious calf, which they ate on the Sabbath. Jewish mystics insist that our patriarch, Abraham, used the same method to create the calf prepared for the three angels who foretold Sarah's pregnancy in the biblical account at Genesis 18:7. All the miraculous creations attributed to other rabbis of the Talmudic era are ascribed to the use of the same book, according to rabbinic commentators," Naomi finished.

"I believe you. But what's got your underwear in a twist?" Abe asked with a hint of a smirk.

"Your mind never leaves my underwear, it seems. What has them in a twist is that the Sefer Yetzirah was likely written in the second century. It's not that old, relatively speaking. It contains instructions on how to make a golem. Different rabbis have different theories on how to make one. Most of these involve sculpting earth into a figure that looks sort of human, then using God's name to bring it to life, since God is the ultimate creator of life."

"Golem, right. A human made of dirt. I had one of those teaching me health last semester."

"McGonigle? Yeah. Balance-beam sniffer for sure. Couple of girls he coached in gymnastics just came forward. I doubt he'll be teaching anyone anything for a long time, creepy pedo. Anyway, yes. A golem is made from inanimate organic materials by rabbis then brought to life to serve or protect them or, as with making an animal, to feed them with its new living flesh. Sort of like the old cartoon about the brooms that come alive and carry water buckets. Those brooms are golems. They end up flooding the sorcerer's world because they are too efficient at it. I mean, yeah, sure, it seems pretty farfetched, but here's the interesting part: the archaeologists working on the Solomon dig are sure they recognize some Paleo-Hebrew words that ended up in the Sefer Yetzirah, words that date back over two-thousand years before it was supposedly written. Crazy, right? We have the Torah, the Talmud—we have the entire Old Testament. Old they are. But this mystic stuff is fairly modern.

"Most theologians believe the Sefer Yetzirah was made up by a few feisty rabbis in relatively recent times. They align writing styles, which change over time. But what did they just unearth? Four-thousand-year-old tablets about golems. I'm just waiting for the high-res pics so I can analyze them myself."

"Totally crazy. I've never said it, but I think it's really cool how deeply you research Judaic history. You probably know more about it than our rabbi. Anyway, now, about those underwear. What color are they today?"

———

"Did you hear the cops questioned Bruce about Frank Watson's suicide?"

"What? No, he hasn't called me since the last day of class. Frank Watson committed suicide?" Sue asked, or more accurately—shouted. Tammy thought she sounded scared.

"Have you been living under a rock? Yes, everyone's talking about it. Blew his head off. His parents found his brains splattered all over their living room wall and a note taped to the microwave. It blamed them . . . and mentioned Bruce."

"Bruce? What the hell did he have to do with it? He didn't hang out with Frank. Oh my God, I can't believe this is happening."

"Yep. Bruce was mentioned. My boss told me. He has Freemason buddies who are cops. They all belong to the same Blue Lodge or something. He asked me if I knew Bruce or Frank. I lied and said no."

"Is he in trouble?"

"Nope, not since he has an alibi. Turns out he, Carmen, and Earl went to get tattoos. Frank had asked to come, too, but they rejected him. He was really hurt by it."

"Bruce got a tattoo? Dear Lord. If mom and dad find out about this, Bruce will never be allowed to set foot on this property again. Why hasn't he called me?"

"Would you be up for sex with all this going on?"

"You make it sound like that's all he wants from me."

"If the pointy shoes curled up at the ends and dunce hat fit . . ."

"Shut up. Okay, hanging up now. I have to at least try to call him."

"C'mon, ya big dope, answer," Sue muttered as Bruce's number rang for the fifth time. *At least his phone is on, and he's not on another call,* she thought. Eight, nine . . . she was about to hang up when finally he answered.

"Hi."

"Hi! Bruce? I haven't heard from you. I'm worried. Are you okay?"

"I'm fine; why, what's up?"

"Well, I . . . I heard about Frank Watson."

"Wasn't a friend."

"I know that, but he mentioned you in his suicide note. And you got a tattoo?"

Silence. "Sue, have you been spying on me?"

"No! I would never! I hear things, is all."

"Bullshit. I know what you did to Sophia. The only reason cops aren't knocking at the Nastro door right now is because I swapped out her tires. Not a good look, Sue."

"But I—"

Don't want to hear it. Listen. I'm not saying we're done-done, but I'm taking a break. My cousin up in Maine asked me if I wanted to earn some really good coin this summer lumberjacking with his crew. Told him I'd think about it."

"You're not seriously considering—"

"I think that little stunt you pulled with Sofia made the decision for me. You and I need a break. You've completely lost your shit. So, yeah, headed north. See you in September."

"Wow, they really work!" Anna said, studying her one-shade lighter teeth in the bathroom mirror.

"What did you say, dear?" came the distant voice downstairs.

God, she has ears like a bat, Anna thought. "Nothing. I'll be down after my shower," she yelled back.

She recognized that never had she felt so happy, hopeful, and optimistic, ever, as she did on that Sunday morning. She brushed, rinsed with antiseptic mouthwash, flossed, then took a quick shower, which included the hastiest-ever armpit-and-leg shave. She took care to wash off all remaining traces of makeup, per her mother's orders. She bounced downstairs in her robe, with her hair up in a towel, and wearing white footie socks. "What's up, Mom?"

"You're not thinking of wearing that new dress to church, I hope."

"Why? It's a fantastic dress and very proper."

"Proper? I can see your neckline and both shoulders. I'd hardly call it proper."

"I'm nearly eighteen. I'll wear whatever I want."

"Mocking God," Margie Dingel muttered. Beady eyes drilled into Anna. "You think you're in the big-time? Okay. Get out. Go live on your own. Then you can wear whatever you like. As long as you're under this roof, you will live by my—our—rules."

"I'll go see what Dad has to say about this."

"Oh, hi, baby doll. Didn't even hear you come in."

Anna knew that when he was working with makeup, he was in his creative zone and peaceful. "Dad, we need to talk about Mother."

He set down his horsehair makeup brush, pulled over two wheeled stools, one for each, and the two sat. "Dad, I don't think I can stay here after graduation."

Face thoughtful, he said, "That bad, is it?"

She nodded. "Yep. That bad."

"Is it about her freak-out over your makeover Friday?"

Again, she nodded. "Well, that, and all her other restrictions. No phone, no computer, no Internet, no boys. Dad, you know none of this could be considered normal even under the strictest Christian guidelines for living. Pastors and priests have email addresses and phones. She believes that all electronics lead to evil; that somehow they invite evil into us. I say things are just . . . things," she said and shrugged. "They can be tools for good or evil, depending on the person using them and to what purpose. And the dress I wore Friday is the most appropriate, conventional dress Naomi and I could find! Everything else was sexier by degrees. Still not good enough for Mother. She wants me continually wearing that hand-me-down piece of crap on Sundays and to dress like a boy for school. Dad, seriously. I am done with this entire scene. I might not last the year before taking off. Might not even last through summer break. Telling you right now, I'm going to go see my friend Timmy's band when they play at the bar. Mother can call the police on me if she wants. I refuse to miss it, not for anything."

He stroked his chin and smiled. "You really did look amazing. Stunning. I couldn't believe I was staring at my little peanut."

She fought it at first but gave in and smiled. "Thanks, Dad." She rose and hugged him tightly before returning to her seat, where she sunk back down into her depthless funk.

"I love you so much. You're the best dad anyone could ask for. I just don't see how you two could have possibly hooked up in the first place and stayed together this long. You're so normal, and she's . . . well. Dad, she's totally nutso, if you want to know the truth. I know it's not just my adolescent brain, wired for rebellion against my parents' wishes. I see other parents interacting with their teenagers. She's not right in the head."

He shook his head. "Anna, I understand you're upset, but please don't say that about your mother. She loves you and wants more than anything to protect you."

"Protect me? From what, *life*? Am I never permitted to live one, as she did?"

He rolled his stool closer and leaned in. "I'm going to tell you a few things, Anna, that may come as a shock to you. This stays completely between you and me. Understand?"

Anna felt a little shiver. She nodded. "Between us, only us, no matter what. Got it."

"Great. Okay, here goes. I'm not her first man."

Anna's mouth hung open. "You mean mother was married before you?"

"No-no-no, not married. You don't have to be married to fall for someone and have sex. She had fallen in with some much older guy when she was your age, lost her virginity to him. That didn't work out, so she went with another guy who lied to her about his other sex partners, and he gave her a venereal disease."

"Mom?" she said a little too loudly.

"Shh. She has ears like a bat."

Anna broke out laughing but slowly collected herself. "I say the exact same thing!"

"Great minds," he said. He playfully knuckled her shoulder. "Anyway, she got banged around by men. Lived with an alcoholic. Every one of them cheated on her; broke her heart. One got her pregnant. He insisted on her getting an abortion, but she just felt that was wrong. Her conscience wouldn't let her. Turns out her body rejected that embryo all on its own. In her depression, she threw herself at the feet of the Lord, got baptized a second time in our church, worked mundane odd jobs to feed herself while spending most of her time in church, either making herself useful or kneeling alone in prayer. That's when I came along. I was a Christian in search of a fresh, new, welcoming fellowship. I started coming to church, and I spotted her. The most beautiful thing I had ever laid eyes on. I think I loved her from that first moment. Anyway, I love her no less today than I did twenty years ago, which is why I'm asking—no, begging—for you to work with me. I understand you're a young woman and need to gain some experiences of your own. Get your heart lifted, thrust down, then lifted again. All I ask is that you remember everything we taught you about the Lord and about being responsible to Him and to yourself. Integrity, fidelity, and above all, love and forgiveness. Love God, then love yourself second."

She fell silent, and his last words hung in the mortuary air. Finally, she said, "Dad, still. I don't know if I can—"

"Do you trust me?"

"Well, yeah. Of course, I trust you."

"Then trust me some more to work on her. To reason things through with her. I'll take full responsibility for your 'evil' behavior, Anna. So don't make me a fool in front of your mother. Will that work?"

"I suppose—"

"You'll get to see your friend play. Just wear whatever she wants you to wear to church. Who cares what those people think of your couture? But outside of church, to school, and wherever else you go, wear makeup. Wear dresses and fancy shoes."

"What about bringing my computer to my room? And a phone? I'm the only kid in school who doesn't have a phone!"

"I'll try to convince her that you need a phone for security purposes, you know, for emergencies and whatnot. As for a computer, I mean, I go through this with her. Dinkel's must maintain a web presence, plus I need it for the business, but she fought me *so hard* on this. Has a real mental block about it. I know she snoops. Checks my browsing history and whatnot."

"I've noticed. She trusts no one. Not even her own family."

"I know, honey. I know. I'll see what I can do on that bit, but no promises, I'm afraid."

They hugged for a long time.

"Sweetie, I've been thinking. If you learn the business, put in your three-thousand hours with me, I should have enough money saved, along with taking a loan, to open a second Dinkel's somewhere near here. Far enough away from home that you'd have complete independence, but close enough that we can all still help each other when needed. I can teach you everything, including the business end of it. Then if you want to get a degree on top of it, you'd be set. Unstoppable. An independent revenue-generating machine."

"Dad, I—"

He held up his hand. "Just planting a seed, baby doll. Maybe once you're out there competing in the corporate world, get yourself banged around, you'll realize what a good business this really is. Sort of like the Monopoly game when you land on those pesky railroads and utilities: they soak you for hundreds every time. So, while others focus on putting hotels on Boardwalk and Park Place, mortuary science is always here for you. It isn't glamorous, but it sure is steady. It's recession-proof, and it's Godly work, helping devastated families, keeping things a little bit orderly and sane for them during their worst times. Compare this work to the vicious corporate jungle. You go ahead and try that insane life if you want. Maybe you won't know what you had till it's gone. And hey—steady supply of customers. People are just—"

"Dying to get in here? Dad. You seriously need some new jokes."

He laughed. "*Need*, you say? Here's one: Need in one hand, shit in the other. Let me know which hand fills up fastest."

She laughed hard, and it felt good. She hugged him again. "Best dad in the world."

Anna ignored her mother's stare. Smiling, she trotted up the stairs, closed and locked her door, then padded over to the toy chest filled with dolls and teddy bears untouched in years, and slid it forward. She had carefully pried up the carpet from the wooden tack along the baseboard, hidden the device, then smoothed it back down. The charger she had hidden near her radio; she now plugged it into the device.

She found the power button and smiled when the screen brightened. The rest was intuitive. *Like it was meant to be.* She smiled as her fingers flew. First, she saved all the photos Naomi had emailed, then set up her Instagram account. The first thing she did was to look up Timmy's profile and also the SpaceJunk band page. Her heart beat faster. She followed both.

Within an hour, she had seventy followers, all guys, mostly strangers. She blocked all, went into settings, and made herself as difficult to find as possible. After choosing the top ten photos of herself in front of the fountain, she posted them. Then, on the band page, she watched videos, song after song. She applauded Timmy's performance.

"Anna, what's going on?"

"Nothing, Mom, just listening to really good new songs on Christian radio."

When she got to the video of Timmy by himself, holding an acoustic guitar, she stopped breathing.

"I started composing this song in class about a special little lady who earned me a detention the last day of school, which is where and when I finished it," he said, smiling into the camera. "She has no social media presence because I hear her parents party like it's 1722, so she'll probably never see this song. Was thinking of naming it 'Prison Blues,' but that was taken." He laughed nervously.

Anna's eyes and mouth opened wide. He started picking a D chord. His fingers moved—glided—without effort; eyes closed, face relaxed, he seamlessly plucked and strummed. Anna had never seen anything like this; someone she knew possessed such ability and talent. Mesmerized, she had to force herself to breathe when his singing started. She did not think it sounded like him, not at all like his speaking voice. *It's like a completely different person has moved into Timmy's body, a confident, mature adult, passion emanating in waves from every note.*

"Burning thoughts possess him, fervor and delirium obsess him; on and on he plans to show her that place in his heart, but she's only his secret love, she's only his secret love . . ."

Through space and time, Timmy bewildered and intoxicated her brain. Captivated, eyes transfixed to the screen, languid warmth seeped through her chest, then fluttered down deep in her belly—and lower still. Soulful sounds and words as he divulged himself; laid his soul bare to her; safe because he believed she would never find out. *Maybe secretly, he wants me to know*, she thought.

A bright beam of rational light shafted through seventeen years of darkness that had overshadowed her spirit and constrained her heart. It caused tingles throughout her body as that sweet, sultry voice—Timmy's voice—cried out *YES!* in affirmation.

"Anna! Bring your wash down and help me fold laundry!"

Anger. Bitter resentment.

Whispered resolutions.

CHAPTER FIVE

Execution

At seven o'clock Tuesday morning, on her back in bed, Anna studied dust motes floating lazily along sunbeams like water currents. She thought only of Timmy's alluring, fathomless eyes that seemed to search ethereal, empty spaces within her. Feeling no pressure, deadlines, or commitments, her brain loosened its grip, which freed her spirit to wander along like the dust. She allowed her thoughts to lead her wherever they whilst—to beautiful, exciting new places, and the familiar—through fresh new eyes.

She threw off her bedsheet, launching pink stuffed animals in sundry directions. Quietly, she padded barefoot to her secret hiding place; she brought the fully charged tablet back to bed. She pulled up Instagram; no new followers. *Patience is a virtue*, she thought. A friend acceptance from Naomi Silver, but still nothing from him. She opened SpaceJunk's page. Before returning to the videos, she clicked the Events tab.

There it was. Saturday night, nine o'clock, at a local tavern known to attract nationally known talent on occasion. *Nothing in Heaven, nor here on Earth, will stop me from going*; her lips formed soundless words. Promises she always kept to herself and others. This felt different somehow. *Not a promise. A declaration of war.*

Halfway through Timmy's song, "Only His Secret Love," she hit pause, overcome with a deluge of unfamiliar feelings, emotional and physical, so ardent and intoxicating that they startled her. She recalled a phrase: 'Childhood ends the moment you know you're going to die.' Raised in a home of the decomposing dead, she strongly doubted this philosophy. She pulled away and examined herself objectively; she suspected a life of artless innocence among the ceaseless rotation of rotting cadavers had led her to this moment.

Love animated her heart, and she would examine its innermost recesses with Timmy Caperila, she decided. She would dissever Anna Joy Dingel, the only child of David and Margaret Dingel, from the millstone these two had draped about her neck; distance the desires of her heart from these two people who had rolled up and hung on her all of their hopes and dreams for themselves—along with their fears, regrets, past mistakes, and guilt for sins she had not yet committed.

Tired of lugging around their baggage. It's my life, dammit. I'll be eighteen in three months.

Childhood had decidedly ended.

———

"Yeah, cousin. I'm gonna do it."

"Bruce, that's awesome, dude! Listen, summertime's best. Believe me; you don't wanna be doin' this shit in February. Maine winters are superbad. Like a special jet stream straight from the Arctic Circle or somethin', I swear. I've seen Northern Lights from here. Moose running around everywhere, bears in summer. They avoid us cause we're noisy with chain saws and big-ass trucks. One thing you need to buy is a shit-ton of 100-percent DEET."

"What's that?"

"Bug repellant. Go to the nearest-closest place that sells hunting shit, and buy gallons of it. Summer woods here are full of mosquitoes and black flies. Damned ferocious. Black flies have driven moose from the woods. If they can bite through moose hide, that tough shit, imagine what they'd do to your lily-white ass."

Bruce Barnette, unafraid of man or beast, still got the message. He knew his far tougher and more fearless felonious cousin's warning tone, subdued though it may be, meant serious harm if he failed to take him seriously. "Done. I'm on it. Anything else I should bring?"

"Leather gloves. Bring a shit-ton a-those, too. They wear through pretty quick in this line of work. You're still pumping iron, right?"

"You bet. I weigh two-twenty now. Benching three-fifty for a few reps, squatting five, deadlifting about the same."

"Damn, son! You'll fit in just fine here. Go buy a few Carhartt coveralls and waterproof work boots. Until sawdust builds up, for half the time, you're working in some muddy-ass terrain. Get a few pair, change 'em out every day 'cause they'll get slopped up and develop cracks for sure."

"Anything fun to do up there when not working?"

Laughter. "Yeah, sleep. This is hard work, buddy, ain't gonna lie to ya. You'll fill a suitcase with cash, more than any of your dumbass friends; but believe you me: you'll earn every shekel, that I promise. Sometimes me, Jonesy, and Clyde will drive down to Portland. There's some action there. And, hell, if you can't seduce it—rent it."

"Ha. Sounds really good, man. Thanks."

"When are you coming up?"

"Sunday. Start work Monday, if that's cool."

"Yep, that'll work. I'll let the foreman know. He'll be over the moon. We're down a man after a little accident last week."

"Accident?"

"Yeah, it was stupid. Rodenbaugh was topping a big one, needed pole spikes to climb up. All the guys learn the right ways to do things, but Rodey's a risk-taker, does stupid shit all the time. Didn't sink both spikes; tree top falls, branch hits him, his one spike can't take the full weight and energy, so he falls. But he has his lifeline holding him pretty close to the trunk as he goes down; dumbass hit every sharp, sliced branch nib with his crotch all the way down. Ripped off a testicle. We call him 'Wingnut' now." He laughed harder than Bruce would have liked.

"Wow! That sucks."

"Sucks for us. We're short a man until he heals up, which could be weeks. Can't get a straight answer out of him as to when he's coming back."

"He plans on coming back after *that*?"

"Hell yeah. Got a young wife and baby girl in a cabin, mouths open like two little birdies. Dude, the top ten percent of us will pocket fifty-two large this year."

"So, if I work as hard as you . . ."

"You'll earn thirteen grand. After gubmint takes its big wet bite out of your ass, you'll be ten thousand dollars wealthier in September than you are right now. Where else can a workin' man pocket that much coin in so short a time? If you know of a way, then cut me in."

"Wow."

"Listen, just follow procedure, and you'll be fine. There's a craft side to it, which you'll learn from me. Don't want some big-ass tree fallin' on me, or do a 'Rodey' and lose a ball for the trouble. Neither do you. I'll teach you how to avoid these little annoyances."

Bruce smiled. "Okay, cuz. I trust you. Listen, I mapped it out based on the coordinates you gave me, the parking lot at the mountain foothill."

"Yep, once you start smelling diesel and seeing crazy truck ruts, you'll know you've found us."

"Cool. Well, okay then. See you Monday."

"We have a cook. Food and beverages provided. You'll burn ten thousand calories a day, easy. Just go get that other shit, seriously."

"Will do. Later, cuz."

"Later."

———

"What are you doing Saturday night, Tamster?"

"Orgy with eleven offensive players from the local university football team, you?"

"Ha. That wouldn't be fair to them. Seriously, what?"

"Nothing."

"We're going to a bar with a live band."

"They'll card us."

"No, any age can come in if you pay the cover charge because of the live music. We'll go early, grab a table, and wait. Guys will come to us, buy us drinks. We won't get interrogated by the help on account of the money being spent on us by the gentlemen."

"They won't card us?"

"No! Been doing this for years, everywhere; New York, Paris, Milan, Madrid. Works the same wherever you go. Just look old enough, and sucker guys do it all for you."

Sigh. "Means I'll have to dress up."

"A little, Tamster, just a little. Throw on some makeup, a skirt, real shoes. I'd give you some of mine, but nothing will fit."

"Because you're a string bean, Suebedoo. Eat a hamburger once in a while, why don't you."

"I'm twelve pounds up, and it ain't muscle I gained. Model's daily diet during Fashion Week: one wheat biscuit, one cube of cheese, champagne, and as much nose candy as you can possibly stand."

"Get out. Are you serious? You never told me this."

"Yeppers, serious."

"Wow. That's super effed up."

"Yeah, well. One must suffer for Fashion. Seriously. That's our mantra."

"Not me. Comfortable Girl here. In fact, Saturday night's ensemble will be yellow drawstring sweatpants, commando of course, with a red hoodie and matching sneakers."

"I'll kill you."

"Ha. I'll try to clean up real nice for ya. Maybe I'll even get lucky. Who knows, some asshat with beer goggles might think I'm a runway model, too."

"They'd have to be like, Hubble Telescope-thick goggles."

"Bite me."

"You're not fashionable enough for that, dear."

———

"Sorry, can't come with . . . Saturday is Sabbath. But *you're* going! So awesome. What did the warden say?"

Instagramming with Naomi, Anna responded, "Band set starts at 9. My mother said no, of course, but my dad manned up and overrode her. One condition . . . I need to be back here by 11:30."

A pause of twenty seconds. "Not too shabby. Two hours of Timmy Caperila. I hope you remember all of Wendy's excellent makeup tips and plan to wear the dress and heels."

Anna replied with a smiley emoji and a thumbs-up. "How's the archae-ological thing coming?"

Immediately, "SO COOL. You don't even know. This discovery changes everything . . . my head is spinning. Will keep you posted."

"When I go to the bar, should I stand, or sit at a table, or sit on a bar stool?"

"Honey, if I were you, I'd sit or stand someplace where Timmy can see you even with stage lights blaring in his eyes."

Anna sent a heart emoji. "He wrote a song and told the world it was for me. I owe him a thank-you, at least."

Naomi replied with a wink face. "I know you will figure out a way."

"Anna! I need a hand!" boomed Dave Dingel's voice from ground level.

Anna sent a blushing-face emoji. "Okay, need to go help my dad."

"Just remember this . . . *always* leave them wanting more. Never seem too anxious. Make him wait a week if he asks you out. Be cool. Always be cool. I'm dead serious. Trust me?"

"I do. You're the bestest bestie. Byes!"

Alone with her fully powered tablet device, soon to be free of all encumbrances, she smiled at the prospect of spending her Thursday evening with Timmy, if only in her mind. She hoped time would pass quickly until she saw him in the flesh. She entwined the device's power cable with others to disguise it before she restored the tablet to its secret corner under the wall-to-wall carpeting. She unlocked her bedroom door, sprung eagerly out of the room, ignored her mother in the kitchen, and bounced down to the mortuary.

Bent over the face of a sixty-something slim female corpse, David Dingel put the finishing touches to the plain-looking face with his magic brush, the dyed copper hair already brushed and smoothed down, while the apprentices looked on. *They're bored*, Anna thought. *Forced to give Dad their compulsory attention.*

Taylor noticed her and looked over. She caught him quick-glancing her down and up.

"What's up? What do you need, Dad?"

Dave looked up, then at his two protégés. "Gents, give us a few minutes, please? Thanks." He set down his makeup brush and wiped his hands on his white coat. Taylor brushed his shoulder against Anna on his way out. *Deliberate*, she thought.

Alone with her, David smiled. "Anna, I may need your help with something important. Have a seat." She pulled up a rolling stool.

"Everything's important, every little detail. Something my daddy taught me. Give it up. What must the indentured servant do now?"

Laughing, he said, "Touché. Well, this has to do with money."

"Oh. Got it. What's up?"

Inhaling through his mouth, exhaling through his nose, he said, "There's a body in the Texas State Penitentiary at Huntsville, Texas. The family lives here in our county. I was recommended to them. Okay, great; work is work. Now, Texas law requires that all bodies held for over twenty-four hours or in transit must be embalmed, refrigerated, or encased in a leak- and odor-proof container. Which is fine; I have a container that will fit in the van."

"Why don't you just have it shipped?"

"Two reasons: One, the prison won't do it. This person was executed; a capital punishment case. They want the body out of there yesterday. I would have to pay another mortician near Huntsville to package the goods and arrange for the flight. We are talking about way more than double my costs alone. The family can afford to pay my standard fees, but not for all that."

Anna nodded. "So, how can I help?"

He pointed to the other two bodies. "As you can see, I have my hands full. Even with the two boys contributing what bits of labor they can while learning the trade, this current load will take two days, and the viewings are scheduled for a week from now. I can't spare the time to drive the van to Huntsville and make sure prison officials load the body properly in our container."

He leaned in close, eyes pleading. "Your mother is too weak to make a long trip on her own—not to mention she's the world's worst driver."

Anna laughed and nodded her agreement. "Yup. Yes, she actually is the world's worst. She'll drive twenty under the limit, and it'll take twice as long."

"And I need the guys here. I have no one else. Will you help me?"

She had known it was coming. The front of her brain accepted the situation, while the back—and every fiber of her being from the neck down—sang 'Only His Secret Love.'

"When would I need to leave? That trip will take a week."

"Saturday?"

Her face flushed. "Absolutely not, Dad. Saturday evening, I'm seeing my friend's band, remember?"

Dawning recognition. "Oh, yes. Yes, I see. Well, if I called the prison and told them you'll be there Tuesday morning, meaning you'd need to hit the road first thing Sunday morning, would that be okay?"

She had imagined many different episodes of the bar scene, each more compelling and romantic than the next. *What if tomorrow evening ends so well he asks me out for coffee or lunch Sunday? But my dad . . . Damn it! I would've executed this prisoner myself with my bare hands if they had asked me two weeks ago when the timing was convenient. As Naomi would say, "The struggle is real."*

Which made her think of Naomi's sage dating advice: *Be cool. Always be cool.* She recalled scenes of Naomi waving off the best-looking Jewish guys in school, forever attaching themselves to her like mosquitoes.

"Okay. Fine. Sunday it is. It'll be the first time I've missed Sunday service since I had the flu that time. Mom will not be pleased."

David Dingel beamed and hugged his daughter. He exhaled deeply. "You saved my bacon, kid," he said. He reached into his coat pocket and handed her an Android phone. "For emergencies only, and don't tell your mother! Hopefully, you won't ever need it. Tell you what: You pull this off for me, I'll give you a gift card for five hundred beans. Go buy more fancy clothes," he said and pressed his lips to her scalp, "Just keep it between us."

She pulled away, smiling, gave him a nod and a complicit wink, and cradled her new phone as if he had handed her the keys to a kingdom made of diamonds and gold.

———

"Sunday. Heading to Maine in the morning," said Bruce.

Carmen wondered if this was a bad dream. *He would abandon us for the entire summer?* "Who does that!" he said into his smartphone.

It came across as a non-sequitur. "Does what?"

"Uh, nothing. So, like, this is for big bucks?"

Slowly, it dawned on Carmen that, without Bruce, his life had no meaning. *He's our warlord, our leader, and our only cool friend in the world.* With no plans after graduation and losing Earl to the US Navy recruiter, the solemnity of Carmen's aimlessness closed around his heart like four blue glacial ice walls.

"Ten grand, buddy. You know what that means, don't you?"

"Um, what?"

"Means I'll be driving your asses to school in a 1969 Dodge Charger Daytona, candy-apple red, two-foot-tall rear wing, flush rear window, long sloped nose cone."

"You can't afford that. Those are like a hundred-fifty grand."

"Bet? This one's beat to shit. Body rust and dents I can take care of, easy. Seats are cherry, dash is clean. I'm buying it for the 426 Hemi engine. The rest just needs a little TLC. Then it'll be worth one-fifty. Some old guy needs to convert his stuff into cash to live. He wanted eighteen-five; I offered twenty, gave him a grand I had saved as a good-faith down-payment if he would take it off the market and wait till Labor Day for full payment. Which means that, as soon as I get back, I need to sell the Z/28. Yo, Carm, picture us pulling up with that 426 growler—*blatta-blatta-blatta-blatta*—like a major yacht docking. Every head will turn. You'll feel it in your balls; this thing will make your ass pucker. Bad-ass or what?"

Carmen could easily imagine its roaring motor making every head turn. *Bruce is a magician with cars, both bodywork and mechanical. But living in boredom for nearly three months, cruising around with Earl in dad's body-rusted Oldsmobile looking like two total pud-pullers: great. Just fuckin great. Thanks, Bruce.*

Bruce sensed it. "Carm. It's one summer. You and Earl carry on the egg raids. I want stories. Send me details."

"How can we ever possibly top egging the cop cars with them inside? Or the blind guy's seeing-eye dog?"

Bruce laughed. "I still say the best was nailing the beatbox, that block party in Fishtown."

Carmen sniggered. "Yeah, totally. When the eggs hit the DJ mixing board like mortars, sprayed his dreadlocks, and those douchebags on either side of them. Holy shit, man. The *faces*! Thank God for green lights all the way to I-76."

Chuckling. "At least fifty people wanted us dead."

Carmen laughed. "Not as much as the guy who chased us through two counties after I egged his wife, and Earl nailed his little daughter in the dress coming out of that church. I will never forget egg goo dripping off the wife's hair and that kid's Sunday dress *covered*; oh *man*, was that freakin' great." Now both laughed uncontrollably.

"Trying to forget that one. I figured for sure the cops would come to the parents' house the next day. Dude had to have gotten my license plate number."

"Tough to top those. But we'll do it. Starting tomorrow night. When are you leaving?"

"Sunday, I said."

"Oh, yeah, right. Well, what's say we do one last raid before you leave?"

Bruce hesitated. "You know what, I'm spinning into sober-land. Thinking my last night in town needs to include alcohol and music."

"They never card you. They always card us."

Bruce sighed. "I know. But I need this. I'm going to the tavern. Space-Junk's playing. D'Alessio's pretty good. Writes decent stuff. Heard 'em play a party once."

"Well . . . call us then, from the road. We'll top all raids. Any ideas?"

Bruce chuckled. "Actually . . ."

"Uh-oh. He's got a plan."

"Heh. Here's a challenge for ya. A dare, maybe. You guys drive to downtown West Chester, to Darlington Street; use Earl's car. Three-quarters down on the left, remember who lives in one of those row homes?"

"The crazy gun guy? The Desert Storm marine survival guy who sold you the AR-15?"

"Yep. Gunnery Sergeant Powell, the Little Green Killer. You know that if you pelt his windows, he'll come out onto the little porch armed. He likes shotguns for home defense. Hit his door, then his windows. Earl's better with stationary targets. You're best with moving targets, so you drive; have him locked and loaded in the back seat. The second he cracks open the door, Earl unloads at least two eggs. Be sure to hit the gun in his hand; that'll piss him off more than a body shot. Now, don't you hesitate. Stand on the accelerator, leave him in a rubber dust cloud so he can't get your plate. Up for it?"

Carmen hesitated. "If we pull this off, we win the biggest balls trophy. The most dangerous caper of our lives."

"Mm-hmm, indeed it is. He'll kill you, that guy. Little Green Killer, Advance Recon unit in Kuwait City. He walked around clearing buildings, shooting men dead like paper targets. He won't hesitate to cap your asses. Don't screw this up. I'd miss y'all too much."

Chortling. "Done. We'll sweeten his Mossberg 500 with hen fruit. Call you Sunday."

CHAPTER SIX

Spirits

"I don't like it. You look like a damned whore!"

"Marge! Stop! She does not!" said David with a hard glare at his wife. After a few seconds, he turned to Anna. She watched the diamond-hard rattlesnake expression soften; noticed a little of the rubicund flush had normalized.

"I think you did a great job, honey. You look just as beautiful now as you did after your makeover." He applauded loudly and wolf-whistled. Margie shot him a disapproving look, which he ignored despite knowing the consequences of his actions would involve a less than cordial evening at home. *I'll work straight through until she gets home*, he thought. *Kill two birds.*

"Now, be very careful. Bar politics are plenty different from real life, baby doll."

Margie said in her most condescending lecture tone, "Alcohol is from the devil. It makes men do horrible things to women and to each other. You're a pork chop walking into a wolf lair, and you're too young and dumb to even know it."

Anna turned red. "I am *not* dumb! You're rude! Just because maybe at some point in your life you did stupid things doesn't mean that it's genetic."

Margie, fuming, took two steps toward her daughter. Her husband's hand clamped down on her shoulder. She spun on him like a feral animal.

In his eyes, Anna saw a side to him completely foreign to her; a determination, decidedness, stubborn resolution had commingled with fire and fury rivaling front-line soldiers charging into battle. Anna glanced at her mother's profile; in it, she perceived surrender etched into its contours.

"As I was saying, you look fabulous, honey. Any problems, you call me. I don't care what's troubling you. No judgment, only immediate and enthusiastic assistance from someone who loves you more than life itself."

Call him, he said, she thought and made a mental inventory of the contents in her new small black Michael Kors Brooklyn leather satchel. *My new phone is at large somewhere inside, no doubt spooning with the keys to my ridiculously high-mileage used Toyota Celica that belches blue smoke and could die at any given moment, but hey, beats walking two miles in heels. Driver's license: check. Small sample of lip gloss and some cash: roger that. Okay, I think we're done here.* She turned and walked to the mud room.

"And be back by eleven-thirty. Don't make me come get you."

She smiled. "Thanks, Dad. I will. I mean, yes, I'll be back by then, and no, you won't need to come looking for me." David and Margie Dingel watched their baby clickety-clack out the door, united in the grim and sudden realization that their little girl was not entirely subject to their wills; not anymore. They beheld, for the first time, a young adult with her own mind.

She could no longer be contained.

"Eight o'clock. An hour early," Anna muttered to herself. She found a parking spot directly under a bright pole lamp, recently vacated. *Close as I can get to the door in case I need to make a run for it*, she thought. She locked the car and nearly tripped as the heel of her new shoe crunched over a stone in the lot. *This fashion crap will definitely take some getting used to. Stop feeling so nervous; you have no reason to feel this nervous.*

She felt more jittery than she had ever felt before. She glanced down. *Yes, girl, you are pretty put-together; as good as it's ever gonna get.* Fingernails matched toenails, which peeked through the black strappy Jimmy Choo heels. Wendy had done the fingernails, still pink from the Naomi Salvation Mission, as she had called it. She painted the toenails herself.

After walking seventy feet, she arrived at the door. Two large, mean-looking bouncers stood outside. She grinned at them as she walked a half-circle around them, aware of eyes burning through the bottom rear of her dress. Inside stood a hostess behind a podium, who appeared at least twelve years older than Anna, alongside another bouncer.

"I.D.?" said the hostess, nametag: Chloe.

"Um, sure," Anna said. She reached into her purse and handed over her license, which the bouncer snapped up and shined a penlight onto. Chloe glanced at the bouncer. He handed her a thin yellow strip.

"Hold out your right hand, please." Anna complied. She watched the woman peel off a white paper backing then close the plasticized yellow band around her thin wrist. "Know what this means, hon?"

Anna shook her head. "No, sorry. That if I go out to my car, I can come back in?"

Chloe grinned. "Well, that, yes. It also means you can't order alcohol. Don't even try. Servers don't bend. Sorry, State law. Now, I'll need eight dollars cover charge."

Anna counted out eight dollars and handed it over with a smile. "No worries. I don't drink. I'm only here to see the band. My friend plays guitar for them."

"Timmy? Oh yeah, mmmhm, he's a cutie, that one."

"If you don't mind me saying, ma'am, you look really good for some-one in her thirties."

Chloe's eyes narrowed. "I'm twenty-four." She snapped the cash out of Anna's hand with nicotine-stained fingers.

Anna took one hesitant step past the hostess stand and scanned the scene before her. To the left, a bar, mostly every stool occupied by older men, some dressed professionally with ties undone, others in dirty cover-alls. One gray-bearded man in a distressed brown leather biker vest with tassels.

All turned to stare as a novel sensation swept through her. *Am I Alice, about to disappear down a rabbit hole?*

Some returned to whatever conversations or thoughts they had going on before her entry. Others continued to stare. She saw only the back of one man, whose bearing seemed more her age. From behind, she observed him; he seemed familiar somehow. The bartender was an incredibly tall, well-built young man in his twenties (she guessed, probably with more accuracy this time), arms covered in unrecognizable tattoos, nonsensical like the graffiti applied to concrete abutments straddling the interstate. He glanced at her, then returned to his focused conversation with the younger patron she could swear she knew. *It's the hair*, she thought. *I know that hair. The only one who hasn't looked at me.*

To the right, booths lined two walls. Tables with chairs, some with seating for two, some four, occupied the center-right portion of the dark tavern. Historic drawings of the community lined the beige plaster walls. Neon beer lights, some red, some blue, some pink, and one green, illuminated each of the many windows. It was obvious to her that two or three hundred years ago, this place was some wealthy German settler's two-story home. Against the far wall was a stage, black plywood, elevated maybe one foot. She saw a drum kit, mics on stands, and amplifiers set up on it. A gang of multi-colored spotlights hung from the ceiling in a black metal trusswork, with only the brightest and whitest of them currently beaming onto the stage. All of the four-person tables were occupied with groups of friends and families, including some with little kids, to her surprise, as were the booths. Directly in front of the stage, flirty new couples occupied the two-person tables. Behind those, there was one small table recently vacated, empty beer mugs and crumpled napkins discordantly cast atop greasy-looking plates. She smiled and turned back.

"Um, Chloe? Did I say it right?"

Chewing gum, Chloe popped a tiny bubble, "Yah. What's up."

"May I sit at that table over there?" She pointed. "It looks empty."

"Yah, sure, kid. Someone will eventually clear it and wipe it down."

Excitement flowed through Anna as she made a beeline for the table, walking as quickly as her awkward footwear allowed. Again she felt people staring at her from every direction. She sat rigidly, knees pressed together, and primly rested her purse on her lap. She dared look left at all the faces and profiles of every stare-bear at the bar. The tall bartender was still conversing with the young man as he turned in her direction. *Bruce Barnette*, she recognized. *And look at that, why don't you*, she thought as she watched the bartender grab a bottle of well tequila and pour some into a small glass. He slid it between Bruce's folded hands, open to receive it. He casually secreted it between the bulk of his forearms to avoid detection. She watched him laugh. Almost every time she glanced over, she watched the bartender slide over shot glass after shot glass and watched the contents of each rapidly disappear down the seventeen-year-old's throat. She examined her yellow armband. *Well, if he can, why can't I?*

A bus girl came by, cloth over her arm, a large, round brown plastic tray in hand, onto which she relocated every utensil, plate, mug, and piece of detritus on the table before her at lightning speed, which impressed Anna. "Wow, you're fast!" she said.

Blank expression on the girl's face. 'Hah, thanks," she said as she sloppily wiped down the table with a moist cloth in three sweeping movements. Then she was gone, soon replaced by an attractive twentysomething, a big-chested and small-waisted blonde in a black T-shirt with the tavern's name in white. She handed Anna a menu. "What can I getcha?"

"Um, a Coke, please?"

"No food?"

"No, no thanks. I ate at home," Anna said and handed back the menu.

With a disgusted eye roll, she said, "Okay," and snatched it from her.

At an angle that afforded a clear line of sight to the stage about twelve feet to her right, also to the bar ahead and slightly left, and the left entrance, she did not know where to look as she waited for the show to start. Bruce Barnette slugging down illegal shots was something to talk about with Naomi, so she decided to analyze the interaction.

Why do so many girls at school find him so attractive? Good-looking face and body, sure, but mean. That whole thing with Frank Watson cinched it if the rumor is true. Just another loudmouthed bully flexing his muscles. Stupid girls confuse that insecure garbage with manliness. The real men are the confident, studious, quiet ones with goals in life, like Abe Jacobs. He'll be a doctor and save lives. And Timmy. He'll make the world a better place through music. What will Bruce do? He's peaking right now and is too stupid to recognize it.

The bartender had to do his job and serve another customer, which left Bruce unattended. She watched him down another shot. As he clacked down the little glass, he glanced right. His eyes met hers. She looked away, but she knew he was still staring. The bartender passed in front of him and stopped. After a brief lean-over to hear Bruce, who never took his eyes off her while speaking directly into his ear, he quickly squirted soda over a glass of ice, then spilled in a generous portion from a bottle he had pulled from underneath. Straw, lemon garnish: Done.

Oh no. Please, bartender-guy, go back to entertaining him, she thought, just as her server's slim hands slapped down a napkin and set a glass of bubbling brown liquid and small ice cubes atop the white paper square. The tiniest paper umbrella jutted up, and a slice of a lemon sat impaled over the lip. The server hustled away, passing Bruce Barnette as he moseyed toward Anna.

"Hi. Seat taken?" he asked, pointing at the chair opposite Anna.

Silence. He sat down anyway and snatched away Anna's Coke which was served in a pint glass. He replaced it with an identical pint glass. "Try this. Way nicer." She frowned at the glass, then over at Bruce. "I want to be alone. I'm only here for the band."

He smiled warmly. "Me too! D'Allessio's a friend of mine. C'mon, try it, you'll like it. I promise."

"What is it? Looks like another Coke."

"Seven and Coke."

"What's Seven?"

He smirked. "Whiskey."

"Alcohol?"

"Shh! Not so loud! In case you haven't noticed, you must be twenty-one to drink legally in this State."

"You're drinking like a fish over there."

Conspiratorial smile. "That's Matt, my friend. I get things for him, so he serves me. Win-win."

"Things?"

"Forget it. C'mon, taste it at least."

With reluctance on her face and in her body language, she reached over, took the glass, put the straw in her mouth, and sipped. Bruce watched. He smiled. "Good, right?"

She took another sip before setting down the glass. She deigned to give him one nod. "Drink up! Hi," he said and reached his right hand across the table. "My name's Bruce. I've never seen you here before. Are you new in town or something?"

She laughed. "Um, yeah, I know who you are, Bruce. The entire school knows. I sat two desks behind you to your right in health class last semester."

He frowned. She watched his puzzlement with great amusement. "Wait. The 'D' row. Dingel? *You're* Anna Dingel? The undertaker's daughter?"

Laughing hard, she nodded. "Yep!" She showed him perfectly straight white teeth, through thin, beautifully formed glossed lips, upturned at the corners. Her smile was radiant and exceptional, which she reserved in her mind for Timmy alone, but the irony of the situation—Bruce Barnette currently working overtime to charm her—rendered it impossible to contain her amusement.

"Holy *shit*! I mean—wow, Anna! You are absolutely gorgeous! How is it possible you and I never got to know each other?"

She took a long sip from the glass and set it down. She shook her head. "Because I was never your type, Bruce, and because you are exactly the inverse of my type."

In the quickness of a fired bullet, his expression changed. At once, she felt glad to be in a public place surrounded by people. "What type is that?" he growled.

"Nice. I only like nice, sweet guys. You know, as in gentlemen? So tell me," she said with alcohol-fueled overconfidence. "Is it true you pushed away Frank Watson in his hour of need?"

His face turned the color of a firetruck. "That's *crap*!" Several nearby patrons turned to look at him. "I don't know who started that rumor, but if I ever find out—"

"Thanks for the drink. Better hurry back before someone steals your stool."

"No one would dare," he said, tone agitated. As he leaped up, the heavy wooden chair scudded and nearly fell backward. "Hey, Dingelberry. You owe me for the drink," he snarled and stalked off. For just that one uncomfortable moment, she felt her blood pressure elevate. She had read enough true stories in the Bible, not to mention world history and some fiction, all of which aligned with her theory. She chalked this moment up to the oldest story of them all: *The unscrupulous taking cheerful advantage of the unwary. Thank you, Lord, for eyes that see and ears that hear.* She recited the Resurrection Prayer in silence.

She raised the glass to her lips and smiled as the languid warmth of liquid anesthetic coursed through her brain and body. The anticipation of seeing Timmy fluttered low in her belly as she removed the straw and chugged the glass down to naked ice.

I can honestly say that I have never felt this good in my life!

A man in his forties, dressed for business, approached Anna's table. "Using this other chair?"

Shaking her head, she said, "Nope. Please take it. I don't want anybody else trying to sit down and distract me." She thought the man was good-looking, shorter than Timmy but with a face that maybe might look a little bit like his in the far, far distant future.

He smiled. "I see. I was going to ask if you wanted to sit with my friends and me, but I suppose you'd rather be alone."

She looked at him. "Maybe later." Having figured out the game quickly, she anticipated correctly what he would say next. "Well, at least let me buy you a drink." He motioned toward the bar, and she held up her yellow-banded wrist. He snickered. "Let me rephrase: What are you drinking?"

"Seven and Coke."

He gave her a snakish grin, then slithered back to his seat. He flagged down the server, who took orders at his table and returned quickly with a full tray. He popped back over and switched out Anna's empty glass with a full one.

"I told her to tell Matt that he gets a bigger tip if he makes it extra strong. Enjoy," he said and handed it to her. She smiled back, giving him a thumbs-up. Immediately she sipped. Then, she gulped.

Oh, yes. Thanks, Matt. This hits the spot, she thought and belched through closed lips. Suddenly, the lighting changed from bright white to dim yellow. A short old man in a Hawaiian shirt and salmon-pink shorts grabbed the microphone.

"Everyone, thanks as always for making it one big happy family here at the tavern! If you dare, try the chef's special tonight—meatloaf with mashed potatoes, absolutely to die for—and don't forget to be generous with your servers working so hard to make this a wonderful evening for you! Now, without further ado, back again to grace us with their newest original songs destined to be hits, please give a warm tavern welcome to . . . SpaceJunk!"

Anna stood, knocked back her chair, applauded vigorously, and smiled until she felt her facial muscles begin to cramp. Someone behind her whistled so loud it hurt her ears; she glanced backward just in time to watch Sue Nastro and Tammy Goldsworth skulk into a vacated booth, and that neither got yellow-banded.

The drummer took up his position at his kit, doing a cool twirly thing with his drumsticks. The bass player, whom she recognized from the music videos but hardly ever saw around school, was even quieter and more invisible than she. Out from behind a curtain strode Timmy Caperila. He strapped on his Gibson Les Paul electric guitar. Her heart pumped out a fast four-four beat as the fully-formed band glanced at the audience, and 'Joda' introduced himself along with the band members. He spoke the name of their first number, into which the four musicians launched with great enthusiasm. All at once, Anna realized she was the only one in the table area still standing and clapping. Feeling a bit embarrassed, demurely, she sat.

Throughout the next forty-five minutes, chewing the ice of her third hand-delivered Seven and Coke, Anna enjoyed the music, tapping her foot and clapping. *Naomi was right. He can't see me past those bright lights in his eyes*, she thought. At fifty minutes past the hour, all lights went dark save for a single blue light focused on Timmy as he stood alone at the mic, in his hands a beat-up old Alvarez acoustic guitar. The room grew hushed.

Able to contain herself no longer, Anna stood. Timmy looked at her. She sensed a confused recognition on his face. She smiled and waved. "Go Timmy!"

He smiled. "Anna?" Her name reverberated around the room and made its way all the way to the corner, to the ears of Sue and Tammy. "There she is, oh my God, it's Anna Dingel!" Every eye in the tavern fell upon her. "You guys, this next song I'm about to perform, she inspired it! This is so crazy, oh man. I don't usually get nervous, but right now, I admit it: I'm a little nervous," he said through a self-conscious smile. At no time did he take his eyes off her. "Anna, this one's for you. Hope you like it."

Like in the video, bathed in blue, Timmy's fingers coaxed sweet and perfectly tuned notes up and down the worn old fretboard. At times he finger-picked, and once he used a metal slide to add Southern flavor to his gumbo of silky-smooth sounds. His eyes, closed during his instrumental lead-in, opened as he started to sing. Anna remained standing. She no longer cared that she was the only one and blocked some people's views.

The only times Timmy broke eye contact with her involved dexterous chord changes and difficult guitar transitions. Her hands remained pressed together over her chest.

She felt levitated in midair, completely weightless as she floated free in an ocean of silken warmth, syrupy and relaxed, yet simultaneously invigorated and aroused. Anna knew eyes bored into her from all around now. She felt this attention was perfectly natural—now she *deserved* to be noticed. She would never again feel stared at. It was as if the world now felt compelled to look upon her, like a wonder of the world.

All because of Timmy. He made it all so. In his eyes, I am something rare, and radiant, and special. Even when I was an ugly duckling.

Nothing else mattered.

As the song concluded, blue light gave way to harsh bright whites. Timmy held his guitar by the neck and waved it high above his right shoulder. He grinned his appreciation, and yet—despite strenuous and gut-felt applause, the loudest by far of the set—he never removed his eyes from Anna. Still holding his guitar, he stepped off the stage and over to her. He leaned in and brushed her mouth tenderly with his lips.

Her first kiss. When his tongue licked her lips, and she licked his tongue, the applause included foot-stomping and wolf-whistles. Her life forever changed there in full public display. He pressed his forehead against hers, eyes locked, and he said above the din, "I need to finish up. Can I see you tomorrow after church, maybe? Take you to lunch?"

Remembering Naomi's words, "Be cool. Always be cool," and the deal made with her dad, she said, "Maybe if you had accepted my Instagram follow request, we could have made plans. Sorry. Maybe some other time." She added a half-smile and a wink.

He closed his eyes and shook his head, but the grin never left his face. As he turned back to the stage, she shouted above the din, "Thanks for the song, Timmy!" and resumed applauding along with the crowd.

As SpaceJunk's set ended at eleven, she thought of driving to Texas, her heart an iron wrecking ball. She rose to leave. Timmy, helping his bandmates dismantle their equipment, kept watching as she walked slowly to the door. Everyone else watched her as well, as she was the only person leaving. She turned and gave him one last wave; she saw him stare at the bar as Bruce Barnette rose from his stool and stormed out behind her. Ten steps into the parking lot, she heard his amplified voice.

"Guys, I'll be right back."

"Dude, c'mon. Chase skirt later; we need to pack up."

"It's not about that," she heard Timmy growl. Anna stood under the bright sodium-vapor lamp, backed against her driver's door. Bruce towered over her, pressed up against her.

Bruce whispered into Anna's ear, then buried his face against her neck. Bruce's hand hiked up her dress and snaked underneath. Anna slapped him. Timmy launched into a full sprint. He ran straight into a powerful right fist to his eye, and he fell down. He shook off the intense, stinging pain and sprung up; he headbutted Bruce, wound up, and unleashed his most powerful right hook. Bruce moved just before face–fist connection; his rock-hard skull took the brunt of the kinetic energy. Timmy's knuckles broke audibly on impact. Seconds later, the two outside bouncers arrived and tackled Bruce Barnette with prejudice.

Anna barked a high, keening scream, then fell to her knees over Timmy, whose eyes were closed in pain, his face a grimace. She held him; told him everything would be okay.

Sue Nastro and Tammy Goldsworth stumbled and swayed outside just then, arms around each other. The wide backs of the bouncers obscured their view of the man they had on the ground, but they did recognize Anna and Timmy, who were obviously wounded.

The volume of their mocking laughter filled the humid and still night air, louder even than the police sirens moving closer.

CHAPTER SEVEN

Old Magic

"Stop talking about it; you're making me hungry. Still hours to go before I can eat lunch." Naomi spoke to Abe's handsome whiskered face on her computer monitor. "Yes, sure, pick me up at eleven. I'm always up for trying new Kosher restaurants, especially since my favorite closed. Yesterday at temple, I heard someone mention it, and it made me sad. No one knows why it closed or where she went."

Abe's face fell. "God knows how I loved Hamifgash. Best Romanian kebabs on the planet. Hummus, too. And shawarma. And shakshuka. And bourekas. No one did falafel and stuffed grape leaves like she did. Her baklava, not too sweet, with the pistachio sprinkles on top . . ."

"Stop, I said!" Her stomach rumbled. "I wonder what happened to her."

Abe shrugged. "She's from Tel Aviv, originally. Maybe she realized Philadelphia has turned sour. Some of our people on Sansom, the die-hards on Jeweler's Row, they'll stay to the bitter end. She's too nice. Not wired for daily warfare. It's why she left Israel originally; she told me once. Tired of the annual rocket launches from Gaza, sick of the politics. Also, she hated being poor, by our standards." He tittered. "She immigrated here seeking peace and to make her fortune."

"Pshaw. Philly allowed her neither. What a loss. Not only to her but to me and you."

"You could learn to cook like she does. I mean, it takes a special man to want to marry a computer hacker."

"Computer scientist, dopey."

"Yeah, whatever. I can't eat software. Make me the happiest man on earth: Go take your free Birthright Israel trip and learn her old-country recipes."

"Hm. Right after you enroll in tech school summer shop and learn how to repair cars, repair electric, plumbing, masonry, and carpentry. You can't even change a tire."

He laughed. "Clever girl."

"Cleverness beyond even a partial comprehension by mere mortals such as you, Abraham Jacobs. Speaking of which, see if your insectile brain can grasp this: The Dead Sea Scrolls included copies of every book of the Old Testament except for Nehemiah and Esther. And guess what? Very little had changed, meaning that the Hebrew Bible had been transmitted with incredible accuracy over a millennium."

"Got it. You know why Jews make the best lawyers? Because they keep crazy detailed records of everything."

Naomi nodded. "Yep. Ancient tribes painted their histories, like on the Cave of Altamira, in Spain. Egyptians wrote curses on tomb walls to prevent body thefts going back thousands of years. Ours isn't the only tribe good at documenting itself and our relationship with God. It's only just that, as his chosen people, we have always fostered envy and resentment wherever we wandered. Got ourselves kicked out of everywhere. Pagan rulers burned us out, including our libraries. So, knucklehead, anytime we find evidence of our history, it is a *really, really* big deal. *Huge.*"

"Right. Which is why you're obsessed with this big dig over at Solomon's mines, yes, I get that. But what is it that my mere mortal ass can't comprehend that your perfectly shaped, luscious, and perky little ass can?"

She grinned and blinked once at him. "The oldest biblical text is on the Hinnom Scrolls, two silver amulets that date to the seventh century BC, rolled-up pieces of silver they found in a series of burial caves at Ketef Hinnom, which they unrolled and translated."

"Seventh century. Pretty far back."

"Wait, further still. There are other ancient texts that allude to the Bible. The tenth-century BC Khirbet Qeiyafa ostracon is similar to Exodus, a Psalm, and Isaiah. The Elephantine "Passover" Papyrus, dating to 419 BC, references the instructions for keeping the Feast of Unleavened Bread found in Exodus. I'm only listing the oldest ones that contain clear sections of Scripture from the Hebrew Old Testament."

"Interesting. I feel ya."

"And other excavations where writing was found support the case for the Bible's accuracy because it meant that, three thousand years ago, the Israelites could record events and transmit the history that was compiled like the Bible several hundred years later. But these tablets they just dug up date back to the time of Abraham, two thousand years BC. Think about it! Some Israelite in the time of Solomon took a lot of care and trouble to find the most secure spot to bury these tablets, already by then a thousand years old, to protect them. Protect them from what? Protect them from whom? Israel was a major power then."

"Yep. This we already know. Now, blow my mind. Blow something, for God's sake."

"Blasphemer!" she said, smiling. "So then, smart guy, riddle me this: How is it possible for the name of the Nazarene—a Jew who wouldn't come along and get Himself crucified until two-thousand years later—end up carved onto one of these tablets?"

———

"So glad you learned how to Web-meet, honey! I can see and hear you! Can you see me?" said Naomi.

"Yes," said Anna.

"The real question is, where the hell are you? That's not your bedroom."

"Motel room somewhere in Tennessee. I saw signs for Chattanooga, but who knows? Had to stop driving. I've heard about hangovers but never experienced one until today. God, I am so tired."

"*What?*"

She nodded. "On my way to Huntsville, Texas. Left later than I needed to this morning due to a very long night."

"Wait. First, why are you going to Texas?"

"To pick up some stiff executed by the State."

"Oh. Lovely. Daddy-o couldn't spring for a box and a few postage stamps?"

Anna smiled weakly. "Long story."

"So, are you ever going tell me what happened last night with Timmy?"

Anna related the story from the scene in the kitchen, where she was told she looked like a 'damned whore,' to the Coke and whiskeys and her first kiss. Naomi's face burst suddenly into pure, triumphant elation. "My work here is done! Wow! Okay you *have to* tell me, not that you have any baseline to compare against, but . . . is Timmy a good kisser?"

Anna nodded. "It was the single greatest moment of my life."

Naomi studied her. "But . . ."

"But then everything went bad—no, terrible, a complete disaster—snap!—in an instant."

She took Naomi through the sexual assault in the parking lot, then Timmy's brave defense, which cost the guitarist a busted-up, now completely useless hand and one very black eye. The bouncers, police taking everyone's statements, and her father showing up at midnight.

"The bouncers had to restrain my father. I think he would have killed Bruce if not for them. I mean it. Seriously. I have never seen him like that . . . he was like, like a wild animal. My *dad*, Naomi. You know him. He's been one way my entire life: Mr. Calm-Cool-Collected. Of course, later, when we got home, my mother smirked and said, 'Tried to warn you. Told you so.' I am so over her."

"Oh. Dear. God. Are you serious? You're not joking?"

"Do I *look* like I am? I should be over the moon right now. They called an ambulance for Timmy. I heard the crunch of bone-on-bone when he punched Bruce's face. He was so incredibly brave."

"God. He's a guitarist."

Anna's face fell. She started to cry.

"Hey! C'mon, bud. He'll heal. Have you spoken to him?"

She shook her head. "I don't even have his phone number."

Naomi was speechless. Anna sobbed nonstop.

"Sorry, but I have to ask because I am so fucking pissed off right now that I can't even find the right words. Tell me this: Where is Bruce Barnette right now?"

Blowing her nose first, she said, "Jail. He's charged with aggravated indecent assault, a second-degree felony. I heard the State Police trooper telling my father he'll likely plead to a misdemeanor charge of the first degree."

"Because he pushed you against your car, and you loudly protested, tried to push him away, and he went ahead and stuck his finger inside you."

Anna nodded and started crying again.

"Yup. That's sexual assault. Boy's in deep shit. Witnesses?"

Anna nodded. "Tavern employees, the bouncers. They are more than willing to testify. Timmy also."

"Oh, he must be out of his mind pissed-off."

Sniffling, Anna nodded. She coughed and took a swig of spring water from a bottle. "The trooper ran his record. No violent priors. He thinks Bruce will spend the summer at the County Correctional Facility, and the judge will let him finish out high school. My dad was about to blow a few holes through him with his .357 Magnum until the two huge bodyguards held him back. This all happened in front of the cops. They checked to make sure he had a concealed-carry permit and talked him down."

"Uh-huh. Bruce Barnette should be executed like the toe-tagger you're about to haul from Texas. Hanged by the neck until dead. Electric chair. Give him the ol' cyanide gas."

Anna nodded and laughed a little. "Wish I could find the words to describe how amazing I felt last night, up until that animal had to go and ruin it. Timmy told everyone his song was written for me. He was beyond shocked to see me there, totally unexpected."

"And, girlfriend, I know you were looking *so* good."

Anna smiled. "Evidently. I had guys buying me drinks and staring at me. Nothing like that has ever happened to me. Young, old, in between. They couldn't take their eyes off me."

Naomi grinned. "I didn't just turn a caterpillar into a butterfly. I turned it into the hottest girl in town—besides me, of course," she said.

Dramatically she blew on her fingernails and polished them on her blouse. "I have the magic in me."

Anna laughed. "Yes, honestly, you do. It felt like I was floating. When he kissed me, I felt things I had never felt before."

"You mean your underwear got a little wet?"

Anna blushed. "Well, yeah. That, for sure. But . . . I mean, I think maybe I felt the beginnings of true love. Is that even possible?"

In a measured way, Naomi said, "Mm-hm, yes. Very possible. It happened fast with me and Abe. But, remember what I told you—"

"Be cool. Always be cool."

"Right! Good! That's right. Always be cool. Leave him wanting more. Don't put your true feelings in words. Make him understand with your body. Actions are green-lighted; words are few and sparing. Be aloof, be reticent. It'll drive him nutso trying to get verbal assurance of your singular devoted affection. Guys want to own us. If they could, they'd piss on us to mark their territory.

Laughter. "Wow. You really have this all figured out."

She nodded. "Yup. Sure do. Abe's the best guy. I love the stupid lug. I really, truly do."

"He loves you back?"

"Oh my gawd, honey. Nuts over me. We'll be true to each other. Jews like us would never marry outside the faith. When it's right, it's right; and with us, it is. We'll get through what we must, school and careers, and we'll do it all together, like a married couple."

"I'm so happy for you two. At the risk of sounding uncool, I kinda-sorta wish something like that might happen to me and Timmy. I've had a crush on him since, like, forever. Until the song, I had no idea he felt this way for me."

"Remember, babe, he had a crush on you back when you were Comfortable Girl, with your giant ear blackheads and bird's nest hair, and jeans washed so many times they were white and frayed. And those ridiculous Converse sneakers and your James Fenimore Cooper log cabin shirts. I mean, who the hell even wears all that? A homeless man wouldn't even look twice at you."

"Gee, thanks. You're all heart."

Naomi grinned. "Actually, what I am is highly logical and pragmatic. I'm a sophisticated, AI-controlled cybernetic organism with a decent face and body."

Anna laughed. "Well, you're my bestie-bot. Love you to death, girl."

Naomi, grinning, interlocked her two index fingers. Anna held up her hands, doing the same. "Besties."

"So. What's next with Timmy Caperila and Anna Dingel? What and when will be the next chapter?"

Anna shrugged. "I really wish I was there to comfort him instead of hungover in a really crappy motel room on my way to pick up a bad lady's leftovers."

"Ew. Yeah, I'll bet."

"After we sign off, I'll check Instagram. I'd told him about trying to follow him, which was right after you gave me the tablet. He still hasn't followed back."

"He's not like you, Anna-banana. He doesn't sit in his room reading American pioneer literature and American history books for fun. Kid has himself something of a real life going on. Maybe he has groupies satisfying all of his manly needs."

"Seriously? You think?"

Naomi laughed. "Uh, no. Joking! Joking. I think I'm a pretty fair judge of character, and I'm here to tell you that boy is a virgin. Pure as the driven snow."

"How do you know? I mean . . . how can you be so sure?"

"When a man is 'in the saddle,'" she said, making quotation marks in the air, "he develops a sort of thousand-yard stare. A swagger, a bounce in his step. His entire bearing changes. Stands straighter. Acts like he doesn't have a care in the world. Your boy ain't that, girlfriend. He's really cute, super-talented, and has a bright future ahead of him, and you guys are the same religion, I assume?"

"I think he might be Catholic."

"Oh boy. Mother Mary help us, or something like that. Well, you're both in the same stadium, which is good. Not worlds apart. Honey, he's been saving himself for you. Seventeen years of pent-up, raging hormones and sexual fantasies just brewing, simmering day and night. Do you think that, if he were there with you right now, you'd toss a spark on that gaso-line, see what happens?"

She grinned and shrugged. "Dunno. Maybe. But pretty sure I'd sleep through most of it."

"Liar! Liar-liar, I can always tell when you're not being completely honest."

"Maybe, I said. I'm not really in touch with that side of myself. I'd never drunk alcohol before last night. Are you supposed to wake up with a headache, sour stomach, and light hurts your eyes a little? A dry mouth that tastes like roadkill?"

Naomi laughed. "Yup. Which is why I rarely touch the stuff. Only maybe a glass of champagne at someone's wedding, that's about it. And that side of yourself, mmhmm, trust me; you're about to be inseparable from your passionate, romantic self. Once Timmy unleashes your inner beast, there ain't no goin' back to life BT."

"Life BT?"

"Before Timmy. Speaking of religion, I have a question for you about all that. Has to do with the little research project I'm doing for fun."

"The ancient Jewish tablets."

"Yup, the tablets. So, my question to you is, what do Christians believe Yeshua of Nazareth really was? A prophet with magic power? God Himself? What, exactly?"

"Okay, wow. Talk about a hard-right turn doing sixty-five."

Naomi laughed. "I know. Trust me; you'll have many hours to dream dreams no mortal ever dared to dream before of you and Timmy Caperila running naked through the daisies together. So, what was He to you?"

"Like most Christians, I believe there is only one God, who is experi-enced as three persons, also known as the Trinity. Three distinct spirits all come from the Father, including the Son, who is Yeshua, also called the living Word of God; then there's the Holy Spirit. You've never asked me about this before. What's this got to do with your rock tablets?"

Naomi smiled. "So, in your mind, God, the same God I worship, obtained the consent of a teenaged Jewish virgin to implant his, uh, godly DNA into her, which resulted in her birthing a being that was in every aspect human, but also divine. When the Romans executed Him—"

"Jews set that up. Romans merely did the deed."

"Mmm, yeah, okay. I'm sure Marge would never let me forget it. Afterward, Yeshua, being a human but also possessing unimaginable power, according to your beliefs, rebooted Himself back as a human, at least for a while, to prove to His loyal followers that He truly is from God. Also, before all that, it is alleged that He restored dead people back to life. Dead for a few days, one of them."

"If He didn't actually restore Lazarus, then why, after the murder of Jesus, did the Pharisees in charge come seeking Lazarus and his sisters and family, to erase all witnesses and kill Lazarus a second time?"

"Hm. Interesting. And what is this Holy Spirit?"

"Counsellor, early converts called it. It was sent here to us by God, same as Yeshua. I've heard it described as the little voice inside your head or dream weaver at night. It causes feelings, or physical signs, to help guide believers. I don't know how to explain it. Like, a guardian angel, maybe. Why, are you jealous that the Little Voices speak only to me?"

Naomi laughed. "Yup. That's it! Now, last question about this: I've heard of faith healers among Christians. Laying on of hands, speaking in tongues, snake-handlers. Sounds pretty far-fetched and weird to me. But do these people believe that invoking the name of Yeshua can heal people? Or restore life to the dead?"

"Ah, well. Sort of. Not restore life to the dead; dead is dead. But only because Christians today lack the true faith of early Christians, that first wave of eyewitnesses. Back then, they had the Spirit burning inside them without limit. But some believe today that invoking Yeshua can heal the sick, cast out demons and stuff, yes. I fact-check this as true."

"That it works?"

"No, only that people believe that it works. I don't really know if it works or not. But we're meant to believe without seeing, right? Faith."

"Hm. Maybe there's a way that we can find out if it works."

"What?"

Naomi shook her head. "Nothing. Just me thinking out loud. The tablets are like—my obsession lately. Can't stop dwelling on them. How many hours of driving left tomorrow?"

"Twelve, probably."

"Ugh. That's a long week. You gonna be okay there, Anna-banana?"

She hesitated, then nodded. "I think so, Naomi-baloney. If mister fingerpicker ever accepts my friend invitation, I will for sure." She smiled.

"Ahhhhh! That smile's worth more than words, girl. For sure, Timmy Hot-Lips has *the* biggest crush on you, girl. All is right with the world. All you need to think about."

"Gonna go check Instagram. Thanks, bestie. Enjoy your tablets and the tongue of Abe Jacobs."

"Tss. Oh, yes. Later gator."

Anna fell asleep quickly. She dreamed nightmare scenes, disjointed. She saw herself running from something through unrecognizable woodlands, which then quickly changed to her father's mortuary. She lay upon the stainless-steel embalming tabletop, naked and still. Every abomination from Hell—eyeless freaks, pallid horrors—lurched stiffly in a circle around her as if in some perverse Maypole dance of the damned. Taylor, her father's apprentice, she recognized among them, although only his face and white coat, which hung open, as did his abdomen, where intestines spilled out like blue and purple snakes on the smooth tile floor. A covetous grin appeared carved into the meat of his face. *Cadaver eyes*, she recognized; that familiar hazy film formed over his eyeballs postmortem, which made them appear gray.

Taylor took one step forward and out of the unhallowed circle toward her. Closer now. The Taylor-thing stood at the end of the table, at her feet. Poking up and out through the disemboweled mess, she saw an erect member pointed at her with urgent interest and singularity of purpose, baptized with blood and gore but unmistakable.

No! Dear God, no . . .

CHAPTER EIGHT

Tetragrammaton

"Took your good old time getting here."

"Sorry, Bruce. The process to get on your Approved Visitors list was a bitch. They took our pictures and charged us five bucks apiece for these badges," Carmen said. Both he and Earl pressed these up to the plexiglass. "Ran background checks. But we're here. And we have fifteen minutes— that's all they gave us this first visit. If you're a model inmate, they'll give us an hour next time. How's it going in there?"

With a glance left then right, Bruce said, "Caperila and Dingel—" and made a throat-slice motion with his right forefinger. He pushed the same finger to his lips. Carmen and Earl nodded their understanding. "Someone is listening to every word, reading all mail. I'm going to speak in code. If you don't understand my words now, you two discuss it later. It'll make sense."

Looking at each other, then back at Bruce, they both nodded.

"Stiffs house. Color of my Z. Only the Dead Live Here, and BB Says You're Next. Use rocks, not eggs. Kristallnacht. Cars, everything. Don't return here until mission accomplished. Don't get caught."

Each nodded his assent. Earl leaned close. "Did anyone get to you? You know. What they say happens in here?"

A large black prison guard tapped Earl on the shoulder. "Rules state no discussion with inmates about prison affairs."

Earl looked at Bruce. "Forget I asked. What's your exact out day so we can plan a party?"

Bruce gave the August date. "It'll be a Saturday morning. And to answer your first question," he said, fists balled, "these guards are worthless pieces of shit. My tax dollars at work. By the end of the first day, my asshole got ripped and bled while these maggots didn't do shit!" he screamed. "I gotta get out of here!" He lowered his voice. Remember your mission. Pay those Dingelberries back!" He pushed away from the security glass and turned toward the prison staff. "When I get out, I'm paying back each one of these useless, good-for-nothing screws; bet your mothers' lives on that! You hear me, screws?"

Two guards immediately arrived behind him, cuffed him, and dragged him out of the visitor's center. "Complete the mission!" echoed through the cinderblock room, then they heard him no longer.

—— — ——

"To Jews, a name is not merely an arbitrary designation or pleasant combination of sounds. The name conveys the nature and essence of the thing named. It represents the history and reputation of that which is named."

Walking through Valley Forge Park, on the paved trail along Route 23, Abe squeezed Naomi's hand. "Do I seem like an Abraham to you? Like our brave and faithful Patriarch, and like our President who preserved the Union and freed the slaves?"

"You seem like Abe Lickersnatch, a porn star name I just made up, most of the time," she said. He tittered. She read from the browser open on her phone. "The most important of God's Names is the four-letter Name represented by the Hebrew letters Yod-Heh-Vav-Heh—YHVH. The Tetragrammaton; The Ineffable Name, the Unutterable Name, or the Distinctive Name. In scripture, this Name is used whenever it goes into God's relationship with human beings and when emphasizing His qualities of lovingkindness and mercy. It is frequently shortened to Yah, Yahu, or Yeho." She searched his face. "Mostly what I hear said in temple sounds like Yahweh."

"Me too."

"Sometimes Elohim or Eloha, El, Eloha, Elohai. And yet, Yeshua—Jesus—is the one name written on the ancient tablets carved by Jewish mystics thousands of years before His birth."

71

"Yeah, that is strange.

"You bet it's strange. Beyond strange."

"Any doubt the tablets are four thousand years old?"

Naomi shook her head. "Nope. Archaeologists worked with lab scientists to carbon-date the tablets. And, too, they tested samples of every material surrounding the tablets buried along with them inside this little time capsule. Also, language analysts have pored over the writing style. Paleo-Hebrew, for sure."

"Have they posted images yet?"

"Yup, sure have. Which reminds me—something Anna told me. A passage from the Sefer Yetzirah, which may have been written two-hundred years before the Nazarene, reads, 'First, is the Spirit of the Living God, blessed and more than blessed be the name of the Living God of Ages. The Holy Spirit is his Voice, his Spirit, and his Word.'

Naomi explained to Abe what Anna had taught her. "They believe God is a Trinity of distinct personalities, including the Father; and the Son, who is also called the Word of God; and the Holy Spirit, which I take to be the part of God choosing to make its home in some people. Weird, huh? That ancient Jews understood the One God has distinct parts all made of the same stuff? Consubstantial was the word she used. Centuries before the man they claim was the Christ made the scene."

"Huh. Weird for sure. So, what do the tablets show?"

"Bits not seen until thousands of years later, words and sentences you later see in the Sefer Yetzira, written by Jewish mystics relatively recently."

"You mean Kabbalists?"

She shook her head. "Before them, but long after these tablets were carved."

"So, they've translated it?"

"Some of it." She pulled up a website. "Like this: 'There is no distinction between God and a righteous person who has no sins, and just as God created the world, so can the righteous. He hath formed, weighed, transmuted, composed, and created with these twenty-two letters every living being, and every soul yet uncreated. Twenty-two letters are formed by the voice, impressed on the air, and audibly uttered in five situations:

in the throat as guttural sounds; in the palate as palatals; by the tongue as linguals; through the teeth as dentals; and by the lips as labial sounds.'

"Abe, the writing on the tablets from the time of Abraham aligns almost letter-for-letter with the Sefer Yetzira. Abraham was said to have created a golem. Some believe that Abraham studied God's teachings and wrote the Sefer Yetzirah. He studied with Shem, son of Noah, and tradition holds that he created souls with this knowledge."

"I think what you're saying is that maybe Abraham really did learn supernatural practices from God, which, in fragments, made their way down through the wormhole of time."

Naomi stopped walking. She looked straight at him. "Yes."

"Making people out of dust or raising the dead. Real people, with souls."

She nodded.

"So then why hasn't someone over the course of, oh, say, the past four thousand years successfully made a person? Or raised the dead?"

"Maybe, Abe, they were using the wrong name for God. Suspend disbelief for just a moment: Suppose there is truth to the Nazarene's reputation of raising Himself or others from the dead; truth to the claim that He was sent from God. If you were Abraham, or a rabbi disciple of Abraham at the time—if you were given a glimpse of the future of our people—in the ceremony, what name for God would you use?"

"Yod-Heh-Vav-Heh?"

She shook her head. "What name was carved in the tablet after 'There is no distinction between God and a righteous person who has no sins, and just as God created the world, so can the righteous? Supposedly, Rava created a man, a golem, using some combination of these twenty-two letters to create every living being and every soul yet uncreated?' Give you one guess."

"Yeshua?"

She nodded. "Yeshua. Who Christians believe is a part of God."

Abe uttered a soft explosion sound in the back of his throat and gestured that his mind was blown. "Speaking of, how is Anna-banana?"

They resumed walking. "She'll be okay. I think she and Timmy make a dreamy match."

"You're a regular shadchanim for goyim."

She laughed. "That's me, matchmaker extraordinaire. Seriously though, she needs to worry about Bruce Barnette. He attacked her and got locked up for it. No doubt he'll be sitting in some of the same classes as Anna this fall. He's emotionally unstable and super pissed-off. Guys like him never learn from mistakes; they only make worse ones. His species compounds their sins until they end up dead or lifers in prison getting 'Born To Lose' tattoos on their knuckles. We all know the type. What are you pointing at?"

"The open door leading into a very dark, private, lonely little log hut replica over there. Let's go check it out," he answered with a smirk.

She shook her head. "What if kids exploring the park suddenly show up?"

"You would deny my American historical curiosity?"

"What do you plan on finding inside? Ghosts of soldiers from The American Revolution?"

"Hm. Maybe. They can watch. I plan on you placing your hands flat against the logs as you bend over at a forty-five-degree angle. I will kneel behind you with my head up your skirt in a sort of Revolutionary War seance. And when you can take no more of that, I might just bump your head against the logs a little."

"You really are a piece of work, Abraham Jacobs."

"Well, all this talk about restoring life to the dead has reanimated my dead bird, thus making this little side trip an imperative," he said as he pulled her toward the structure. She giggled and smiled, then surrendered.

Standing aside the open rear doors of her van at the loading dock of Texas State Penitentiary, Anna wondered if skydiving into an active volcano might feel cooler. "Hey there, little miss: What are the internal dimensions of the transfer case? And what's it made of?"

"Twenty and a quarter, by seventy-four point five, by eleven point three seven five. Uses a channel gasket in the lid and is hermetically sealed with screws. Twenty-gauge zinc-coated steel construction. I have a Phillips screwdriver if you need it. Happy?"

The prison guard looked her up and down, laughed a little, nodded, then scribbled in his notebook. He unclipped a walkie-talkie from his thick brown leather belt; speaking into it, he repeated what Anna had just said. After about fifteen seconds, she heard the word 'clear.' He looked at her and nodded.

"Miss, you are by far the youngest and prettiest body-snatcher ever to pull up to this dock, and as for me, been here twenty years."

She smiled. "Thanks. So, tell me: What did this chick do to end up in my container? Since we'll become best friends riding together for the next two days, I feel like I should get to know her a little."

A huge toothy smile suddenly animated his stern, clean-shaven black face. "Well, first of all, this here little lady," he said, jabbing his left thumb over his left shoulder, "was convicted in the murder and robbery of an eighty-year-old man in his home. Probably near about your age when she did the dirty. Sat on Death Row for twenty-three years and eleven months until her final appeal got squashed. Governor got tired of her file crossin' his desk, photos of the butchered old guy in his face."

"Butchered? How, exactly?"

He cast a glance back at his three younger colleagues. They nodded. He turned back to Anna. "I mean, she really did a number on him. Frail old guy, they found him with defensive wounds on his hands and arms. Helpless as he was, this bitch laid into him like a dervish. Stabbed him nearly sixty times with a paring knife, a butcher knife, a grapefruit knife, and a fork. She also whacked his head with a hammer and shoved a foot-long lamp pole more than eight inches down his throat. Still alive, he lay there bleedin' out and suffocating. Before he passed, she sliced off his ears and nose. Poor old guy felt every bit of that."

Anna's mouth opened in horror. "God forgive us."

"Mmhmm, my thoughts exactly, miss. And you know, maybe the worst part is, she was an exceptionally attractive young lady. If she had chosen a different path, that little darlin' would've made someone a trophy wife, pumpin' out little trophy babies. Everything's a decision."

She nodded. "From the moment our eyes open in the delivery room until God closes them one last time, everything we do is our choice. Something my dad drilled into me since I was a kid."

"Ha. You're still a kid. And your daddy sounds like a wise man. Okay, she's screwed in. Do us a favor and stand over there," he said, pointing to the driver's side door, "give us some elbow room. We'll load her. Then you two can get acquainted. After you sign right here."

"How did she die?"

"'lectric chair. Old Sparky. She rode the lightnin'."

"They still do that here? I thought Texas switched to lethal injection."

"The state shut down Old Sparky 'cept for the condemned whose capital crimes happened prior to March 31, 1998; also when they choose death by electrocution rather than death by lethal injection, or if lethal injection is declared unconstitutional by a court. She was grandfathered into the old method."

"What was it like for her at the end?"

"Your need to know, right?"

"More or less." She smiled charmingly, "I really appreciate it, Officer . . ."

The guard, flattered, chuckled and shifted his weight. "Lieutenant Austin Randall," he replied. "Everyone just calls me Rand."

She reached up. His hand swallowed hers in a gentle two-pump. "Good to meet you, Rand; Anna. And yeah, I'm really curious about how a pretty lady could end up like this. Seems a bit extreme. Nor cruel and unusual punishments inflicted: Constitution, Amendment Eight, and all that."

He nodded. "You can decide if the state's squeeze fit her juice. They brought her over last Monday mornin' from the Mountain View Unit; that's where they keep Death Row women. So we dusted off Sparky, searched her body cavities, kept her in a cell directly across from the execution chamber. She had all day to stare at her fate. Come six o'clock, we stripped her, packed her ass with a few dozen tampons so she wouldn't shit herself so that we'd all have to smell it; redressed her, shaved the top of her head, wet the sponge with saline for a good solid connection, strapped her in, then lit her up. She fought the current, that I can tell you. Tough kill. Bled out of her eyes a little. At least she didn't vomit like many do. She had turned down her last meal. The ladies always do, for some reason."

Tendrils of fear arced up and down her spine. She fought it and shook her head. "My dad's not going to like the shaved scalp bit."

"Why not?"

"He's an embalmer who likes working with natural hair. He's going to have to find hair roughly the same color, like a wig-maker, and glue it on or something. Might even have to dye the whole head so that the glued bit matches. I just know he won't like it."

"Sorry about that, miss. I don't think the young lady in the box liked it all that much either." He handed over his clipboard and pen. Cargo loaded, sheet signed, Anna opened her window to wave. She saw in the driver-side mirror four hands waving.

"They were nice," she said to herself. Air conditioner on full blast, she flipped through radio stations seeking one that came in clear. "This place sucks," she muttered and gave up trying, forced to settle for the Firestone Symphony of rubber meeting highway, the engine, and fan-forced air. The combination made her drowsy, fast. She reached back and rapped on the metal container. "Hey there, killah-chick. Let's have us a talk, shall we? Great! I'll begin. My name is Anna Joy Dingel. I'm eighteen years old. Well, that's not true: I'm about to turn eighteen this fall. And I think I'm in love. What's he like, you ask? Oh, well, let me tell you. He's tall and thin with bulges in all the right places. Long wavy brown hair and wide-set brown eyes. And wow, what an amazing kisser! It's like everything roiling away inside him, a fortune in feelings and passion he can only express two ways. First, through his music—which is *so* unbelievably good, by the way. The other is with his tongue, which I have tasted, and oh girl, did it taste good! Better than all the chocolate in Belgium. Better than all the vanilla in Madagascar. You feelin' me there, Crispy Mary?

Annoyed by radio signal fading to static as miles wore on, she switched off the radio. She thought of the container behind her. *What went through her mind in that final hour? That body back there is all she had in this world. Strangers poking stuff up her ass: God, how humiliating! Strapped into that chair, knowing she'd never stand again. Did she think of Heaven and Hell, what might come next? Did that disgusting-hideous murder scene loop in her mind? Did she beg the Lord for forgiveness while she still could? Or did she see Satan, big fat red grin on his face, arms wide open? All those amps and volts inside her! Must've felt kinda like being roasted alive. . . .*"

She made a left turn and heard a thump behind her, then another. And another. *What the hell was that?* Unusually alarmed, harried mind spinning in novel new directions, she pulled over. She reached for the Phillips screwdriver, grabbed the plastic handle, and froze. *Anna, what are you doing? You know it's only just a vacated shell back there. Dead means dead. Ain't no coming back from dead.* Though she chalked it up to sounds from a tired old transmission, of this, she wasn't so sure.

"Might as well stay at the same crappy motel. The devil you know is better than the devil you don't, right?" She pulled into the same drab, rundown, dusty lot somewhere in Tennessee. "Be right back!" She rapped on the van three times. "I'd bring you along to the lobby for check-in for security reasons, but now that I think of it, who on earth would want to steal you?"

Form filled out, cash handed over, key in hand, back at the van, Anna removed her knapsack of clothes and toiletry items and locked the white van with 'Dingel Funeral Home' in blue lettering. The color blue always reminded her of death, even when glowing prettily among Christmas light strings. She rapped thrice, bidding goodnight to the lone occupant, and entered her new room, an exact copy of her old room except for two doors farther down to the left.

"Mm. Love the smell of mildew when I'm trying to sleep!" She kicked off her sneakers, pulled down the bedclothes, and sat on the sheets, as per her father's warning that bedspreads are microorganism breeding grounds. She opened her knapsack and fired up the forbidden tablet, relieved to find she had a strong Wi-Fi connection. One email from Naomi, with a selfie of her and Abe in front of one of the Valley Forge National Park log huts, a naughty smirk adorning each of their faces. No message, but a subject line: 'Public Sex Revolution.'

Laughing, she shook her head. Finally, she dared to open Instagram.

And there it was. A little heart. She clicked on it. Timmy Caperila. She balled up her fists and shook them before her, "*Yessss! Yesssssss!*" She clicked on his name, opened his profile, clicked Message, and wrote the first thing on her mind. 'Greetings from Tennessee!'

Setting the PC on the nightstand, she went into the bathroom and took a long, hot shower. The older model showerhead flowed fast and jetted hard; she allowed the water to relax the muscles of her neck and shoulders, knotted and tense from driving for well over a full day. *Dad's not paying for this water. Think I'll stay in here as long as I like until I use up all the hot water in the whole place.* Fifty-one minutes later, a towel wrapped around her; she jumped into bed, turned off the light, lay on her back, closed her eyes, and imagined Timmy's response to her message. *'Anna, I want you. Anna, I need you. Won't you give your love to me?'*

Having teased herself into a preposterous frenzy, she opened her eyes and grabbed the device, which came awake as she did. Instagram opened where she'd left it, on Timmy's page. Her eyes widened. A return message indicator dot. The tablet slipped out of her hands as she scrambled to finger it open. Back in control, she took a deep breath and opened the message.

First, a ten-digit phone number. Then: Call home asap. Barnette had someone trash your dad's funeral home.

CHAPTER NINE

Necro

A single scoop of peace swept like a cool blessing through her all-consuming hot tension as she guided the van along familiar roads, almost home, with the mandarin orange sunset behind. Her father's business came into view, her cherished home since birth.

Her gut knotted. Where they weren't shattered completely, fist-sized holes had been punched through every window on both stories; car windows cracked and useless. Bloodred painted words across the white siding dripped down in places. 'Only The Dead Live Here and BB Says U R Next.'

She pulled into the driveway, maneuvered the van into park, and killed the engine. Unable to move, she sat and wept . . . for her childhood home, for all the memories within, most of them sweet. She wiped her eyes on her shirt collar, pulled the key from the ignition, flung open the van door, and rushed to the kitchen entrance. She found her parents at the kitchen table, file folders spread out on top. Her father was on the phone, talking about business insurance versus homeowner's insurance.

Then she noticed the enormous purple bruise around her father's eye.

"Mom! Come here!" she whispered loudly, motioning with her hand while stepping backward. Together, back in the mudroom, Anna spoke in low tones. "Mom, what happened to Dad? His face?"

Margie made the mocking 'tssht' sound of disapproval. Anna suddenly realized how much she hated that awful, degrading noise. "It didn't take Scotland Yard to figure out who 'BB' was, now, did it?"

"Bruce Barnette."

Margie nodded. "Your father drove over to the boy's house to confront his parents. No sooner had he gotten the first words across, standing there on the front stoop, that the father launched a ham-handed sucker punch to your dad's face. Back in the car, he called the State Police. They arrested the father. Simple assault charges pending, or some such. Meanwhile, your father's attorney is all over this, planning this lawsuit and that lawsuit."

"Mom, do they think they know who destroyed our home?"

"Oh yes, they know. The Barnette kid's friends, Carmen and Earl. They did it."

"How do they know?"

"The bank across the street from us is loaded with security cameras, even in the cash machine. The police watched them do it from every angle."

"So, what's happened to them?"

"Arrested. Two insurance appraisers were already out. Our property damage is in excess of ten thousand dollars. Felony in the third degree. These boys could get up to seven years in jail and fines up to fifteen thousand dollars. But the State Police think that because it's a first offense—and also the District Attorney is soft on kids—these miscreants will return to school this semester. Same with the Barnette boy. All three of these young devils will end up with the same light sentence."

"Wow. That's great. I mean, great that they caught them and that they'll be punished, as in life-ruining punishment, with a permanent criminal record following them around. Barnette will have the sex crime label, but . . . I wish he'd gone away for seven years."

"You could be spending your senior year passing all three of these reprobates in the hallways and lunchroom. Your father suggested the idea of sending you to a prep school for your final year."

"*What?* No!" she screamed. Margie motioned with her hand to keep it down. Anna was not about to admit the reason why that move could never happen. "I'll be okay, Mom. They wouldn't dare try hurting me in public. Are we covered? I mean, will insurance take care of all this?"

"Your father thinks so. He's working it out now."

Anna toed the manufactured tile under her sneakered foot. "Well, mission accomplished. I have the body in the van."

"Go let the interns know. They'll carry it down."

"Then I need to eat something, like, right away. Starving."

"We ordered pizza. There's still half a veggie flatbread pie left. I could warm it up for you."

"Don't bother. I'll eat it cold."

She trudged down the steps to the mortuary and wondered about the fall semester. *What will I say when I see these cretins? What will I do? Take back hallways . . . slink around like a mouse avoiding a barn cat?* As she entered the embalming room, Grant and Taylor stopped what they were doing and stood at stiff attention. When they saw it was only Anna, they visibly relaxed and smiled. Both waved at the same time, which struck her as funny.

"You guys are here late."

Taylor responded. "Yeah, well, we were waiting for you, actually. Mr. Dingel said you would arrive this evening with a little gift."

"Hah, right. If you want to call it that. Your next customer awaits you upstairs in the van." She handed the key fob to Taylor, who took it and made sure to touch her palm with his fingertips, looking intensely at her eyes as he did. "Well, allrighty then. What condition is the customer in, do you know?"

"A little bald on top. Blood leaked from her eyes, and she has a butt full of tampons. Might be a little crispy. Died in the Texas electric chair. A real charmer, she was. A great listener, I'll give that much. Anyway, enjoy. I need to feed."

———

"Hello?"

"Timmy? It's me."

"Who is 'me'?"

"Anna."

Silence. "Oh my God! Anna! Sorry, sorry, I didn't recognize the number."

"Note to self: He receives many calls from girls at night."

He laughed. "Yep, that's it exactly. Wait. Which Anna are you? I juggle so many."

"Well, I'm the one you got detention over, the last day of school before break, and then the one you kissed at the tavern and whose honor you nobly defended in the parking lot. Seriously, Timmy, that was the bravest act I have ever seen. He has about a hundred pounds on you, yet you didn't even hesitate. I'm just sorry you got injured."

She heard him exhale through a closed mouth. "Yeah. Me too. I can't play guitar. I'm glad you called because it sucks to type into the little message window. Besides, I love hearing your voice."

"Really? What do you love about my voice?"

"Well, there's an answer for that." He laughed—nervously? "It's kind of a music-geek answer. The pitch range for men's voices typically runs somewhere between sixty and one hundred eighty hertz. The pitch range of women's voices falls between one hundred sixty and three hundred hertz. I'm thinking yours is around one-twenty."

"So, you're saying I sound like a man? And that's good because secretly you like men?"

Laughter again. "Stop, you're killing me. Okay, put it this way. Along with your timbre, which is slightly on the nasally end of things, your pitch makes you sound more grown up. Like a real woman."

"As opposed to a really fake woman."

"I should just shut up."

She giggled. "The only voice that matters here is yours. It's gold, Timmy—pure gold. I love listening to you sing."

"Well, if you'll let me take you to lunch this Saturday, I'll give you lots of Timmy-voice. Nobody else will be listening to it for at least the next month."

"Geez. That long?"

"According to the docs, yeppers. I'll miss four SpaceJunk shows over decking that jerk—worth it, by the way."

"Such a wonderful evening he ruined. For what he did to us, I want Bruce Barnette gone, forever."

"As in life in prison?"

"Umm, more like . . . the other kind of forever."

"Yeah. We need a witch to put a maloik on him."

She blinked. "A what?"

"A curse; a hex. The evil eye. My grandfather from Italy taught me about the dark side of the spirit world. Listen, it wasn't a total ruin. I mean, here we are, just a man asking a woman out on a date, and she's not accepting . . ."

To the soundtrack of Naomi's trusted advice playing—'actions, not words'—she shoved aside noisy years of messaging from her mother and from the pulpit that pre-marital sex is a grievous sin. "Accepted! Where are you taking me?"

"Your choice. You get to drive us—because I'm not allowed to operate heavy machinery with my hand in a cast. You could drive us to the Chinese buffet, which I can afford, or allow me to make us a picnic lunch, and we take it to this really cool spot I know."

"Hm," she said. She struggled to tamp down waves of electric excitement. She pretended to be caught up in an authentic decision process. "A picnic sounds nice. Can I bring anything?"

"Actually, yes. McGonigle tossed your note back at you, which is why I didn't have your phone number. I wanted to call you and let you know when and where we were playing."

"Thought you'd forgotten me. Besides, I didn't have my own number. My dad would've answered. Awkward!"

"Forget you? Never happen. Anyway, if you could bring that note, great. Let's see if I remember what it said: If your band plays near here before my curfew of eleven, text me, I'll come."

Giggles. "Why do you want it? I might still have it."

"Oh, I'm a *total* scrapbooker. Hah, obviously. Who knows, maybe one day in the far-far distant future, I'll show it to our kids and say, 'This is how your mother and I first came together.'"

Laugher. "I had to make the first move. You're not exactly the pushy type."

"Well, I . . . well, no. I guess I'm not a brave guy."

"Timmy. What you did for me after the show is the definition of brave. You're just not . . . showy about it. That's exactly what I love most about you. Dumb girls in school chase the loud, obnoxious guys; they confuse flirtatious and pushy with masculine. I'm not dumb, in case you haven't noticed. You are the manliest man in that school. You put your inner self out there for the world to accept or reject, which takes real courage. And you're smart and talented. Don't ever change."

A pregnant pause. "I want to know you better, Anna. Always have. I mean, with that basso voice of yours, if you could only grow a five o'clock shadow and hairy chest, you'd be my dream girl."

She laughed so loud that her mother screamed up the stairs. "Oh geez. I disturbed the beast. My mother. Anyway, message me your address; I'll pick you up there Saturday at eleven-thirty, then bring you back here super-quick to meet my folks. My mother's a real Bible-banging Baptist, so she might ask a few questions about what church you attend."

"St. Paul's RCC."

"I don't know which is worse to her: Catholics or devil-worshippers. Just slide past it and say, 'I will go to any church that welcomes me because I love Christ more than I love my life, ma'am,' or some such. She'll back off."

"Wow. Thanks for the tip. Sounds like a trip, your mom. Are you like her, with all that?"

"God, no. Any congregation devoted to Christ is fine by me. I really don't care about the differences. But I thought all rock-n-rollers were devil-worshippers."

"I did, too, until I stopped drinking blood and sacrificing virgin high school girls to Baphomet. I wanted to be the world's first Christian pagan musician."

Laughter so loud, this time, it brought a knock on her bedroom door.

"Gotta go, pick you up Saturday, bye!"

———

"That little bitch."

"Wait . . . who? What's up?"

"Open up Instagram."

"Done."

"Enter: Anna Joy Dingel."

"Wow!" said Tammy, genuinely astonished. "Same hot-girl outfit she wore to the tavern that night. Great dress. Boobs are super small, but her waist is so tiny it doesn't seem to matter. Great ass, hips, and legs, like, super-slim. I could break her in half with one tackle. Built like a twelve-year-old girl, she is."

"You see those shoes? Those cost about six-hundred bucks. I have a closet full of Louboutins and Blahniks and Choos—I damned well know what they cost. I'm the only one in a fifty square-mile radius who wears proper fashion—and looks awesome doing it."

"Hmph. Not anymore, Suebeedoo. She looks freakin' hot."

"Tammy. Listen to yourself. You think she's anywhere close to my level? For real?"

Hesitation. "Judging from these pics, I'd have to say our little Christcunt is running a close second. Definitely, a tie if you saw yourself that night tossing your cookies by the car."

"Shut up. You're the one who dared me to do shots."

"Yeah, whatever. So, what's the problem?"

"What's the—are you kidding me? She stole Bruce from me!"

"Wait. Because he followed her outside and tried to rape her in the parking lot and went to jail for it, you call that stealing? She's all-in on Timmy Caperila. A blind fool can see that."

"She's the reason he's in jail. And did you hear Carmen and Earl got sent there too? Each got the same sentence as Bruce."

"No? Holy crap, what'd they do?"

"They defended Bruce by trashing that haunted house."

"Wow. Sucks."

"She's the cause of all this."

"I don't see how—"

"Shut up. You know she is. And I'm going to get some payback."

"What are you gonna do, slice her tires? How well did that work out for you last time? Sue, the guy dumped you, then tried to rape a girl. Forget him. Word to the wise."

"Whatever. Hey, does your mom still have that awesome digital camera with the telephoto lens for bird pics?"

"Ah, yeah. Why?"

"Because I have an idea."

———

"I can't pay you time-and-a-half or anything, Taylor. We're working on low margins this year."

"That's okay, Mr. Dingel; I'm not asking for more than straight rate for the overtime. I want to help. If I quit around one in the morning, between now and then, I can make headway with this new one. Go be with your family. You guys have been through hell this week. Grant said he'll be here normal time in the morning. I might be an hour or so late tomorrow, just to catch some extra z's."

He clasped a hand down on the younger man's shoulder. "Good man. You'll go far in this business with that kind of worth ethic."

He smiled and waved as Dingel closed the door, waited until he heard the familiar creak of wooden kitchen floorboards above.

Taylor unzipped the plastic body bag to a whiff of decomposition. *Not bad. I've smelled a whole lot worse.* It took him three minutes to wrestle the nude body into position on the mortuary table. He placed the head in the plastic mold and saw the bald spot. *Not insurmountable, maybe seven-point-six centimeters in diameter. Beautiful long hair, except for that. Hell, I can just give her a haircut and repurpose it over the spot; perfect match.* He stretched her limbs, then stood at her feet to take in the view.

"Beautiful," he told her. The facial muscles seemed locked in a strained position. He had never seen this before, as all muscles, including involuntary, always relax completely at the moment of death. *Poor girl. You died hard.* He moved behind her head and massaged her face to work the muscles back into a relaxed state. He stared at her chest, flat stomach, and light brown pubic mound. He leaned down to massage the breasts, heft and knead, to pinch the sallow, unresponsive nipples. The stomach felt firm underneath the smooth skin. He paused to hold his ear against the door. Satisfied all was quiet up there in Dingel-World, he moved down to the feet to play with and rotate each toe. He pressed his nose to each foot pad and inhaled deeply. *Mmm.* He pried apart the legs and massaged the silken inner thighs. He pressed his nose over the pudenda and inhaled. *Oh, girl, you are fresh.* Fully aroused, he removed his coat, pants, and finally, his tighty-whities.

Taylor Rydell climbed atop the corpse and penetrated it vigorously. Eyes locked onto the spiritless face, he kissed the blue lips and thrust fast and hard. Sweat dripped onto her ashy blue-white face. After five minutes, he let go—climaxed hard—mindful not to groan too loudly.

Two rapid light knocks on the door, then it opened, "Taylor, I left my folder—"

Both men froze. Dingel launched at him. He clapped both hands onto Taylor's ears and ripped him off the table down to the tiled floor. He shifted nearly his full weight to his foot and pressed down against the intern's gurgling neck. For the briefest moment, an image of himself grabbing a scalpel and opening the man's jugular flashed into his brain.

Then, words from the last nightmare scene crossed his mind: Deviant sexual assault. It had been one of the State Troopers who said it. He decided in a split-second what his next course of action would be. Reaching into his pocket, he entered 911, pressed the green phone icon, and held it to his ear, voice strained. "Connect me with the State Police. David Dingel, yes, funeral director, yes. Abuse of corpse. Yes, I'm holding the suspect under citizen's arrest. Yes, okay." He waited a moment, listening to the operator on the line, and then ended the call.

"Mr. Rydell, abuse of a corpse is a misdemeanor in the second degree here in Pennsylvania. You're looking at two years in a room with no doors. I will officially blackball you from every mortuary science school and from my profession. I'd ask you if it was worth it, but I'm not lifting my foot from your neck until the police arrive to take you away to face the rest of your accursed, sick life. Fight me, and I'll claim self-defense for whatever follows."

"Dad, what's going o—"

"Honey, go upstairs and wait for the police. Send them down when they arrive."

"Oh my God," Anna screeched through hands over her mouth. She understood at a glance what was happening. "Oh my God—oh my God," she muttered. An unwanted thought blobbed up like a lava lamp: She recalled herself on the interns' first day, wondering what Taylor looked like naked from the waist down. *Now I know*, she thought and fought to push the remembrance back down into its hole. "Oh God, I think I'm going to throw up." She turned and ran upstairs, almost knocking down Margie, who was on her way downstairs. "Mom, do *not* go down there. Come with me." She clamped a hand around her mother's arm and pulled.

CHAPTER TEN

Maidenhood

"My dad can't catch a break."

Timmy shook his head. "Such a nice guy, too. What is it they say, nice guys finish last?"

"Actually, I've heard it said that the nicest guy gets the girl." She turned to look at him. Their eyes locked.

"Hey, watch the road," he said. Anna hit the brakes hard to an abrupt stop a foot from the pick-up truck in front that had suddenly slowed down for no apparent reason. Anna smacked her horn and stuck her middle finger out the driver's window. She glanced in her rearview mirror; the driver of a blue Ford Mustang also had to brake hard to avoid hitting her.

"I'd like to snap that finger off and shove it up his nose. Guy nearly causes a three-car pileup. Asshole could've killed me!"

Timmy laughed. "Interesting look. Full-time nose-picker."

Laughter. He reached over, pressed his left index finger into her ear, and wiggled it. She cringed away and laughed harder. "Well," he said, "I suppose a dead girl is a cheap date, at least there's that. Never talks back, always says yes, no guilt trips if you forget an anniversary. I should look into it. Can I have her number?"

"Stop, I can't," Anna managed to choke out through raucous laughter.

"Slow down; the entrance will be on your left, easy to miss."

"How do you even know about this place? I mean, nobody's ever heard of this."

"My cubmaster knew about it. He took us hiking here one time. Said it's the best-kept secret in the area. Privately owned, but the owners died years ago, and so the land is caught in some kind of legal limbo; a bunch of lawyers year after year try to figure out how somebody can make money off selling it to a developer. I like to come here and enjoy the unspoiled, private beauty while I still can. The general public doesn't know about it. The exact spot I'm taking you is where I brought my acoustic guitar and picked out the melody for 'Only His Secret Love.' It's an inspiring spot. I always imagined you there with me."

Anna smiled, reached over, and brushed his cheek with the back of her index finger. "You shaved. For me?"

He blushed. "Well, yeah. Kind of. I mean, if you were to kiss me like you did at the tavern, I wouldn't want your tender skin to get brush-burned."

"Wait. *I* kissed *you* at the tavern? You frenched me in front of an audience, Chester Molester."

He nodded, unsmiling eyes on the road. "And I wouldn't swap that moment for a record deal and national tour. Eyes on the road, I said! Look, there it is, ahead on the left—see that metal barrier? That's it. Park anywhere in front of that; we'll get out here and hike in."

He discovered that lugging the Igloo plastic cooler in his uninjured left hand felt awkward, used to carrying loads with his right. The coordination now required by the seldom-used left side of his body felt entirely foreign, and it showed. She carried the thick white cotton-acrylic king-size bed comforter, rolled up tightly and tied with twine, which he supplied. Walking at his pace, they crossed a large flat gravel area, which both assumed had been a house or structure at one time long ago. Now, enormous weeds grew up through the stones. "Life finding its way, Earth reclaiming what men had temporarily borrowed from her," Timmy said.

"You're a deep thinker, Caperila, I'll give you that."

The relentless July sun had baked the ground hard; this midday, it bore down on them like a pyroclastic cloud. High humidity caused Anna's floral print summer dress to cling in unexpected places from sweat. Her white flats with embroidered flowers felt slick inside. Timmy wiped stinging drips from his eyes with his casted right hand. Both blew jets of air before them, attempting to disperse small clouds of gnats attracted to their salty perspiration. A path entrance appeared at the edge of a thickly wooded area. Under the canopy of trees, the ambient temperature suddenly dropped from the nineties to the upper seventies in the shade.

"So quiet here," she said. She thought of her life, of the incessant noise that comes with being part of a society that quiets at night but never completely. Here, all she heard were the sounds of their footfalls, tweeting birds, and the distant burbling of water over mossy rocks. "And no bugs!"

Timmy turned halfway back, on his face a righteous grin as he spoke over his shoulder. "Told ya. Our own little private slice of Paradise." She followed him another ninety yards along the wooded path until he slowed. The source of the sound presented itself to her.

"Timmy, wow. Never had any idea there was something this beautiful so close to home."

"Few do. If not for Scouting, I would never have known."

Looking around, she said, "What if a troop shows up and spoils our private picnic?"

He smiled. "I checked every Troop website in the County. No hikes planned."

He set the cooler down atop two thick exposed tree roots. Branches overhead formed a dense canopy over a fifteen-foot-wide natural rock pool, kept full by an artesian spring. Water flowed gently from the pool into a narrow stream percolating eastward; she followed it with her eyes as it wound stealthily about in mazy courses until it was lost from view. The pool lay at the foot of a rock overhang twenty-five feet high. Forest understory shielded the dark pool from all but a few anemic leaf-filtered sunbeams.

"So beautiful. Really perfect. How deep do you think it is?"

"Hm. Good question. A couple of feet at least."

"Think anything lives in it?"

"Oh, I imagine so, yes. Crayfish and minnows, sunfish, a few turtles. Eels and leeches. Maybe a great white shark. Let's find out!" he said. Suddenly he scooped her against him, lifted and carried her to the water's edge, his face a sardonic smirk.

She pretend-pounded her fists against his back. "Stop! Put me down—big dumb animal!" she yelled, laughing. Several birds noisily took flight. He did, pressed an affectionate kiss to her forehead, then awkwardly used his left hand to untie the comforter. She helped him lay it against the leafy ground all the way to the pool's edge. He swung the Igloo to the left corner, slipped off his sneakers, and left them on the roots where the cooler was. Anna handed him her flats. He opened the cooler and withdrew two plastic water bottles. He handed one to Anna: both chugged greedily after the quarter-mile hike.

From the cooler, he removed the picnic lunch. Sandwiches, plastic utensils, napkins, foil condiment packets, paper salt-and-pepper packets, and plastic containers of potato salad, cole slaw, and pickled beets.

She smiled. "Looks like you thought of everything! Did you put all this together yourself?" She looked at him with one raised eyebrow. Just then, her stomach made a goinging, boinging sound. She laughed. He smiled.

"Well, mostly. My mom makes the best salads and slaw; that much is hers. But I made the sandwiches. Not knowing what you like, I made two egg salad, two ham and cheese, two BLTs, two Lebanon bologna sandwiches, and two falafel and hummus wraps."

"Impressive, wow! Actually, I'm vegan, so if you don't mind," she said, lying down and propping her head with her elbow, "I would love a veggie wrap." He handed her one of the plastic-encased wraps on a thick paper plate with a napkin and took one for himself. "Wait, are you vegan, too?"

He smiled. "I am today." He lay down across from her, salad containers between them. They ate their meal in silence and listened to the hushing influence in the water's flow, lulled by soft sounds, together at last, safe within the protection and serenity of their private piece of Heaven. Perspiration dried; heartbeats slowed.

The spirit of inevitability overcame her in due course, and in that knowledge, she realized that there would be room for none other in her heart. Gazing into the depths of his consecrated eyes, she thought only of them—and of him.

"Only His Secret Love," the lyrics and music looped inside of her by day, and sometimes, even in nocturnal dreams. *He poured out his whole soul in tears at my feet, with the entire world as witness, advertising and forever enshrining his heart's most private yearning, bowing down at my footstool without a struggle, in the most ardent, in the most abject worship of adoration. Me! Fugly little Snaggle. He saw what nobody else could.*

Her head felt like an upstairs room after a fresh sea breeze had blown in on a hot and horribly muggy afternoon. A marvelous, helpless joy filled her. She saw it reflected in his eyes.

"Put your hands on me, Timmy."

She noticed the hairs on his arms stir and tried to stand up. A single shaft of light outlined her in spectral radiance where she lay. With his injured right hand, he swept the picnic remnants away from the soft white space between them. He wormed closer, face now inches from hers. He pressed his lips against her mouth, eyes half open. With his casted hand against the back of her neck, he pulled more of himself into her. She stroked his hair, then explored his body with her hands. The reality of his taut arms, chest, and shoulder muscles exceeded all of her fantasies. She felt and tasted him with all of the madness in her soul.

Her fingertips traced the contours of his manhood, hot and urgent, straining the zipper of his blue jeans. As he pulled back, his fevered eyes met hers. He grinned. "Something I have always dreamed about doing with you." She sensed a form of ecstasy rise within him, suffused in a glow of wonder and happiness. He offered her his left hand; she clasped it in hers and squeezed it fiercely.

Both of his hands gently pressed her shoulders flat against the comforter. He kissed her front as he went all the way down. "Raise your hips for me." She did, and he pushed up her dress. With his left hand and teeth, he slid her light blue underwear down her legs to her ankles, where she kicked them off. Both laughed when they landed in the black rock water pool. "Guess you're spending the rest of your Saturday commando." His big brown eyes smiled kindly, a dichotomy to the lupine appetite written into the rest of his visage and the urgency manifested in his crotch. As he gazed down at his long-anticipated meal, he licked his lips.

About what would happen next, she had no doubt.

She closed her eyes, on her face, a peaceful smile. She gave herself over to the solemnity of the moment, to the intimacy, and to this new world of pleasurable sensations she had never known existed. The word 'orgasm' had always remained merely a concept, something she was aware happened to people but never once to her, given her mother's effective guilt sermons about the evils of masturbation. Deep tingles, electric and poignant, steadily increased until her body reached a point of no return. She exhaled through tightly-pursed lips. With her right hand, she grabbed his thick hair and pulled him against her tighter, trapping him with greedy urgency.

White pinpoints of light, red explosions behind her eyelids, thighs involuntarily clamped vicelike around Timmy's face getting battered and smothered with her hip undulations. She squeezed his hand. Surging power, which seemed to go on for nearly a full minute. When all tension had fled her body, her thighs fell away to either side of him. Adrift in the warm sea of love that now elated her heart, she opened her eyes half-mast. The triumphantly grinning wolf stared up at her, his face one inch above her most private door. She smiled, big and bright, teeth as white as sun-bleached desert bone.

He could take it no longer and released her hand. He stood between her legs. She watched, at peace and with rapt interest, as he pulled off his tee shirt, wriggled out of his jeans, and at the same time, his boxer briefs. Eyes widened as she beheld the enormously fat, long, strident serpent pointed at her with great interest. A flicker of fear illuminated her face, and he noticed. "It's okay," he said. He bent down and retrieved a little foil square from his rear right pocket. "Be prepared. Scout motto." He ripped open the foil with his teeth, spat aside the little metallic strip, then tossed down the remaining square. She watched him completely encase his rebarbative organ. She never took his eyes off it as he knelt between her legs and pushed both knees against her chest. With a playful preamble of a few ownership taps to her engorged parts, he pinned her wrists above her head, flat-licked her chest—and then plunged deep inside her. She gasped at the entirely novel, momentarily painful, then incredibly wonderful new sensation. Low guttural sounds escaped both throats until her sounds commutated to a high, breathless whistle, sometimes descending to a bass roar before glissading up to a whooping scream.

Tammy stepped on a medium-size branch, snapping it in two with a crack so loud that birds took flight. "Shh! I told you to be quiet, you fucking rhino!" whispered Sue. "They definitely heard that! No way they couldn't!"

"They seem a little preoccupied," whispered Tammy.

"He's Catholic. I'm certain of it."

"How can you be so sure, Marge? And so what if he is?"

"Dave, evidently, I know your daughter better than you do. She's completely taken with this boy."

"Great! I like him. Nice kid. Articulate, intelligent, clean-shaven. What's not to like?"

She shook her head. "What if she *marries* him? He's Roman Catholic. Their pope is subject to demonic rule. They worship graven images. You want your daughter to become Anna Caperila, the Catholic?"

"Tut. I don't care if she becomes Anna McGillicuddy or Anna Stradivarius. Seriously, Marge, if you cared so much about last names, you would not have stopped at one child and given me a son."

Teeth bared. "Bless your heart. Everybody knows it's sperm that decides gender."

"Oh, is that right? Since when have we become reproductive scientists?"

"There's no talking to you."

"Maybe that's because you only ever talk *at* me."

"You have something to say? Then just say it."

"Marge, she's a senior in high school or about to be. She has time yet. Yes, I see her interest in the boy. I'm not blind; I see. Her first love; everybody has one. How many end up paired for life with their first? Hmm? Not many. For the purposes of argument here, let's just say these two make it to marriage. Say it turns out to be a Catholic wedding—"

"God, no! Don't even say it!"

"Marge, Anna is her own person. You must accept that anything can happen. And despite all Protestant objections, Catholics fervently worship the same Savior as we do. Maybe they go about it a little differently, with their statues—"

"Graven images."

"No, Marge, statues. Baptist worship services are plain, stripped-down to bare wood, and boring, except for the sermons. Sure, we do attract some talented and fiery ministers preaching the Word. Catholics have incense, art, stained glass; their services have a magical element to them, regardless of what homilies and readings happen or the public speaking talent of who's reading them. The very same Jesus Christ lives in both houses. If you can't accept that, Mrs. Dingel, well, then I can't help you. No one can."

Fierce eyes focused on Dave like acetylene torches. "I had a dream last night; a nightmare."

"Another one? About whom, or what, this time?"

"Anna. Always about Anna. This one really rocked me," she said. She poured herself another cup of coffee and sat at the kitchen table.

"What about her? It's okay. Tell me." Dave knew his wife believed dreams are when souls are laid bare to the spirit world. And he had to credit her source: even in the Bible, dreams directly affected reality—the Angel Gabriel appearing in dreams to Mary and Joseph set into motion the chain of events upon which the entire religion of Christianity was founded.

She shook her head. "Lately, it's never good.."

He nodded. "Dreams can certainly be predictors or carry heavy meaning, of course, but it doesn't mean every dream and nightmare means a visitation from that other place or needs to have a biblical effect."

"Dear sweet Lord, give me the wisdom to know the difference."

"What was it?"

Her eyes filled with tears. "Only a fragment of the dream is still with me. But, Dave, it's like a memory of an actual event. My waking mind cannot tell the difference. There was a sign, red and bright and flashing, like the signs you see in front of those scary rundown motels in Jersey."

Dave nodded. "What did the sign say?"

"VENGEANCE. Red, blinking, and ominous. Everyone was laughing at my Anna. Students, teachers. Her heart was broken, Dave. And anger. The spirit of hate found its opening in her at that very moment. It moved in and set up shop. Our little baby was destroyed. And somehow, it all goes back to that boy."

"Timmy? C'mon, Marge. That boy doesn't have it in him to hurt our baby."

"Not *him*. That Barnette demon."

"Oh. Him."

"Dave, I know she's against a move. School starts up again in two weeks. If you and I look really hard and make some calls, I'm confident we could get her placed at a private academy. Her grades are fantastic, and she's . . . different. Schools like that love diversity and kids with odd backgrounds. What could be stranger than growing up in this," she said, with a dramatic sweep of her hand, "this house of ten thousand corpses?"

He eyed her narrowly and swallowed bile. He decided to shove aside his wife's biting negativity and focus his thoughts on Anna. "Okay. Maybe it's for her own good. Put some distance between her and these thugs. But you know why she wants to stay."

She nodded. "Timmy. Timmy the Roman Catholic. And the Jew girl, Naomi."

"Marge, I never knew you to be so intolerant."

"I'm not. Only of devil-worshippers and Christ-crucifiers."

"He shook his head. "Wow. You really are prejudiced. And I don't like it. Why?"

"It's about Roman Catholicism, Dave! He descends from a long line of brainwashed Papists, I'm sure. Why? Because these are cults, that's why. I won't have my baby sucked into a cult."

"Geez. Not this again. Where do you get these ideas?"

"Televangelists."

"Which?"

"None of your business."

"Have you spoken with our pastor about this?"

"No, and why should I? Let him dig as I dig. Whatever knowledge he failed to pick up after divinity college is on him to gain."

"Tell you what, Marge. I know a way out of Hell for you."

"Excuse me, what?"

"I will enroll Anna in the local Catholic high school."

"*No!* Absolutely not!" said Marge in the unmistakable tone of a veteran contradictor.

Elbows on the table, Dave Dingel's fingers drummed lightly against his closed-eyes, his head bowed against steepled hands. Carefully, he considered all angles. His eyes opened. He had come to a decision.

"Yes."

CHAPTER ELEVEN

Out Day

Alone together in the mortuary, seated on stools, Dave lowered his head, inhaled, then exhaled, meeting her eyes. "I spoke with the principal, Father Sweeney. It's been arranged."

"No! How can you do this to me, Dad? Oh my God! Is this really happening?"

Though he had steeled himself against emotions he had fully anticipated, nevertheless, Dave felt his spirit sinking lower than it had in a very long time.

"It's for your safety, darling. These violent young men mean to do you—us, our family—a whole lot of harm. For whatever reason. Nothing that we did. I mean, look around you. Look at your friend Timmy. Is there not one sacred aspect to your life that they haven't wounded?"

Anna wept. "I know, it's true. But I can take care of myself, Dad!"

"Honey, I know how strong you are; believe me, I know. I had no hesitation sending you all the way to Texas alone, did I? But I would be a failure as a father if I let you spend all day locked inside a cage with these animals. Maybe it's because my eyes have seen more than yours. Some people . . . it's like they were born with great big wide holes running straight through their middles; dark empty places that can only be filled, just a little, by other people's pain."

He paused, a thoughtful expression: "Hate. The spirit of hate is real; we know this. As Christians, we recognize Satan and his works in people. We know he's the source, the eternal opponent of God, a liar and murderer, and thief, mutated from the beautiful creation he was in the beginning. These boys and their families, for whatever reasons, provide aid and comfort to the enemy. They embrace hate in their homes; foster it, feed it. Hate runs them. Bullies are the same everywhere in the world, doesn't matter where, or what race they are, or what religion they proclaim. They come in all ages, young to old. In school, they seek out differences, flaws, openings to exploit to cause others pain. Maybe it's pimples or being short or fat; could be ill-fitting or outdated clothing. Could be bad haircuts or personal hygiene flaws.

"You see, Anna, it really doesn't matter to haters. The substance never does. It's only a surface excuse to unleash what's inside them, that spirit of hate forever goading them. Like the young lady you brought me from Texas. What on earth could ever possess a kid like her to do the awful, unimaginably hideous things she did one fateful day? What came over her at that very moment? What overshadowed all basic human drives of compassion, doubt, fear, mercy, pity, remorse—that ultimately led to the State having to end her life for what she did? There's only one answer, and it's the same old answer. Hate. It's real. It is a spirit driven to try and claim each and every one of us living down here in its Principality. And God, in His infinite wisdom, gives us the free will to choose it; to let it in and run us. Those who are weak in the Lord are the most vulnerable. It's like electricity, in a way; always right there, a powerful current pulsing just beneath the switch, waiting for us to flick it on."

Anna nodded.

"For whatever reason, and it's not at all your fault, the Barnette kid hates you. And he's looped others into his dark orbit and will continue to."

"He came on to me at the bar. I rejected him. I brought up the rumor that, somehow, he was responsible for Frank Watson's suicide. He walked away mad."

"So? Is that cause for attempted rape?"

"No."

"Exactly what I just said. Rape was only an excuse, the one trigger that the spirit of hate, living strong within him, needed. One little opening. In the parking lot, the beast within him ran him, lock, stock, and barrel. You see now? Why you must distance yourself from all that?"

Anna hesitated. She nodded. "But you know what, Dad? There's another way to look at this, too."

"What's that, babe?"

"You're teaching me that the only way to deal with my problems is to run from them."

Dave smiled. "Our Lord was grabbed by temple priests who meant to deliver him up to Caiaphas, but He cut and ran. In fact, He had several documented close calls like that, and probably many more that were not recorded as He went around expositing Satan within people. He is the wisest person to have ever walked this earth. Was He running from his problems? Or was He obeying His Father's Spirit in every move that He made and every word that He spoke?"

"He was waiting for the right time to deliver Himself into their hands."

"Right. There are times when we pick our battles and times when we negotiate a truce with a stronger enemy to retreat from certain death. I believe this is one of those latter times, baby. These are convicted haters, violent young men, and they will never stop trying to hurt you. There has only ever been one way to deal with Barnette's species, and since the law can't protect us, I have to. I can protect you inside these walls, but when you're out there, I cannot." He stood and opened his arms. "I would never forgive myself if anything bad ever happened to my little Anna."

Burying her face in his chest, Anna cried. He held her until his white coat showed a large wet patch.

Saturday morning, August twenty-ninth, disclosed more activity than usual at County Correctional, as families queued up in a lot, anxious to reunite with loved ones on their last day of sentences served. A special exit was used to escort the processed and released inmates. It was outside that entrance that Sue Nastro, in her blue Ford Mustang, waited nervously. She swiveled and constantly fidgeted, not knowing if Bruce's parents would be there to pick him up or not. Thus far, she had not spotted the father, Frank Barnette, in his big beat-up silver Dodge Ram or the mother's, Heidi's, black Trans Am. She'd been waiting for over an hour already, bladder long past throbbing point after several coffees chased with a bottle and a half of water. She flipped the radio on and off. When on, she scanned through satellite radio stations. Nothing would calm her, not in the slightest measure. She grappled with the idea of leaving to find a public toilet—but then she spotted him in the distance, height and form unmistakable.

She unlatched the door and swung her leg over. The act of standing cramped her bladder all the worse. She straightened the wrinkles on the midsection and hips of her mid-thigh rose-embroidered Rebecca Taylor summer dress. She left the door open and studied his face through crystal clear sunglasses as he walked closer. *I wonder if the place has changed him much. Looks the same as before.* A guard flanked him on either side, though his hands were not cuffed.

Will he be overjoyed to see me? In there, did he dream of me?

His head faced down until he got to within fifty feet from the parking lot, at which point, he raised it. With his right hand, he shielded his eyes from the intense morning sun in what looked to her like a smart military salute. Then his gaze fell upon her. She waved; he waved back. Visual confirmation of someone there to pick him up achieved, the guards muttered something, turned, and reversed course along the same walkway.

"Bruce! Oh my God!" she yelled. He did not respond, only continued walking toward her. When he stood within twelve feet of her Mustang, he stopped. Excitedly, she trotted toward him, hips and body in constant lithe movement, heels clacking against the asphalt. A foot away, she beamed him a model smile.

"Hi, Sue. Thanks for coming to pick me up," he said, face inscrutable. "My dad knew the right time. They would not have released me if I did not have a ride pre-arranged. The old bastard stood me up. He had told the screws that he'd be happy to grab all three of us."

Behind him, she noticed Carmen, also flanked by two guards, then Earl behind them. Bruce turned briefly to see what she was looking at. "Do you mind giving all three of us a ride home?"

"Um, well, I was kinda-sorta hoping to take you to breakfast—"

"It'll have to be all of us, then."

"Um, well. Okay. I know a good breakfast buffet around here."

"Great, thanks."

"Can I get a hug at least? Aren't you happy to see me?"

"Sure," he said, and she threw her arms around him.

Bruce Barnette did not hug her back.

———

"Shabbat Shalom, bestie."

"Anna-banana! Shabbat Shalom to you, too! Hey, what's wrong? You look like you've been crying," said Naomi

"You can see that through this screen?"

"Honey, I have eyes like a hawk and the nose of a bloodhound. Nothing gets past me. What's up? How did your date with Timmy go?" She gasped, "We're not mad at him, are we?"

Anna smiled, laughed a little, and wiped at her eyes. "No. The most perfect date ever in the history of dating." She paused, blushing.

"Oh. My. *God*. You got laid! My little banana is a virgin no longer!"

"Girl, please! You make it sound so common."

"Face it, chica. You got laid!"

Anna laughed and nodded. "No, Naomi. I made love for the first time. And I am decidedly and most definitely, hopelessly *in* love, thank you for asking."

Naomi tittered excitedly. "Aww, you're a woman now, a full-fledged, card-carrying member of the Sisterhood! This is *so* awesome!"

"Don't tell anybody."

"Seriously, are you crazy? Don't hurt me like that. Like I would ever tell a soul."

"Better not. If my mother found out, I think I'd be living under a highway bridge abutment."

"Margie, hey, it's me, Naomi. Your little slut daughter got nailed between the legs, yep, impaled like a museum insect. Marge, really, you should've seen her flapping her little limbs, all sweaty and hot—"

"Shut *up*! You total sicko!"

"So, on a scale of one to ten, one being 'meh, it hurt but I kinda liked it,' ten being 'my world is rocked, he's a porn star, I want this all day every day for the rest of my days,' where does our boy Timmy fall?"

"Honestly? I have no experience with porn, but still, I'd have to rate him a million. Off the charts. I've never felt so good. But then, I mean, for a few days after, I was sore like you couldn't believe. It hurt to sit, hurt to walk. Not that I'm complaining! I'd do it again in a heartbeat. I guess maybe it's that I'm kind of small down there?"

"And let me guess: He's big down there."

Anna motioned with her hands, left to right, then formed a circle. "Oh. Geez. That's like way bigger than Abe. Ginormous!"

"Really?"

"Uh-huh. Wow, girl. You're a trooper."

"Didn't know I had it in me, did you? Me either, to tell the truth."

"Anna, I am *so* happy for you! And now, after all that, you most certainly have nothing to cry about."

Anna's face fell. "I won't be coming back to school Monday."

"What?"

Anna nodded. "Dad enrolled me at a Catholic school. I start there Monday."

"Wait. Catholic? Your mother hates Catholics."

"*Right*? My world is spinning out of control. Flipped upside down."

"Because of Barnette. And those other two devils."

She nodded. "Sick, right? I won't get to see you and Timmy every day. Funny how stuff we consider guaranteed in this world suddenly gets taken away for no reason; at least none that I can think of. Why am I paying for crap I didn't earn? No matter what bullshit this world deals me, I need you two."

"Oh, honey. We'll be with you! We are only an email or chat window or text message away. And we'll see each other in off-times like always. No big deal," said Naomi. Her face grew thoughtful. "Actually, absence makes the heart grow fonder. Not seeing Timmy every day could be a very good thing."

"How so?"

"When you do see him, nights and weekends, you two will have missed each other so much that every date will feel like the first . . . with that same passion and energy."

"Hm. You may have a point."

"Don't I always?"

"So, your dad really thinks Barnette's still a threat to you. Hey, I agree completely. Guys like him never learn. They only get worse with time. But it sucks that this is all so . . . real."

"Exactly what my dad says. Hate eats away at them, builds up inside. Takes over their days and nights. And it is very, very real."

"Are you going to have to wear one of those cute little Catholic school girl uniforms?"

Anna nodded. "Blue-gray skirts, white collared shirts, black sweaters, tights, and those ridiculous shoes."

"Oh, you can work with that, honey. Go commando one day underneath all that bulky cotton and polyester. Tell Timmy; nobody knows but he and you. Then wear the uniform on one of your dates. Tell Marge and Dave you have to meet with five other girls for a group project assignment. Really, you'll meet with him. Seriously. He will all but tear you apart. Those outfits are meant to homogenize everyone, but they have the unintended effect of driving the boys wild, always wondering what's underneath that sets each girl apart from the next. And the suggestion of what's just so close, so untouchably close, just up under that skirt."

"Mmhmm, like we discussed at the mall. This could be fun."

Naomi laughed. "Oh, believe me, it will be."

"Do you think all the drama with Bruce Barnette will be over now that I won't be in his face every day?"

Naomi hesitated. "I hope so."

"You hope so. You don't think so?"

After a time, she shook her head. "No, babe. He'll keep coming at you."

"But I didn't do anything to him!"

"Of course, you didn't. None of that matters to a twisted mind like his. The criminal blames everyone but himself for the steadily worsening consequences of his actions, for his world closing in on him. No, I really don't think it's over. Not with a hater like him."

———

While Carmen and Earl each dug into the third plate of scrambled eggs, home fries, biscuits, and gravy, Bruce, with Sue holding her phone in front of him, scrolled through photographs. "So dark, these."

She snatched the phone from him. He watched her fingers dance across the glass. "Now look."

Studying one of the photos, his eyes widened. "I can see her face. And his face. Yes, that's really Caperila and Dingel." He continued sweeping left to right. "No. *Shit*. Hey guys, check this out," he said. Greasy fingers clutched the phone as he held it up.

"Is that Dingelberry's pussy getting pounded?" asked Carmen.

"See her face, can't you?" Sue said with a smirk.

Earl nodded. "Damn. She's got herself one hot little bod. Hella good shots, Sue. And look at Caperila's ding-dong. Boy's hung like a porn star."

Bruce glared at him. "Just sayin'," Earl muttered. Bruce stared until Earl returned to his arteriosclerosis happy meal.

He took the phone back to himself and continued to swipe. He studied the different expressions on Anna's face, the milky pale thinness of her unblemished skin and body, presented here in amazing clarity. It felt as if Sue and the other two were no long present as he witnessed Anna's innocence lost. It reminded him of what he almost had but which had escaped him—and also cost him a new muscle car and a summer in jail.

After seeing the last pic from Sue's set of twenty-two, he handed the device back to her. "Be right back." He stood and walked to the single-occupancy men's room. He locked the door and stood before the urinal, where he masturbated to completion. He zipped up and then studied himself in the mirror. *It's decided. Anna Dingel's getting impaled. And nobody's getting between us. Not again, not this time*, he thought.

Back at the table, seated again beside Sue, he looked at her. "Good work. You know she lied about the parking lot scene. I was wasted. She came on to me. I pushed her away and then got jumped."

"I know, Bruce. She's evil. Happy to punish her."

He smirked. "Okay, here's what you're going to do next. . . ."

———

"Sorry to hear that, Anna. But in a way, I'm not," Timmy said.

"Wait. *What*? Why not?"

"Because Barnette can't be trusted, and I can't watch out for you every second we're in school. At least there, nobody can get at you. Catholic schools are stricter. They don't tolerate any nonsense. He can't get you there."

"I thought you were about to say you'll be happy to be apart from me most of the time."

Holding his cell phone voice port as close to his mouth as possible without tasting it, he announced: "Anna Dingel. I'm going to marry you."

She giggled. "Stop. You don't mean that. I'm only your first."

"And my last. Anna, I'm serious. You know I still haven't showered since our date."

Giggles turned to laughter. "Why not?"

"Because my skin still smells like yours, and I can't get enough of it. The scent is fading . . . but I can't wait to refresh it soon. Oh, by the way, I think I may have some big news of my own."

"Really? Do tell."

"So, this guy in Nashville, a real power-broker, he's like super-famous in the behind-the-scenes music world; a mogul, right? Gordon Shomacher, you can look him up. Guy is worth half a billion or more. He's the one responsible for the last three big boy bands; he's like the wizard behind the curtain. Well, get this: Somebody sent him a link to my 'Only His Secret Love' vid. Anna—Mr. Big called me! Not one of his people: *him*! He actually called the house—my cell phone is unlisted—so my mom screams up the stairs at me; I come running downstairs, grab the phone. At first, I thought it was a prank."

"Really? That's amazing, Timmy! Wow. What did he want?"

"So he's putting together another boy band. He said he has auditioned hundreds of young guys. He thinks I might have the 'X' factor, as he called it. Sent me a round-trip ticket, first class, for next weekend. Wants to throw me into a few situations and see how I do."

"Situations?"

"Musically. With other guys like me he's considering."

"Wow! Oh my God! Timmy, this is unbelievable!"

"Um, why? Why can't you believe it? You don't think I'm that good?"

Laughter. "You know what I mean, lug-head. But . . ."

"Yeah. I know. What becomes of us?"

"Mmhmm."

"Cross that bridge when we come to it, I guess, but I can't see anything coming between what we have, Anna. I asked him about school, and he said he'd pay for tutors so that I can graduate if it comes to that. I could tell him part of the deal is that he must do the same for my wife."

"Silly."

"Why? Why is that silly?"

"Once you become rich and famous, you'll have girls way prettier than me throwing their underwear at you. You'll forget all about the undertaker's little ol' daughter."

"*No.* No way, Anna. We'll both be eighteen when school starts again. We'll marry—I'm serious! I ran all this past my parents."

"Even the part about marrying me?"

"*Especially* that part. What little they know of you, they love. They want to meet you right away, of course, but they blessed my decision completely. They've always trusted that when I want something, I'm certain of it. There's just one thing . . ."

"What? Tell me, what's the catch? There's always a catch."

"No catch! Er, well . . . it's sort of more of a condition. You told me about your mom—how she is. They said you'd have to agree to get married in the Catholic church and that if we have kids, we will raise them Catholic."

"Seriously?"

"Serious as cancer."

She hesitated, then broke out laughing.

"What's so funny?"

"Nothing. Just that, well, yes, absolutely, I would agree to both of their terms. I'm laughing at what this announcement would do to my mother. I can see her face," she choked out hysterically.

"She'll try to block us?"

She sniffed, then calmed her storm. "Long story. God, it's so sick that someone else's parents even need to put conditions on our relationship just to protect us from my insane mother . . ." She sighed and softened a little. "She just doesn't understand Catholicism, that's all."

"We'll make her understand."

"First, you need to pass the audition and get an offer."

"Right. True."

"And, God forbid, you don't get an offer. What then?"

"Marrying you anyway. Wherever I go, you go."

A pause. Then, "I'm in. I'm with you, Timothy Caperila. Always have been, I think. Maybe even before we first met. Someday, maybe, you'll figure out exactly what that means."

"Anna, why do you love me?"

"Didn't say that I did," she teased. "Why do you want to marry me?"

"Because you're special. Different from all the rest. There's a light inside you—I can see it. Feel its warmth. And I want it, all to myself."

Call ended, electronics on her bed, she laid down and stared at the ceiling. Shallow sleep pulled her down into a dream. She recognized the rows of lockers in her high school hallway; murals, posters, and sports trophy cases she'd passed hundreds of times. Student faces were blurred, until several came into focus. Sue Nastro, bent over laughing, pointing at her. Tammy, Bruce, Carmen and Earl flanked her, all laughing. Dozens of unidentifiable faces, teeth bared in laughter so loud she feared permanent hearing loss. "What are you laughing at?" she screamed. This only increased the volume as dozens more joined in the laughing and pointing. She could make out the school principal standing beside that awful McGonigle, eyebrows raised, smirking. She looked down at her bare legs and feet. All at once, her total nakedness registered. She felt the blood in her veins hit the boiling point as though her entire skin, especially her face, was melting off. Her eyes opened wide in her room, as they did in her dream.

She wept until it hurt. She whispered, "Thank God, it was only a nightmare."

CHAPTER TWELVE

Maelstrom

It felt strange but good. A crucifix hung atop every door. All the other girls were dressed exactly as she was. Students here carried themselves with a bearing superior and more mature by far than back in her public high school. *Far more cerebral and less emotional*, she thought. *Better behaved.* She held a pretend conversation with Naomi inside her mind. *People are here to teach, others here to learn. Hey, what a concept. So this is what school was meant to be like. Far fewer petty games, no one-upmanship with the clothing. No makeup, no crazy jewelry, no t-shirts from famous bands, nipples pushing through. A girl could get used to this.*

Day one's first few classes flew by. It was lunchtime. She wished cell phones or devices were allowed. Her heart ached to connect with Timmy, and Naomi, too; to tell them that she thinks she'll be okay and that she's grateful to her father for making a unilateral decision on her behalf. That, once again, his wisdom proved to be bigger than hers.

Afternoon classes rolled by just as quickly. She understood the material laid out by each teacher, expectations set and felt that it aligned with subjects she already learned well in public school, with the addition of theology courses. She thought that—given all that had been pounded into her since birth, also what she'd learned from the Bible, which she read over and over on her own time—not only would she enjoy these classes, but she would ace every test, too.

And the news from Timmy astounded her still. She fought to blot down the excitement but also her heavy doubts. *What if it happens? Would*

I really just up and leave this all behind, get married, and move with him to Nashville? Finish up schooling with tutors; while he enjoys fame and fortune, I'll sit in some trailer or hotel room preparing a home-cooked meal for him while the other guys go out and party like rock stars? How long would it last, with Timmy beset by temptations on all sides every night?

With everything happening so fast, much of it bad but some of it so intoxicating it made her ears tingle and toes curl, she found it difficult to listen to the teacher.

And there was something else, too. A feeling nagged at her. She had come to trust her Little Voices over the years, like a warning signal from nature; a peal of thunder, clear evidence of the coming storm.

Right now, somewhere, something bad was happening to someone she loved. She could not say how she knew this. But, decidedly, she knew it.

Three o'clock, final bell. Briskly she walked to her car, keyed it open, and was met with a blast of air so hot that it closed her eyes and knocked her back a foot. She opened the rear driver's side door; from under the seat, she fished out her tablet and pressed the power button. The screen lit for a moment; then she saw the power indicator warning flash red just before the screen went dark. "Dammit. How could it be drained? It was completely powered up this morning when I left."

She pulled her phone from the plastic door pocket, turned it on, and saw a similar power drain, also two attempted calls; Timmy and Naomi. Quickly prioritizing based on gut instinct, she sat in the driver's seat and switched on the ignition with the air conditioner blasting and phone charger plugged in. She called Naomi.

"Just get out of class?"

"Yeah. In the car. What's up? Looks like you tried calling.."

"Yes, sorry, I'd forgotten about your new school's policy on no phones in the house. Listen. We have a serious problem."

Anna felt her gut drop. *That nagging doom feeling over the second part of day, the Holy Spirit working inside me, warning me, is now affirmed.* "What problem?"

"Okay. God, Anna, I hate to have to be the one to break the awful news."

"Naomi, please. I'm a big girl; I've been to hell and back this summer. Whatever it is, I can handle it."

"Okay. Then I'll just tell you. On your date, when you and Timmy found your hiding place in the woods, did you happen to notice a blue Ford Mustang behind you at any point?"

Anna thought hard, thinking back to when she picked up Timmy, introduced him to Dave and Margie, through the drive while she navigated his turn-by-turn directions. She remembered giving the finger after slamming on her brakes. She recalled Timmy's warning and glancing at the side mirror. A blue Mustang behind her, a California-blonde chick at the wheel, big sunglasses. "Yes. Why?"

"Because Sue Nastro and her guard dog Tammy Goldsworth evidently tailed you and Timmy to that secret woods of yours. They must've very quietly hiked in after you and hidden in some spot slightly elevated above you two."

"Dear God. They *saw* us?"

"So much worse than that."

"What? Tell me!"

"Honey, they photographed you guys—*in the act*. Lots of high-res pics, lightened, sharpened."

Anna inhaled. She did not exhale until twelve seconds later; her mind and spirit spun widdershins as if caught in a whirlpool of magma threatening to pull her straight down to Hell. "You mean, our faces are in them?"

Naomi hesitated. "Yes, both of you. Sue compiled them in an email and blasted it out to about four hundred people from a burner email account untraceable back to her. But word on the street is it was her and Tammy. Bruce's buddies haven't learned to keep their mouths shut, apparently."

"Who got the email?"

"Students, mostly. Administration and faculty, too, pretty sure. But she used blind-copy, so it could've gone anywhere."

Anna swallowed hard. "Did you see them?"

Silence.

"*Did you?*"

"Yes. Someone forwarded them to me. Which is when I ran outside of the classroom to the bathroom and tried calling you."

"How bad?"

"Full close-up porn. I don't know what kind of camera they used, but it was powerful and expensive, that much I can tell you."

"I have to go." Anna threw up in her mouth a little and swallowed the burning acid back down.

"I know, honey. Again I am *so* sorry to be the one to break the news. I love you, Anna-banana."

"Love you too, bye."

Anna's fingers flew across the screen as she hung up with Naomi and called Timmy in one fluid motion. After one ring: "Timmy?"

"Anna. Oh my God."

"You heard."

"Everyone under age nineteen has, for sure," he said dryly.

"Our parents?"

"Mine haven't yet. Yours?"

"I haven't gotten home yet. Guess I'm about to find out."

"I called Mr. Shomacher—Gordon, the band producer. I told him what happened. I wanted to be proactive in case something like this could ever surface and come back to haunt me later. I was pretty sure he was going to tell me 'thanks but no thanks' to the audition after this."

"What did he say?"

"My heart was in my throat when I choked out the confession. What does he do? He laughs hard, actually, then he says, 'Good goin', kid. You have a gut for showbiz. The raunchier the photos, the better.' Says it's good PR. I didn't know whether to reach through the phone and smack his corrupt face or thank him. Tried to keep a cool head; keep it professional. I mean, it was my mistake."

"Yes, it was." She heard him gasp. "I don't mean we are a mistake; just that spot you chose, holy crap. So how did you leave it?"

I was like, 'Okay, then. Thanks, see ya Saturday.' I mean, Anna, but as for you . . . this could really mess you up. The new school, your parents—"

"Was it worth it?"

She heard his smile through the phone. "My only question is, when can we do it again, and can you make damned sure we never *ever* stop doing it? I love you, Anna. This changes nothing between us. I would ask you the same question. Was it worth it?"

She tried to smile. "Have you seen them? The photos?"

"Mmhmm, yes. One of my bandmates forwarded the email."

"Is it bad?"

"Well, I look weird. Didn't even know I looked like that. But you—oh, Anna. You are just so perfect. You look great, my love. Absolutely flawless. Being with you, in that moment, was worth everything I will ever own. I'd sell everything just to do it again, one more time."

"And you wanted that note from class to show our kids one day. Will you show them this, too?" she asked timidly.

Timmy sighed. "Anna, I know. This will follow us our entire lives. I feel like I'm to blame. I was certain we were alone there. Do you blame me? Even a little, for this? Maybe for all of it?"

She considered the question. Had he sprung for a motel room, they wouldn't be in this mess. It really was a secluded and seldom-traveled spot, his little oasis. It would never have crossed her mind that someone could sneak around in there without giving some kind of warning.

"I did hear a branch crack and birds flittering away. But I suppose I was too caught up with all that you were doing to me—and I mean all of it— and watching your face as you and I, you know . . . at the same time—oh my God, it was glorious . . . I just didn't give a second thought to anything that was going on around us, outside of our, our little pleasure bubble. So, I guess it's as much my fault as anybody else's." She sighed. "We screwed up bigtime, Timmy. We're in the Big-league Screw-up Hall of Fame now. Like the druggies who overdose and end up in rehab; like the couples who get pregnant while still in school. I can't believe my life. So much evil. So messed up. And it's all a consequence of my decisions, one bad one after another. Nobody's fault but mine."

Several seconds of silence. "Is that what I am? Coming to see me at the bar started all this. Am I your life's mistake?" His tone had seemed to change; hard, tense.

"God, *no*, Timmy—not what I meant at all. You may be the greatest thing that ever happened to me. You might even be my future, as in, the forever kind. All this remains to be seen. I just don't know what to do next. How can something so beautiful and perfect have caused such ruin? I'm just really, really scared right now." Anna began to cry.

"Shh. It'll be all right. Things have a way of working out for those who put Christ first in our hearts. Go home, pray about it. If possible, let's meet up for an hour tonight, get some ice cream. That is, if you can pick me up. I should be getting this stupid cast off in like a week. Then I can pick you up, like a good boyfriend."

"Are you my boyfriend, Timmy?"

"Pfft. No."

"No?"

"I'm your fiancé, Dingel-dongle. Anna Caperila. Get used to saying it. In fact, your assignment tomorrow is, in each class, I want you to scribble your soon-to-be new name—Anna Joy Caperila—all over your notebooks. Then when we get together next, I'll check your work for completeness."

"What happens if I don't?"

"Remember what I did to you with my tongue?"

"Mmm, yes."

"I'll do it but only right to the edge. I won't allow you to cross over. You'll go mad, end up in a straightjacket. Which could be fun, I must admit. She has nowhere to run, no place to hide. Could be my next song."

A few small laughs. "Cruel. Okay. Let me go see what shitstorm awaits at home. Stay tuned to Instagram. Mom doesn't know I have this phone. We can chat in silence."

"Done. See you soon, Anna C."

"Bye, babe."

She drove with suspended emotions until the funeral home came into view; the feeling of impending dread returned. She pulled into her spot at the rearmost section of the lot, parked, and approached the side entrance. The weight in her stomach suddenly blew up from a golf ball into a bowling ball. *Something is off. Vibe isn't right.* In the mudroom, she toed off her clodhopper black school shoes, wriggled her toes in relief, and entered the kitchen.

David and Margaret Dingel were seated at the kitchen table. In front of them were screen prints of images and a course catalog with the name St. Anne's-Belfield School. They looked up at her with narrowed eyes. Her mother motioned to the chair opposite them. Three quick strides until Anna was seated across from them. Nobody said a word. It was like a staring contest.

Finally, Dave broke the silence. "A friend of mine with a daughter in your school forwarded the email. I only looked at the first two when you still had some modesty; then, after the third, I could go no further. Anna, the most terrible aspect of all this is my personal feeling of abject failure as your father. Please let me ask: What did I—did we—" he included his wife with a small, tired hand-gesture, "ever do to you that could possibly earn this obscene level of disrespect? Can you please tell us that?"

Anna sobbed. Through it, she managed to choke out, "Dad, Mom, I am *so sorry*. I messed up so bad." Exhaustion overcame her. *God, I am tired*, she thought.

"You most certainly did. This has destroyed our standing at the church. We can never go back and face those good people of God ever again. My business will likely suffer. After the vandalism, people took pity on the hardworking undertaker hit by evil. But now? This? Who on *earth* would ever entrust their loved ones to a man who cannot even influence his own home?" he said with a shrug.

"But, by far, *you*, Anna: *You* will bear the full brunt of this. Anything released to the web is forever. You can never put this toothpaste back in the tube. When you are thirty, picking up your little boy at school, and he asks you, 'Mommy, some of the boys are calling you a hot piece of ass and a slut, and then they showed me these pics'—what will be your response? Don't you see, Anna, the far-reaching effects of what you've done and how it will affect anyone who tries to get close to you? Forever?"

Crying openly, Anna nodded. "I—I know, Dad. Don't you think I know all this? I just found out twenty minutes ago. My world is crashing down on me."

"I told you not to go to that bar, to see that boy," her mother grumbled.

As suddenly as the crying started, it stopped. "Mom, *'that boy'* wants to marry me. And I want to marry him. We're going to get married in a Catholic church and raise Catholic kids far away from here. Away from you—" Marge Dingel cut off her daughter with a crisp right slap to her left cheek. It left finger marks.

"Go ahead, Little Miss Bigshot. Think you're in the big time? I sat where you are, once. Let's see how you handle it out there, you godless little sinner, you. You can try to run, but you can never hide from what's inside of you. First, before you do anything else, you need to fix your infected soul. Get right with God."

Anna was unaware that the fingernails of both her hands were curled inward, dug into her satin-soft palms. "God didn't try to rape me in a parking lot. God didn't punch Dad's face. God didn't throw rocks through our windows and paint hate messages on our home. And God didn't follow me and Timmy into the woods with a high-resolution telephoto camera. God didn't email pics of me losing my virginity to the young man I'm going to marry. And God didn't just slap my face. *You* did. Whatever *you* are, Margaret Dingel."

Another slap, harder this time.

"Marge, Marge. Calm down, take it easy. She's been through a lot."

"*She's* been through—w*hat about me*? What has she put *me* through? *Us*, Dave? How is any of this fair to us?"

"This isn't about you or us right now, Marge. We need to focus on our daughter. Please calm down. Or get up and leave the table, please."

Which, after facially projecting a range of equally unsavory emotions at them both, Marge sprang up and left Anna alone with her father.

"Honey, I'm sorry. Sorry for everything that has happened to you lately. And I agree, this was the devil's hand working through a bunch of dumb kids. You're a perfectly normal, wonderful, smart, beautiful kid, healthy inside and out. I only want what's best for you in this life. Which is why," he said, as he slid school materials across the table toward her, "you're going to make a fresh start here, at a private boarding school in Charlottesville, Virginia. Great reputation."

"Dad, *no*! I just started in a school, and I like it!"

His face fell. Inhaling deeply, he said, "The head of the school called me. The email circulated there already. He believes your presence there poses too great a risk of social disturbance. He has agreed to refund my tuition payment in full and expresses his deep sorrow for our situation."

"Oh my God."

He nodded. "Yes, baby. Pray about it. Because it's really, really, *really* bad."

After showering, she discovered that she had no appetite for dinner. She brought her knapsack up from the car, freed the tablet charger from its tangle by the radio, plugged it into the receptacle by her bed, lay down with a wet head, and powered on the device, still warm from its entombment in her hot-box vehicle. As the home screen appeared, she tapped the Instagram icon. *A message from Timmy.* With the heaviest heart of her life, she opened it, hoping beyond all that it was not a sudden change of heart on his end about her, now that he had had more time to ruminate over their dire situation.

My parents know. I'm sure yours do, too. You're in Hell right now. Just know that you are safe in my arms, and my heart, always and forever, Anna Caperila.

Smiling weakly, she replied: *Just nail the audition. We need to GTFO of Dodge. Dad's sending me away to a boarding school six hours from here.*

It seemed to be taking him a long time. Either he was composing a textbook or editing and revising his thoughts. Finally: *Then I'm coming with you to that school. Wherever you go, I go.*

She paused to compose a reply. *What about SpaceJunk? What about your parents? Would they agree to it?*

A long pause. *I've outgrown the band. I have a serious music business tycoon calling me personally. SpaceJunk ends anyway when D'Alessio goes off to Berklee. It was never more than a short rideshare trip for any of us. Not a valid professional vehicle or anything. And my parents dote on me. They'll do it to make me happy. One year of private school—yeah, they can afford that, knowing that eventually, I will pay them back.*

She typed quickly. *I could never ask you to do that.*

His response was instant. She could sense the weighty, binary nature of it; also the consequences should she answer incorrectly. *Anna. Do you not want me to follow you?*

Instantly: *Of course I do. I want to be with you twenty-four-seven, Timmy. You've lived inside my head, my heart, my soul for a long time now. Longer than you know.*

Smiley and heart emojis. *Together. No matter what.*

Two hearts, a rose, and a skull-and-crossbones emoji. *Done deal. Until death do us part. Let me ask your thoughts on something. Barnette and his cabal of demons have ruined my life. If you were me, would you be worried that it's not over? That he might attack me again when I least expect it, maybe even in Charlottesville?*

117

A pause. *Then I will end him. The forever kind.*

She frantically typed, *No, Timmy. I don't want to drag you into this any further. So the answer is yes. You're still worried about him coming at me again.*

His measured response: *He's psycho. Him and his fellow inmates and his trash girlfriend, the model. Yeah, a little worried. I put nothing past any of them.*

CHAPTER THIRTEEN

Full Moon

Back in the mortuary, seated upon opposing stools, Dave said, "Paperwork for STAB—"

"Wait, STAB? What's that?"

"It's what everyone calls your next school. St. Anne's-Belfield, abbreviated. The paperwork is taking longer than I had hoped. You'll have to miss your first week of school there."

"Gee. Heartbreaking."

He wore a face of deep displeasure. "I need you to drive back to Texas State Penitentiary this week. Make yourself useful, at least. You do know that STAB costs twice that of the Catholic school."

Anna exhaled. "Okay, packing the bags; Dad's sending me on a guilt trip."

"You bet I am."

"Fine. Today's Tuesday; I should be back Friday."

"Same everything. And, baby, please try to stay out of trouble, won't you?"

"Forget guilt trip; I'm now living on a guilt farm."

Her backpack ready, the white Dingel Funeral Home van's fuel tank full, device batteries charged to the max, she drove the van back along familiar roads to the Pennsylvania Turnpike, her gateway to the Southwest. This time, the miles seemed to pass far more slowly, making them feel longer than miles. Time drew out like an endless tunnel of razor wire. *I wonder if this is what major clinical depression feels like*, she thought. Aside from some bathroom stops and for snacks and coffee whenever she felt herself nodding off behind the wheel, she drove straight through until night, anxious to settle in and communicate with the only two people on earth who made her feel safe and sane.

The scene with Timmy in the woods looped prominently within her. She had never felt so good. *There's no going back to feeling like I did before Timmy. That girl is long dead to me now. Those days of walking alone in Valley Forge Park, reading James Fennimore Cooper's exciting adventures of pioneer American men and women in their struggles against Native American tribes and warring colonial powers: It's done. Onward and upward.*

"Been there, done that," she said aloud to herself. "Share all of myself with him. Dreams, fantasies, fears . . . and know everything about him. That's real freedom. Free to be ourselves. Now *that* is living, man. Forget taking over the funeral biz. That's out. Timmy's never going to stick around Pennsylvania; too slow-lane for that rocket."

Her cell phone rang as she turned from I-81 South onto exit 2, headed West on I-24 toward Chattanooga. She fumbled it a few times until she answered the call on the seventh ring. She pushed the speaker button and laid it down on the passenger seat. "Hey, Naomi. Sup?"

"What ya doin'?"

"Drivin'. Hey, did you see all the pics?"

"None of the dick pics. Abe and I made a pact not to look."

"You didn't study them like all the creepers."

"Got that right. What has been seen can never be unseen. I would never look at things you would never want me to see. What's private to you is private to me."

"I love you so much."

"And I, you, banana-head. So, salty-girl, where you at now?"

Sigh. "Tennessee, turning into the same seedy little motel as last time."

"Color me JOMO. The old Burgess is putting you to work before sending you off to a Virginia penal colony?"

"Yeah, pretty much. You know, as I'm driving and thinking about Timmy, to take my mind off this pathetic little life of mine which, as you know, is currently swirling down the toilet bowl: Now that I have you with me, can we talk about eliminating the source of all my pain for just a minute?"

"Oh yes. Let's. You know us Jews. We forgive those who ask. But those who never do and never will: Those unrepentant enemies are the ones we pay back. Jews make it a point to always give more than what was given to us. We're generous that way. Just ask the Israeli Mossad."

"Then maybe I need to convert. Because I'm not clever in these matters. I don't know the first thing about solving mortal threat problems or paying back sworn enemies. Not in my DNA, I'm afraid. Dave and Marge raised a pacifist. Forgive thy enemies."

"Hah. Sure it is. A few weeks ago, you never thought that being the most sexually-interesting woman on the planet was in your DNA, and well. Look at you now."

"Yeah, right. Interesting to two guys, one of whom is a convicted sex offender."

Laughter. "Are you kidding? Girlfriend, every guy in school is now obsessed with you. I'm talking about the entire male student body beating-off to your photos. If you had stayed in school, you would have graduated Most Likely to Become A Trophy Wife.

"And by the way, everyone is pissed at the them for what they did to you guys. It's universal. Normal people can relate to an egregious and malicious invasion of privacy. Barnette, Nastro, Goldsworth: Everyone knows it was them, and now kids avoid them like the plague. Timmy's a different story altogether. He's like . . . I mean, he's already a rock star. Every girl in school is making at eyes at him; it's hysterical. Wish you could be here to see it."

"Is he making eyes back?"

"Hell no. Boy's walking around with eyes like glazed donuts. Looks like he hasn't showered in forever. He makes eye contact with nobody."

"Well, he'll need to shower before he flies to Nashville Friday night."

"What?"

"Long story, but anyway, this big music guy is interested in him. Saw his video, the song about me, 'Only His Secret Love.' Deeply serious buzz in some very high places about our Timmy."

"*Really*? Wow! That is just frickin' *amazing*! And oh gawd, yes. Boy needs to clean himself up and eat a burger. Appears to be wasting away a little."

"Seriously? Well, I shouldn't sound surprised. I kind of relate. Naomi, do you think I'm a good person? What I mean is, I've never done anything to anybody. I love God, and America, and my parents, and you. And now I love Timmy more than anything in this world. I don't feel like I've earned everything bad that's happening to me right now."

"Oh, girl. Rebuking a horn-dog coming on to you at a bar who had plied you with illegal alcohol with the intent of getting you drunk enough not to fight back when he rapes you? Was that your sin, do you think? C'mon."

Anna considered it. "No. I did nothing wrong. Nothing to deserve the shitstorm that landed on me and just refuses to blow away. It only keeps getting worse. And I'm afraid it will follow me and Timmy."

"The pics, you mean?"

"Well, those. That's a given. No, I mean Bruce, Sue, and Tammy. They seem to want me dead. Or locked in an asylum."

"So, what do we do about them?"

"What would you do if you were in my shoes?"

Silence. Then suddenly: "I would neutralize the threat, like Israel's Iron Dome. Nothing personal; just neutralize."

"Sorry, babe. I have no clue what that even means."

"What it means, is . . . what it means, is . . . it means that I would make sure they know there is a heavy penalty to pay for every untoward action taken against me. It means with what measure ye mete, it shall be measured to you again. I would deliver to them equal or greater pain."

"I'm barely a hundred pounds soaking wet. What do you propose I do? Punch them out? I have no telephoto lens camera, and Sue's been half-naked already on fashion runways anyway. Spray paint their houses? Throw rocks through their windows?"

"Uh-uh, no. Whatever you do can never trace back to you. I know a little something about computer science. PoPo is smarter than everyone, with their Palantir software and databases." Naomi spoke from deep knowledge of the subject, with a decided finality in her tone.

"It would have to be someone unconnected to me entirely," said Anna.

"Exactly right, homegirl."

"You mean, like hiring a hit man?"

"Shh! Smartphones are *not* secure."

"Oh yeah. Right."

Naomi paused. "You cray? I may give better than I get, but I'm not a killah chick. But we gotta get this squad off your back. I mean, bye, Felicia: gonzo. Why should you be the one scared out of town? Listen, I may have a crazy idea brewing that I would not want to mention over an unsecured line. It's an extreme long-shot at best. Tell you about it when you return . . . Friday, is it? Hey, that's your birthday! The big one-eight! Can I maybe pop over, take you for ice cream? I mean, if Dave and Marge haven't Amished you."

"Sure. Wow, yes, I'd love that. I'm sure if it's a quick trip, Dave'll give it the nod."

"What about Timmy? Won't he get bent about me taking up one of your last evenings in town?"

She spotted the motel sign up ahead on the left and had temporarily she lost her train of thought. "Where was I? Sorry. Oh, yes. About Timmy. He said that if the boy-band guy's audition doesn't work out, he'll have his parents send him to STAB. He would sentence himself to the same school where I'm going, in Charlottesville. I mean, he said that."

"What if the audition does work out and he receives an offer but has to move to Nashville or some other big city?"

"He said the suits would hire tutors for him so that he could graduate on time."

"Great for him, but what about you?"

"Said he would marry me. I'd get tutored, too. Wherever he goes, I'd go. But, I mean, let's be real. He's great, and I know he wants us to stay together. That boy's crazy in love with me, just like you said he is. But there are so many *ifs* and scary unknowns over the course of the next year. Meanwhile, I'll be the only far-flung satellite, separated from the loves of my life by a six-hour drive."

Hot tears rolled down both cheeks.

"Did you say it to him? 'I love you too'?"

She wiped her eyes with a paper napkin and sniffled back her runny nose. "No! You told me not to. I'm playing it cool, just like Mama Naomi said. My old Jewish mother knows stuff."

Laughter. "Well then, Friday. It's a date. Can't wait to share a few ideas with you. Know this, my little goy: We are going to pay them back, every last one of them, with interest. Like Pavlov, we'll associate fear inside their hater brains with every future thought of doing evil things. That is the only way to control this species. Big fish eats smaller fish. We're about to become megalodons."

"God, Naomi. I do hope you're right."

"When am I ever wrong? See ya."

"Byes for now."

———

"You again. Hey, look, guys, the cute kid is back!" Under a scorching morning sun, having backed the Dingel Funeral Home van into the exact same spot outside the loading dock of Texas State Penitentiary, Anna stepped down and out. She stretched her skinny arms up to the sky, then bent over to touch her toes. She flexed her stiff, road-weary muscles and gave a big sweeping left-to-right wave to the same crew as last time, like painting a rainbow in the air.

"You guys are lucky."

"How do ya figure, little miss?" said Lieutenant Austin Randall, holding the same clipboard.

"Because you never have to decide what to wear every day. Never need to burn brain cells, expend energy. You just go to your closet and grab a clean copy of what you wore the day before."

He beamed. "You know—never quite thought of it that way. You definitely makin' a good point there, miss," he said, and halfway to the other three guards. "Hain't she?" Anna saw them all nod, which suggested to her that the man who did all the talking was an employee of some weight or perhaps the longest-tenured.

"So, I hear you have another traveling companion for me."

"Well, little miss, as a matter of fact, we do. How was the last companion? Give you any trouble, did she? Talk your ear off? Frequent bathroom stops?" The three guards authentically laughed at this.

An image of Taylor lying naked on the ground, penis covered with dead-vagina slime, neck crushed by her father's shoe, flashed across her eyes. Quickly recovering from the vision: "Rand! Gotta tell ya, she was an absolutely *dreamy* companion! I did most of the talking. Very sympathetic to my needs. I think she'd make a fantastic therapist." The volume of laughter from the three increased to a dull roar. Randall let himself go and laughed along with them, white teeth, large and straight, in stark relief to his ebon-black skin. She liked him. *Wish I could hire you as my bodyguard. Barnette wouldn't stand a chance against you.*

"Oh my, oh my. You're a real piece of work," he said through laughter. "You may be a bit dewy-eyed, kid, but I'll tell ya—ya got grit. Hey miss, tell me again the internal dimensions of your case?"

"Twenty and a quarter, by seventy-four point five, by eleven point three seven five. Same one as last trip."

His face grew thoughtful. He stroked his chin. "Hmm," he said and searched the other three, who shrugged in response. "Well, I suppose we could try it." Turning back to this crew, "Don't suppose any of ya happen to have a chainsaw floatin' round in yo back pocket, do ya?"

"My dad—Mr. Dingel—didn't give me any info at all about this one. Why, is the body too large for the case?"

He nodded. "Mayhab. He's a biggun, for sure. Eighty-one inches tall, two-ninety lean, shoulders like a linebacker," he said and sighed. "I guess we can try . . . well, *foldin'* him in there. Might be a little cramped up by the time he gets back to Pennsylvania. I hear his family back there is celebrating his execution—at least his lawyer made it seem that way. The funeral is just a formality, mostly for the mama bear."

"Really? Interesting. Why, did the lawyer say?"

"Sorta hinted at it. You see, Marcus Midlothian was quite prolly the worst killer we ever had on the Row. Real sick bastard. Bein' kin to something like him, well, can't imagine that bein' easy. Those nice folks prolly had reporters and such crawlin' all over 'em for a couple years now. When you're related to someone that bad, people, well, they tend to make your life a living Hell.

"His appeals ran out quick. He only been a guest at the Polunsky Unit, where they hold male Death Row inmates, for twenty-six months. Give you some perspective: The average time on Death Row is over ten years, and the shortest time anyone ever awaited execution was two-hundred fifty-two days. Ask me, I think ole Lucifer musta had hisself an open position down there for a real, real bad individual to help torture souls, so he sped things up. Either that or this world, evil as it is, pushed Marcus Midlothian out of it quick, the way a body pushes out a splinter."

"Geez. What the heck did this guy do?"

First looking back at the guards, who glanced at Anna, he shrugged. As he turned to her, she noticed that his face had taken on a distanced expression, like that of a surgeon about to deliver some very bad news to loved ones in the waiting room. "You sure?"

Anna nodded. "Reminder: I'm the undertaker's daughter. Please believe me when I say that I have heard it all before and have actually seen it all, too, up close and gory. Dazzle me."

A flicker of a smile. Warmth in his eyes. Anna could tell she had charmed him.

"Caucasian guy, born and raised up near ya'll somewhere, drifted down here as a kid when his folks divorced. Twenty-nine years old on arrest day. Graduates high school with average grades, gets hisself hired at a meat packing plant. No criminal record. Then one day, something snaps loose inside." He simultaneously clicked his tongue and snapped his enormous fingers.

"He goes and murders seven people. Now, that alone ain't overly unusual. Normal pattern killers—did I just say normal? You know what I mean—usually they have a 'type.' Little girls, maybe, or little boys, but usually not both, at least as far as I can tell. Teenie-boppers, cheerleaders, college students joggin'. Hell, old ladies that remind them of their cruel mamas. Who really knows? But you get the point. Some fantasy they carry around with 'em, trapped inside 'em since they was kids. And then they get big, get a few muscles, get some testosterone. That's when whatever's inside 'em cuts loose; makes 'em act out them bad dreams.

"See, ole Marcus here, well, he did boys and girls young and old. Happens sometimes; victims tend to be at the wrong place-wrong time. Still though, it ain't usual, so that right there threw off the local detectives. And so then he does a guy in his mid-forties, and a lady who was," he said, turning to one of his colleagues who mouthed something, "fifty-two. See? He was all over the place for a sexual killer."

"Sexual killer?"

The others nodded. "Okay, here's where it gets weird, miss. He never robbed or stole from 'em. Law enforcement always found 'em nekkid, least

126

from the waist down, they assholes all tore up. As in—shredded. Marcus Midlothian's pecker was sized to fit the resta him. Your daddy the undertaker, he gonna see that for hisself, lemme tell you. Now, around front, they'd find 'em partway or completely gutted, you know, like a deer. Always the same: Butts tore up, and bellies gutted. Keys, wallets, purses, jewelry, everything still on or near 'em. And he'd do it outside, always at night, in or near woods or parks, like maybe the fresh air and stars made him feel extra randy or somethin'. Oh, yeah: Always on full moons. Never any other time, like he a werewolf . . . thinkin' he Lon Chaney Jr. or somethin'. See, that partially 'splains how he was able to avoid gettin' ID'd for so long. Homicide detectives had security and ATM cam footage to search, and there was never a clue found on any o' dat."

"Yeah, wow. What a mega-dick." Several of the guards smiled at this, coming from Anna, and even she snickered at her own pun; though Randall's story had made her feel a little light-headed.

"So he remained invisible to the long arm of the law. No patterns, left no evidence. I mean, yeah, semen shot way high up inside lower intestines, but since ole Marcus never before crossed wit the law, he ain't never mailed his spit to one a dem astrology labs—"

"Ancestry?"

Nodding, "Shucks, I meant dat, yeah, for sure. So DNA weren't a thing they could use to catch 'im, you see. So this one night, the cops, see—they get smart. They pick this young female officer, dressed her up all sexy-like, kinda usin' her like bait, movin' her around to different parks every full moon. Nothin'; zippo, for months . . . until this one time, out of the woods, shambling out slow like some big old bear, comes Marcus Midlothian, chasin' after this pretty little police officer. He's got that giant dick o' his unzipped and a sharp blade in his hand. She fires on him, hits him above the right pec." Pointing at a spot on his chest, he showed Anna the exact location of the bullet entry wound. She made a mental note to look at the scar once the body was in the mortuary.

"The rest, as they say, is history. Except, well, you don't really wanna hear this part."

Anna folded her arms. She stared and tapped her right foot.

"You a little pistol. Okay, so when detectives had him chained up in the interrogation room, with a lawyer present and everythin', they asks him why he done 'em the way he did 'em. And so he says, "Asses be tight, and slippery from bleedin', but it weren't till he reached 'round and stuck the knife in their bellies that it felt right. Involuntary muscles inside these poor souls, all scared and shakin', as you can imagine. At that very same moment, his blade pierced skin, severin' nerves, partin' deep muscle tissue and such, those intestinal muscles and sphincters would clamp down on his pecker. See, the deeper and worse he'd cut 'em, the harder they screamed tryin' to escape that awful pecker in the butt and blade in their bellies, both at the same time. They be beggin' and prayin' for a salvation that would never come, knowin' they's definitely gonna die. The more they suffered, the nicer it'd feel to him."

Anna turned pale. She managed to swallow the lump that suddenly formed deep down in her throat.

"The detective asks, 'What did you do, Mr. Midlothian, after you ejaculated inside the victim?' And so he says, 'If they were still alive, I'd sit and watch the lights go out in their eyes. With moonlight reflecting, it was something really special.'"

Anna shook her head. She searched for the naive self she used to be, before learning the details of her father's latest guest. She tried to blink herself back to the present.

"I know, miss. It's his world out there, and don't I know it."

"Whose?"

"The debbil. Satan. See, we here," he said, gesturing to himself, his colleagues, and at her, "we all just be passin' through here on our way to Jesus, tryin' to live right, do right by people. Maybe even leave this place a little cleaner than when we found it. But folks comin' through this penitentiary who earned deyselves a lethal cocktail or a ride on Old Sparky, well. They headin' someplace else, ain't they? Maybe they always knowed it, too; like, since birth. Instead of resistin' like we all do, they bought in to the debbil's lies."

She nodded. "My dad says exactly the same thing. Did Midlothian get electrocuted, like the last one?"

"Oh no, not Marcus Midlothian. He got sentenced long after the cut-off. He got the injection. Families of his victims were there watchin' the whole thing. Marcus was upright. Tilted, lookin' out at the audience. The tilt-table malfunctioned, stuck in position; never did get laid flat. That ain't enough of a malfunction to stop the execution, though, you see. Last thing he saw were families who got they loved ones taken by this monster."

He turned to the others. Everyone knew he had arrived at the most unseemly part of the Marcus Midlothian saga. They nodded; he turned back to Anna. "Died with angel lust—death priapism, permanent hard-on, blood pooled there, like they say used to happen with hanged men. You daddy ain't never gonna forget this customer, not for the rest of his days."

"Eww. So gross. All of this."

Anna figured, like undertakers, prison employees relied on dark humor for emotional survival; in their case, a career that continually pushed them up close and personal with some of the evilest people society would reject. Lieutenant Randall offered Anna a warm grin. "So I guess you and Marcus got just about nothin' to say to one another. You're so darned pretty that I'm sure any o' these fine young gents back here'd be willing to take his place for the ride."

As two, then finally, six thumbs went up, Anna smiled at them. This brief reminder of harmless flirtations and respected social boundaries made her feel fully recovered from the appalling story of Marcus Midlothian.

"Did Marcus have any last words? Just curious."

Randall nodded, face grave. "Last words were, 'I'll be back for every one of you. Look up at the full moon and remember my words.'"

For a moment, she stared across a blacktop of rippling ghosts, air above the asphalt frying-pan distorted from absurd heat.

Anna shivered.

Driving, she remained silent, feeling no great desire to converse with Marcus Midlothian. She wondered what plan Naomi could possibly be hatching to end the threat and keep her close to home. She thought of Timmy and his audition; what the future could look like for them. She pushed out thoughts of him. *Too many unknowns. I don't think my heart could stand to get smashed.* She glanced over her shoulder at the locked case. *What spirit could possess a man to do what he did? Only one that I can think of. Unrepentant to the bitter end.* She thought of his reason for killing the way he did. Of his angel lust. She remembered the full moon, that he'd be back.

She adjusted the rearview mirror to see the whole of the temporary coffin. *Can evil on a scale like his rub off? What if it escapes through a micro-crack in the gasket and jumps into me? No, I don't believe in ghosts . . . but evil spirits? Oh yeah: in those, I believe; Bible doesn't lie.* Empathy for his victims. "God, I trust you welcomed them into Your Kingdom with open arms after what they suffered," she said aloud.

Though she resisted, she felt inexplicably transplanted into the body of a Texas teen girl, under a full moon, in the moment. Abject fear and panic as giant hands shredded her jeans and underwear. No time to feel humiliated. Must escape! She kicked backward to no effect. An iron bar heated to glowing shoved inside her. The pain! Excruciating! Blood ran warm down naked thighs. The blade inserted in her abdomen pushed deeper. Resistance from abdominal muscles. Hard push. She could feel the blade separate denser meat, the blade-tip now about three-quarters of an inch inside her. With the focused strength and decided calm of a surgeon despite his exertions, he carved her into a state of pain and shock somewhere past insanity.

Her head jerked up, eyes flew open, her mouth a rictus of shock and suffering. At once, the silence of the moonlit scene got replaced by an aberrant shriek. What followed were extraordinarily noisome, outrageous, and violent screams. Anna felt herself pour forth her agonies as she dripped blood. "Somebody help me, please!" she begged, hyperventilating. As she lay dying, the most evil eyes she had ever seen bored into hers.

"Where did that come from?" she screeched, hoarse from crying, as she pulled into the motel lot. She felt herself coming back from a waking nightmare that had inexplicably swallowed her. She decided never to have anything to do with the mortuary business after graduation. She became convinced that Dave's dream, this rarely-spoken lie between them, had now completely lost its influence over her.

She thought of a meme she'd spotted on Instagram. 'Surround Yourself With Nice Things' which featured a kitten and puppy at play with a pretty potted orchid nearby. *How can I, when my life is havoc; a swamp of not-nice things?* Relieved to finally put distance between herself and the corpse, walking from the van to the motel office, she looked down at her shadow. *Like it's desperately trying to hide beneath my feet.*

CHAPTER FOURTEEN

Ice Cream

"Nothing over the phone. Meet me at the spot in ten."

Carmen had never shown Bruce even one smidgen of insubordination because it simply was not in him. Ever since grade school, he had felt special, only because a handsome and popular guy like Bruce had deigned to reach down and elevate him to a level of importance and visibility that he knew would have never happened otherwise.

He knew what the 'spot' meant. He borrowed his father's truck and drove to meet Bruce at the nearby Valley Forge National Park, which forbade visitors after dark. Just outside of it, he parked at the gas station on Valley Forge Road; from there, he hiked off-road through wooded areas until he arrived at Varnum's Redoubt, a defensive bulwark built by Revolutionary army soldiers over two centuries prior as a defensive firing point against potential British or Hessian invasion. The middle of the roughly triangular-shaped earthwork was a hollow, grass-covered indent. Park Rangers, roving about in their SUVs, would shine spotlights right over their heads and never see them. They felt more secure here than anywhere else.

"You've brought girls here?"

Bruce nodded. He sat on the grass within the indented bowl, smoking cigarettes while awaiting the arrival of his conspirator. "Several. They think it's romantic in here when it's raining in summer. Clothes come right off."

Carmen sniggered. "Hey, so what's the 4-1-1 here? Top secret, whatever it is—I got that much."

"Matt? Bodybuilder? Mister Universe is a meth tweaker? No shit!"

"Carm."

"I know, I know. Total secret to the grave."

Bruce nodded. "This goes to why he must do exactly what I tell him, say only what I want him to say, and otherwise keep his lips zipped. At exactly the right time—and this is why it's critical for you to find the routine Dingel and her Jew follow—Matt slips around back, flips the power switch to the security cams off for ten seconds. I slip out the deck entrance, which bouncers don't cover. Earl takes my place. You follow? Out I go, in he comes, both of us with our heads down, letting the bills of our Deere hats hide our faces in shadow. They keep that place as dark as shit anyway when there's no band. I guess they call that 'ambience,'" he chuckled.

"Earl sits with his back to the cam. Matt flips the cams back on. Later, when cops check my alibi, they'll see a temporary little flicker, nothing but a blip, and so when that cam powers back on, it's still looking at the back of my head same as before. Everybody in their places, same customers. Plus, Matt will say I'd been there for hours. So will the servers because Matt will convince them to."

"What about your car? They'll see it come and go."

Bruce grinned. "Knew you could be smart when you apply yourself. The Camaro won't move. Lot cams will prove it. Earl and I will be using a car I'll 'borrow' from the shop, license plate smeared with grease. We'll meet up at the gas station where we're currently parked at eleven sharp. Earl drives the borrowed car back to the shop; I pick him up, drop him at home, then I'll return home and wait for the cops. My parents will say I just got in because of my midnight curfew. They'll ask where I've been. I'll tell 'em. They'll say, 'Can you prove it?'" Bruce laughed. "Hells yeah, officer!"

"She'll know it was you; her whole family will."

Bruce smirked. "I surely hope so. Let them try to prove it. Interrogate me six ways from Sunday. Toss the tavern for evidence. Track down and take statements from every single person in there. Good luck with that."

A side of Carmen enjoyed inflicting pain in others, which, up until this point, the worst of it consisted of egg raids. He recalled to mind Sue and Tammy's photos. *Damn right, Dingel is hot. Who knew?* Hot enough that her photos gave him a boner at breakfast, but he also remembered feeling uneasy, like a voyeur. *I felt like a creeper.* Not the same as looking at porn—a favorite pastime. Porn people *want* you to look at them; Anna and Tim clearly did not. Another side of him knew that, deep down, Anna Dingel had never done anything to anybody. She was, up until the beginning of break, the least visible and most forgettable skinny little keep-to-herself mouse he'd seen scamper through halls and stairwells his entire life, clutching books and keeping her head down. Nobody made moves to befriend her. People rarely used her name in a sentence, and on those rare occasions when they did, heard most often were 'Bible-banger,' 'God-squad,' and 'Dances with Corpses.'

He swatted a mosquito from the thin skin on the back of his left hand.

"Bruce, man. You know this doesn't feel right. Bad karma. Serious question: What did she ever do to you that could possibly deserve the rough treatment?"

In the quick of a knife, Bruce launched himself from a seated position to kneeling before Carmen, collaring both sides of the neck of his t-shirt, yanking upward—which caught Carmen completely off guard. No longer speaking, now snarling, he said, "She told me I'm responsible for Frank's death. She took my drinks, knowing damned well what she owed for my hospitality, and then cried rape. She got me sent to prison. *Deserve?* Ask me again, you little—"

Bruce raised his right hand, ready to whip it down hard against the side of Carmen's terrified face—but something stopped him. He lowered his hand, then spoke in a tone Carmen internalized as an unquestionable authority. "She is the root cause of all this. I lost a thousand-dollar deposit and a once-in-a-lifetime chance to turn a beat-up Dodge Charger Daytona into one hundred fifty thousand in gold. I would've been truly rich. That little cunt stole everything from me; from us, Carm. Now my cousin and his crew hate me; when I never showed, it forced them all to work crazy overtime. Dad said he's kicking me out of the house the day I graduate. Mom's washing down Oxycodones with gin; she says it's all because of me. Get it, Carm?

"All of that must come out of Anna Dingel's ass. I demand my pound of flesh. And you're going to help make this right. Yes? I mean, look-it: She's even trying to come between *us*. You guys did time for her. What we went through in there. Remember what happened to us in there, Carm."

"Trying to forget, actually."

"I think we are owed a little payback. Don't you, bro?"

Carmen made his decision in the dark on Varnum's Redoubt. Part of him craved acceptance, affirmation, acknowledgment. He ached to belong to something more remarkable than his peer group. This need overshadowed most others. Though a part of him loudly, strenuously objected to Bruce's scheme. It shrieked out warnings in the form of a queasy stomach and spine tingles on a warm night. Spoken words, in his own voice, looped in his mind: "What did Anna Dingel ever do to you, to me, to anyone?" He remembered the photos, how pretty she looked. But, all decisions are final; a man gives his word but also keeps it. His loyalty to Bruce won the internal argument and sealed his future.

"Happy birthday, Banana!"

"Hmmpf. Doesn't feel too freakin' happy."

Anna and Naomi sat together on a rough wooden picnic bench outside the ice cream store underneath an overhanging lamp that had just flickered on. "Thank God it's Friday," said Naomi. "You know, in all the years I've known you, there's this question I've been dying to ask you."

Spooning chocolate ice cream blended with peanut butter cups into her mouth like someone who had not eaten in a few days, Anna stopped, intrigued. Swallowing, she regarded Naomi through eyes still glazed from the almost narcotic effect of the sugary treat, seldom indulged. "Oh my gosh, girl. You know you can ask me anything and I won't get offended. We're besties! What is it?"

Naomi glanced up into the rapidly darkening evening sky and gathered herself. "Hm. Okay. So, what I've always been curious about is, growing up in a place that was constantly populated with dead people, were you ever scared? You know, ghosts?"

Anna laughed hard. Spooning another gob of cold brown goo into her mouth, she spoke as it slowly melted against her tongue. "God, no. Not once."

"Not even when you were little?"

She shook her head. "Not even. I mean, you have to understand what we believe. Jews believe the Resurrection will happen to dead bodies, which is why you guys don't embalm, right? That on that magical day, life will return to your actual remains?"

"Something like that. What do you guys believe?"

Around another spoonful, Anna said, "We believe this body is nothing but a shell. Like, computers." She lightly touched Naomi's forehead. "This is your PC and hard-drive and memory chip." She touched her chest. "This is your power supply. But what runs it, the operating system and programs, that's what's here," she said, tapping her head and heart. "You cannot see a program. How do you even know a computer program or operating system exists? What happens to those when the box finally breaks down, shits the bed, or gets smashed? When the human box dies, the spirit enters sleep-mode. It's all there, every memory, but it's dormant. Doesn't even know it's asleep."

"Our souls go into screensaver mode? You believe that?"

Anna nodded, not quite ready to swallow the deliciousness on her tongue. "Mmhmm, yup—like screensavers, maybe! Good analogy. Then on the magic day when Christ returns with His legions of angels to gather up His harvest of sleeping programs that belong to Him, He takes them back to the Great Programmer in His Kingdom of Heaven, where they came from, to begin with. Each is given a new box, one that never wears out. Hey, who knows? Maybe we are all silver-colored there. Snap!—no more racism. Anyway, we believe this animated meat we're currently occupying is of little value. Like the empty shells coming through my house. The programs that once vitalized them are sleeping, like in animated suspension . . . dreaming, somewhere, until Christ comes for the ones given to Him by the Father."

"Hm. Interesting. Never knew that. So, like, what happens to the unwanted programs? You said Christ takes with Him only the ones given to Him."

Anna frowned. "Now, that part is scary. I don't like to think about it."

"Hell, you mean?"

Anna nodded, scooping up all remaining traces from deep inside the cup. "Hell. Hades. The place of eternal damnation."

"Fire and sulfur for eternity?"

Anna appeared thoughtful. "Don't know. Maybe. But sometimes I think Hell is separation from God and everyone you love here on earth.

And if it's not your actual loved ones, copies of them are there with you, being violated and tortured, crying and begging for you to please save them. Imagine everyone you love, like Abe, down there pointing fingers at you, saying you're the reason they're here; because in the flesh, you chose to deny Christ and instead embrace the prince of this world and his hateful ways, and so now they are paying the cost for your mistakes. You get to watch this every day, all day, for eternity."

"God, Anna. You are one dark, twisted little sister."

She grinned. "Ayup, that's me. But sometimes I think Hell might simply be darkness, with the sky on the Eastern horizon just starting to lighten, you know, that navy blue color just before the dawn; except that there, the sun never rises. Solitary confinement with added layers of teasing and torment, which is bad enough . . . but to me, it's the eternal rejection, the separation from the love of God that scares me more than anything." She shivered. "You don't believe in Hell?"

Naomi shook her head. "Nope."

"But you do believe in evil, yes?"

She nodded. "Evil spirits, fallen angels, demons: absolutely."

"Me too. I didn't think much about it until I picked up two executed murderers and heard about their hideous crimes. What an eye-opener. I believe the Holy Spirit and Satan are with us, all of us, all the time. Maybe some people are born evil. Some, like Bruce Barnette, hear it knocking and invite it in; give in to it."

"Anna, about Bruce—"

"Oh. Yeah. What you didn't want to tell me over your traceable, unsecured, possibly NSA-tapped cell phone connection."

"Laugh all you want; we computer nerd-herders know stuff mere mortals do not. Those little packets of info bounce around then get snapped up by shady government agencies to be used against you in a court of law."

"Did not know that."

Naomi nodded, expression sober. "He'll keep coming. You know that."

Anna's eyes teared up.

"Oh, honey, I'm sorry. I don't mean to scare you. But then again, maybe I do. You need to understand like I understand. The enemy does not repent. He is not humble before God. He does not even acknowledge the concept of sin. And the enemy must be neutralized before it . . . kills us."

"Bruce is not going to kill me."

Naomi's eyes moved rapidly in their sockets as she stared at her friend, a clear sign to Anna of serious analytics going on behind them. Naomi finally said, "No, probably not kill you. But he'll fuck you up badly for sure. He means to inflict serious bodily harm. He has proven himself capable and more than willing. Do you not see that?"

"I've tried to put it out of my head, but—" she relived the grotesque feeling of his hot alcohol breath washing over her face, big finger snaking under her underwear, then down . . . then in.

She nodded. "He will. I agree. And I trust you, Naomi, truly I do. You're the most logical person I know, calculating odds and probability with a brain like Watson. So, now that we know, again, I ask: What the hell can I do about it? Dad's sending me far away from you and Timmy all because of Bruce. It's only a matter of time until somehow, through the whisper-stream, he'll find out about STAB. One dark night, he'll show up. Unless Dad sends me to school in Somalia, I wouldn't put it past Bruce to—"

"Neither would I. We must end it, Anna, here and now. No matter what happens. Think about your future with Timmy and the safety of your parents. We are going to solve the problem like Israel solves its Gaza problem."

"And how's that?"

"A good plan, executed immediately and violently."

Anna's eyes flew open wide. She searched Naomi's face for signs of satire and found none. "I'm afraid to ask. Naomi, I'm not a fighter."

"Nor am I."

"Are you suggesting we find someone who is physically strong enough to make him think twice about pursuing me? Like, a biker or somebody?"

"No. Bringing another person into this would land us both in County. Three can keep a secret only when one is dead."

"How, then?"

Naomi hesitated. "Anna-banana: You and I are going to make a golem."

CHAPTER FIFTEEN

Abraham

Anna tilted her head. "A what? Go Lem? What?"

"In Hebrew, 'golem' means 'shapeless mass.' The Talmud uses the word as 'unformed' and sometimes to mean 'imperfect.' According to Talmudic legend, Adam is called a golem, which, in that context, meant a body without a soul."

Anna shook her head. "Sorry, babe, not following. Adam: The first man. Got that part. But the rest is . . . literally foreign to me."

"The Talmud is one of the Jewish holy books. In it, there's this tale of rabbis who got hungry while on a journey, so they created a calf out of earth, brought it to life, and ate it for dinner. The kabbalists—Jewish mystics—decided that these rabbis pulled off this supernatural act by means of permuting language. They had applied formulas found in the Sefer Yetzirah or Book of Creation. Just as God speaks and creates in the Genesis story, so, too, can the mystic.

"You've heard the magic word 'abracadabra,' like a million times, right? It comes from 'avra k'davra,' Aramaic for 'I create as I speak.' Anyway, I grew up believing that, under the rarest of circumstances, a human being may imbue lifeless matter with that intangible but essential spark of life: the soul. Back to your relatable analogy earlier, it would mean that Jewish mystics using ancient magic can grab a program from the 'Great Programmer' as you called him, YHWH, and install it inside a man-shaped form of their own making."

"Wait. I thought you just drank chocolate ice cream."

Naomi blinked. "Um, I did . . . why . . ."

Straight-faced, Anna said, "Because now I'm pretty sure you ordered the psychedelic shake." She laughed heartily at her own joke.

Naomi's dark eyes just then reminded Anna of some small, fierce animal, a wolverine, perhaps. "You're the one with the security problem. I'm only trying to help here."

Anna's eyes watered. "Oh, God, Naomi! I thought this was some kind of elaborate joke, and you were setting me up for an awesome punchline! I *so* didn't mean—"

Head down, hand up. "No worries. I know how strange all this must sound to a non-Jew," she said and resumed eye contact. "I suppose if I were in your shoes, I might feel the same. But Anna, listen to me now, ask questions later, okay?"

Anna nodded emphatically. "Mmhmm."

"Okay. The Sefer Yezirah—think of it as a guide to supernatural usage by some Western European Jews in the Middle Ages—contains instructions on how to make a golem. Several rabbis, in their analysis and commentaries of the Sefer Yezirah, have come up with different understandings of the directions on how to make a golem. Most versions include shaping the golem into a figure resembling a human being and using God's name to bring it to life since God is the ultimate creator of life."

Anna's hand shot up as if in class. Naomi, slightly annoyed, said, "Yes?"

"Shaping it out of what?"

"Earth. Organic material. Clay. Like making a snowman out of dirt. One rabbi says that to make a golem come alive, you would shape it out of soil, then walk or dance around it, speaking combinations of letters from the Hebrew alphabet and the secret name of God."

"Wow. Scary. Does a golem have a kill switch? I mean, think about it. They must, otherwise, we would have seen one by now. It would never run out of power like we humans do."

Naomi nodded. "To kill the golem, its creators would walk in the opposite direction around it while speaking the same words in reverse order. The Hebrew word '*galmi*,' meaning an 'unformed mass,' first appears in Psalm 139:16. You know Abraham, of course, right?"

Anna nodded. "Nearly sacrificed his own son for God. Yeah, half of our religion is based on yours."

Naomi's eyes sparkled. "Yes! The father of three world religions, he was. Bet you can guess what he made."

"A golem?"

"Yes!"

"Huh. Why don't I know this?"

Naomi shrugged. "All quite real nonetheless. I believe Abraham studied God's teachings and wrote the Sefer Yetzirah four thousand years ago. We never had any proof of that until recently."

"The big dig into Solomon's mines?"

Naomi nodded. "Mmhmm, exactly. The Sefer Yetzirah contains the secrets to how the entire universe was created. Abraham, and his teacher, Shem, the son of Noah, connected to God in a way no other human ever has. Abraham transmitted the Sefer Yetzirah to his son, Isaac; Isaac to Jacob; Jacob to Joseph; and thus, it was carried from generation to generation. The mystery of Creation is contained in the twenty-two letters of the original Egyptian hieroglyphs making up the Proto-Sinaitic alphabet, and in the various names of God which can be combined from them."

"So this is what you do in your spare time."

Naomi ignored Anna's comment. She noticed that the parents of rambunctious little kids at the wooden table beside theirs kept looking over. She lowered her voice and moved closer to Anna. "Other sources claim that once the golem had been formed, the creator needed to write on its forehead the letters Aleph, Mem, Shin—Fire, Water, Air—the three mothers from whom all fathers were created, in the order of Mem-Aleph-Shin, which makes the golem male; also Emet, which means 'truth.' And, most importantly, the secret name of God. Then, the golem would come alive.

"Erase the Aleph from Emet, and it means 'death.' That was thought to be the means to reverse it. That's the kill switch. Another way to bring a golem to life was to write the words and also God's secret name on a shem and stick it in the mouth under the tongue. Want to deactivate the golem? Simply yank the shem out of its mouth."

"Shem?"

"A little parchment rolled up with the words of life written on it."

"Quick question."

"Shoot."

"Why make a golem, and why kill it?"

Naomi nodded. "Two excellent questions. A golem is designed to obey its creator without question. No need to feed it. Never sleeps. Also, its strength is supposed to be super-human. So why end it? Jewish folktales about manlike golems tell what happens when things go awry—when the power, the life force, goes astray. Often with tragic and unpredictable results."

"Give me a for-instance."

"Suppose Timmy was a golem, and you told him to never stop kissing you. He'd take it literally and kiss you even after you had died of asphyxiation or dehydration. There's no way you could overpower Timmy, the golem. Get it?"

Flustered, glancing at the time on her phone, Anna exhaled. "Naomi. If you don't believe the golem stories, then why tell me all this? We were talking about solving the Bruce Barnette problem."

"Just because I don't believe the common era tales does not mean I don't believe in our holy books, Anna. Or that I don't believe Abraham made a golem," she said. Anna watched her tense up as though steeling herself before a confession.

"Archaeologists have been working in Timna Valley, this ancient dig site in southern Israel dating back to King Solomon. Well, they found something that was deliberately hidden. Something very old, dating back to the time of Abraham."

Anna appeared as she felt—astonished. She knew the stories of Solomon and, further back, Abraham, although, to her, it all felt so abstract, like Noah's Ark or Adam and Eve. None of these stories felt as real as the more recent parts of the Holy Bible. "You keep talking about it, please, tell me: What did they find?"

"Tablets of stone with paleo-Hebrew writing etched into them, still visible four thousand years later. Whoever created the tablets went through a whole lot of trouble—did some seriously deep and truly forward thinking—in order to find a place secure both from human theft and natural geologic destructive forces. They protected these tablets with the same vigor as our military today would take hiding their nuclear arsenal deep underground. They knew the power of it and couldn't possibly allow it to fall into the wrong hands."

"Wow. Incredible. I had no idea about this dig."

"It's not interesting news to the mainstream. Artifacts of my people's history get unearthed all the time, along with Christian finds, too. But you really have to do some digging of your own to find out about them. Mainstream media rarely makes any kind of big deal about it. Which is what I've been doing in all my spare time."

"Why?"

Above, Naomi saw the first stars of the evening, pinpoints of light in the gathering gloom. "Because I love my tribe, girl. Though this world never has, in case you haven't noticed."

Anna nodded. "Anti-Semitism. Alive and well."

"Got that right. So many enemies. People say the history of our tribe is a myth. It's difficult to prove that the Old Testament dates back over four thousand years because the ancient world was so violent. Anything my ancestors wrote down inevitably got torched by one enemy or another. Burned to a crisp. Oral tradition had to suffice until our holy books could be rewritten after our survivors got to safety. This happened over and over. Ours is a history of wars and persecution, Banana. Haters claim that our Holy Scripture is inaccurate—that eyewitness accounts got embellished over the generations, which resulted in key facts getting lost in translation. Each time an archaeology team carbon-dates a new scrap of writing dating back before the common era, and it exactly matches the scripture and holy books we have today . . . well. Let's just say it feels like vindication. Validation. It helps me to know exactly who I am and where I come from."

Anna nodded. "I totally get it. So tell me—I'm super-excited—what's on the tablets? Have you seen them?"

"I have!" Naomi barked, ignoring alarmed stares from the other patrons. Her brown eyes blazed under the bright overhead parking lot lights, around which insects unsuccessfully tried to merge with the warm false suns within.

The moon, Anna noticed, was nearly full.

"The tablets are sections, word for word, of the Sefer Yetzirah that many claim only goes back to, at most, about two hundred years BC, and many claim it was only authored in the common era. *Wrong* and *wrong*! It was written in the time of Abraham, and the tablets are physical proof!"

"Wow! Oh my God, Naomi, that is *so cool*!"

She laughed. "Right? I've been over the moon about this all summer; you don't even know."

"But how does this relate to making a golem?"

"Right. How does it? There's an answer to that, and here's where it gets weird. The real name of the Jew you worship every Sunday is not Jesus. His mother, Mary, did not call young Jesus to dinner—she called Yeshua."

Anna nodded. "I've heard that, yes."

Naomi raised her eyebrows. "Cool. So, I haven't told you all the steps from the Sefer Yetzirah needed to make a golem, but I did tell you that part of the formula is the secret name of God, passed from God to Noah, and on and on. For thousands of years, Jews have tried and failed to make a golem, and again, I don't buy the common-era folklore. I think I know why they failed. But now, today, in the age of NASA and robotic surgery, my people stopped trying. We, as a people, as a society even, have completely lost interest in the old magic. Most don't believe in it anymore."

"Why did they fail?"

With a face possessed of intense certainty: "Because they got the secret name all wrong."

Anna recognized the absolute conviction in Naomi's voice. It would haunt her forever, no matter what lay ahead.

———

"Dad, I am so very sorry. Your best friend, John, was a really sweet man. I thought of him as an uncle. I know you two were like brothers, almost."

Dave Dingel supported himself with a tight grip on the chair back like his knees might collapse under him. He inhaled deeply, exhaled slowly. Marge stood behind him, holding his arm, her head down. "Yes," he answered his daughter. "He was my brother, if not in blood, then forever joined at the heart and spirit. God knows I love him. Not in the past tense; for though his body may be dead, for certain, his spirit lives on. If all my faith leads me only to one wish fulfilled, it is for God to let me see him again, and never part again, forever."

Despite his best effort, she watched her father unleash a torrent of tears. Anna realized that this was the first time she had ever seen her father openly cry. She hugged him. He held her, face buried in her hair, body wracked with intense grief.

"Anna, your father and I need to fly to Memphis early tomorrow morning to pay our respects. Which means leaving you alone. Your father has given Grant the weekend off. We discussed it. We don't want anyone else coming over, and we don't want you going out."

As usual, Anna thought; Marge Dingel, with her condescending tone of voice and the finality of it, always; in this case, she destroyed a tender moment between father and daughter. Inside, Anna boiled. For her father's sake, she kept these red, angry thoughts at bay within her heart.

From her father, she sensed rigidness. He came back to himself and wiped his face on his white coat sleeve. "What is it, sweetheart?"

"It's just that I hadn't planned on being locked inside this place all alone during my last weekend in Pennsylvania for a long time."

"She wants to be with that boy, Dave," Marge interrupted again.

"Oh. Yes, that. School. St. Anne's-Belfield's admissions head called me this morning before I got the news about J—"

"It's okay, Dad. Take your time."

"Margie, can you hand me a paper towel or napkin or something, please?" Scowling, head down, she tore a sheet from the paper towel roll mounted on a bar under the sink and, closing the cabinet, thrust it at her husband. "They can't take you there for another week. They were full up when I had first called, jam-packed to capacity, but then some Korean kid decided her family needs her back in Seoul, so when she flies home, you are to fill her slot."

Anna felt her insides dancing the *paso doble*, but she hid it and congratulated herself on just how well she was hiding it. She hoped that her pupils weren't saucers, giving her away. "Well, you don't need to worry about Timmy; he's in Nashville all weekend. But what if Naomi stops over Saturday night? I'll stay inside all day Saturday. Sunday, I'll drive myself to church. Everyone will see me there. Then straight home. That's it, nowhere else, I promise. Dad, please. I don't want to be trapped in here alone with Marcus Midlothian all weekend. He truly creeps me out."

Without consulting his wife with a glance, he replied, "Yes. It's fine."

"Dave! I really would prefer if the girl didn't come by, corrupting our daughter with unchristian ideas—"

"Margie! Naomi Silver and her family are good people!" He shot Anna a wry glance. "Yes, Anna. She can keep you company. But I want her out by curfew; and no boys."

"God forgive you, Dave Dingel," said Margie. She shuffled into the hallway and out of sight.

He kissed Anna's head, then gazed down at her. She stood looking up at him through eyes wet with empathy for being wedded to a woman like her mother; and, more so, sympathy for one of the greatest losses of his life. She felt the bond between them that night was restored in full. All sins were forgiven.

———

"Yes. As for our latest guest, the job is nearly finished. Grant and I completed the embalming. He's a resourceful one, our Grant: He found a suit in a thrift store that more or less fits the giant. Not a cheap suit, either; a really expensive cast-off, maybe a donation from an Eagles defensive lineman or something. I have never in my life handled a suit or a guest that large."

Anna shivered. "Did you happen to see a bullet entrance wound right about . . . here?" she asked and pressed her right index finger above his left pectoral.

He frowned. "Yes, as a matter of fact. But how—"

"I asked the prison guy. I'm curious about something else he mentioned; I wonder if he was playing with me. Did he also have . . . angel-lust?"

"Anna! That guard should not have—"

"Dad. I asked. I interrogated them. Don't be calling the prison. They're really nice guys. So, did he?"

Dave nodded. "It happens sometimes. To females, too, if they happen to pass while lying face-down or somehow fixed in a vertical position at the time of death. Dead blood pools. It soaks into vessels and capillaries, swelling whatever parts happen to face down or are situated below the heart. It seeps into the flesh, making it purple-colored, sometimes blue. So, yes. The man is quite a unique specimen. Unlike any I have ever seen. I'm guessing that in life, he could've smacked down any of those Eagles linemen if he had put his mind to it. What a shame. Life is decisions, kiddo."

"Yep." She nodded. "And, Dad, I'm sorry for everything my decisions this summer have put you through. I never meant to hurt you . . . or anybody else."

He smiled and affectionately ruffled her hair. "Couple of hundred years ago, I was a teenager myself. It was a confusing time; for everyone, I should think."

She gave back a smile of such radiant warmth that he felt the intense pain in his heart ease a measure. "You're the best dad in the world. I love you so much," and she hugged him again.

He stood there patting her back, holding her. Then, he whispered, "Please be careful, whatever you do, while I'm gone. A kind of darkness has fallen over this house, like a pall. There's evil in this world, sweetheart. Lately, it seems to have taken an awfully keen interest in you."

CHAPTER SIXTEEN

Fear

"My flight leaves at eight. Gordon said he'll have someone waiting for me in baggage claim to pick me up."

"Timmy, just be yourself. Don't try to ham it up. Just . . . be that guy you were in the music video: That's the Timmy they noticed. Be him at all times. If you're feeling down or not at your best, think of me, like you did in the video. Okay?"

She heard him smiling as he thanked her. "No matter what happens, you have my whole heart, Anna Caperila. There's room in it for none other."

"Who's dropping you at the airport?"

"Dad. He's an early riser."

"When are you back home?"

"Sunday night. Just enough time to shower, hit the pillow, and grab a few hours of sleep before school Monday. I might not get to talk with you at all until Monday. I feel like I'm sliding fast down a long chute."

"Timmy, never feel like you owe me anything. I mean that. What we have needs no words. Anything you want to tell me, you will, when there's time in your warp speed life."

"It's true. I feel you thinking of me. No words needed. God knows, I love you, Anna."

"Go get 'em, tiger."

"See you soon, babe. Bye for now."

"Bye."

———

"Tomorrow's Sabbath. I'll go to temple, then we'll sit at table, lunching at home. Then we'll pretty much just hunker down, doing our own things. We don't normally go out. But this is different. I can't think of anything more . . . Jewish. I'll tell my family that I'm meeting with a girlfriend to review and discuss the findings in Timna Valley, which is true, so they'll believe me. But didn't yours lay rules on you about having no one over?"

"They did," Anna typed into the chat window. "But I fought and won the right for you to come over. You just need to be out by curfew. What'd you have in mind?"

"Wow. I feel honored. Can't divulge plans here. Not secure. Tell you when I get there. Eight o'clock sound good?"

"Yep, perfect."

"You haven't told him yet, have you? That you are crazy mad in love with him?"

"*No*! You taught me not to! You said to prove it with my body, but don't say it."

"What a bright pupil you are, Anna-banana. Does he tell you that he loves you?"

"Yes. Every time we communicate."

"Smirking over here. I believe that I have created a monster."

———

"They had ice cream. Sat together on one of the benches, talking. Then they split up."

Bruce felt his pulse quicken. "Where's Silver now?"

"Synagogue in the morning, otherwise, home. I've driven past it once every hour. It's Saturday. They're Jews, man. This is their holy day of rest, or prayer, or some shit. They ain't goin' nowhere, man."

"So Dingel's home? Her parents' cars—they both in the lot?"

"Yep. Started cruisin' past the haunted house at eight this morning. All Dingels are present and accounted for. All day. Nothing has moved. Now it's nearly eight at night—twelve hours of this mind-numbing bullshit. I'm kinda starvin'. Starin' at Casa de Corpse right now, in fact. What do you want me to do?"

Bruce rubbed his head. "Not happening today then. Just keep studying Dingel's house until nine; let me know if anything changes. Unless she leaves, then today's a total bust."

"What about tomorrow?"

Bruce exhaled. "Unlikely. Sunday's church day for the Dingelberries. The time when they beg forgiveness for sins they have no idea their precious daughter is about to commit."

Carmen nodded. "Anna might go out. Maybe she'll make a date with Timmy C. He'll be ready for you this time. Have you thought this all the way through? Maybe you should take some time. Think about it."

Bruce sniffed. "Had a whole summer behind bars to think about it. I'll break his other hand. He can play guitar with his tongue, like Jimi Hendrix. Besides, Caperila won't want her after I get through with her. I'll ruin that bitch for life. Just keep on Dingel and Silver. The right opportunity always presents itself. I've heard it said that the key to success is patiently preparing to seize it when opportunity knocks. Trust me, Carm: I am not asking you to waste your time. It'll happen, trust me."

"I trust you, man. Hey, hang on. . . ."

"What is it?"

"Silver's car, I think. *Yes!* That is definitely her car. I recognize the ADL sticker on the bumper."

"She's over there?"

"Mmhmm. I see her getting out . . . now walking to the back door, the one only the family uses."

"Keep eyes on it till nine. Maybe Dingel plans on following her somewhere. She may be grounded over the sex pics. If Silver is still there at nine, bail. We'll know she's grounded. Girls don't sit home on a Saturday night."

"But I'm starving, man."

"Carm. Are you actually thinking about letting me down?"

"No! Hell no. Staying till nine, man."

"If those two leave together in Silver's car, tail 'em. I need to know where they go. I know they like to go out at night for ice cream."

"Got it. Call you at nine with an update."

"*No.* I will call you."

In the mudroom, Anna and Naomi hugged. "What's that on your head?"

"A tichel. It's a headscarf Orthodox Jewish women wear when they're married. Some rabbis believe that hair covering is an absolute obligation for Jewish women, originating from Moses at Sinai, while others say it is a standard of modesty defined by the Jewish community."

"You're not married, or did something happen since we chatted online this morning?"

Naomi laughed. "I wish. I'm trying to be as modest as I can before the eyes of almighty God. With my Abe, well. I couldn't possibly be any more immodest." Anna shot her a conspiratorial smirk. "For this to work, you must also cover your head." She handed Anna a black tichel.

"Um, can you do it?" Standing behind her, Naomi wrapped and tied the headscarf for Anna. "How do I look?"

"Makes your blue eyes appear turquoise. We'll make you into a Jewish American princess yet, dear."

Anna smiled. "I'm on Team Yeshua."

Naomi nodded. "I'm beginning to see why, maybe. Listen, if this works, tonight, I want to come with you to your church service. Read things I was told never ever to read."

Anna blinked rapidly, confused. "Is this a joke?"

Naomi shook her head. "Remember me asking you about Yeshua, what He means to you?" Anna nodded. "Yeshua of Nazareth was born two thousand years *after* Abraham wrote the Sefer Yezirah, the Book of Creation, which breaks down the formulas God used to create the universe and everything in it. Anna, I believe in God completely. My faith is unassailable. I believe in the Sefer Yezirah; and now we have physical proof that it ties back to stories in the Book of Genesis just after the Great Flood.

"I believe that God touched Abraham, tested him, and found him worthy; He entrusted him with certain knowledge, which became the Sefer Yezirah. And I was raised to believe that the Messiah, or Christ, has not yet come; that the man you worship was only just a man, with no special power; and that His followers made up all those crazy stories of raising the dead. 'Black Magic' is what common-era rabbis claimed about those so-called *miracles* that apparently affected thousands of people.

"So then, can someone please explain how Yeshua's name ended up carved over four thousand years ago into stone tablet bearing the secrets of creation? That name didn't even exist at that time. It would be like finding Walt Disney's name beside some cartoon mice carved into a four-thousand-year-old rock. And explain to me why common-era rabbis continually failed to raise a golem?"

Anna shrugged. "I'm following, like, totally, but I don't know the answers to your questions. You told me about Hebrew words and dancing around men made of earth and about carving the words and the secret name of God into the clay-man's forehead. Writing it on a shim and sticking it under the tongue."

"Shem."

"Right; shem. So, rabbis either got the words wrong, or the secret name of God wrong, or the dance wrong?"

"Possibly, but *how* did a name that the world had never heard of until thousands of years later end up on the tablet? Don't you see? Like finding a perfect scale model airplane inside Tut's tomb."

"So, we believe Jesus—Yeshua—is a part of God; came from God; was sent here by God to deliver His word, and also asked by God to become the sacrificial lamb for all of mankind's sins. Any person from that moment on who simply believed this really happened, and who loved Yeshua for His loving sacrifice for us, would be saved."

"What happens postmortem if you do believe it's all true?"

"You only die once; bodily death. Your eternal soul, or 'program,' if you like, goes back to live happily ever after with the eternal Programmer. Get it?"

Naomi nodded. "Why do you believe so strongly? I mean for me; I was well trained. Besides, I don't believe in random. All of this . . . life, this world, didn't just happen. Couldn't have. A supermind with a great big heart is behind it. It's logical. Same for you? Trained?"

Anna slowly shook her head. "I never cared much for Marge's rants and the boring pastor's interpretations. So I picked up and read The Gospels for myself. That's what convinced me. The words and actions of His Apostles, the eyewitnesses, how they peacefully handed themselves over to be tortured, murdered—silenced—rather than to shut up and stop telling the world what they had seen and lived with, from a supernatural origin. If they did not believe it, fully, a thousand percent, they would not have walked away from their families and comfortable lives to go spread the Good News, knowing that doing so was guaranteed to end in horrifying torture and bodily death. This I believe, completely."

"Yeshua, in Hebrew, the name. Do you know what it means?"

Anna shook her head.

"It means 'to deliver, save, or rescue.' This word, which two thousand years later became someone's name, did not even exist in the time of Abraham."

Anna grinned. "There you go! Maybe we'll make a Christian American princess out of you yet."

Naomi smirked. "I'm with Team Moses."

Anna blinked, bewildered. "Wait. If what works? You're not thinking of trying out your theory on a figure made of dirt, for real . . . are you?"

"Did you think I was joking around?"

"Well, no. But I didn't think you meant for us to do this, like, now. Tonight. I can't leave, remember? And I don't think Dad will appreciate it all that much if he comes home to find the yard or landscaping all dug up."

Naomi placed both hands on Anna's shoulders. "Organic material . . . shaped like a man." She recognized the solid-state hard drive whirring hot behind Anna's bright blue eyes. Then she saw it find the file it was searching for.

"No! Are you *kidding me*? Oh, dear God. If Dad comes home and finds Hebrew names carved into the forehead of his latest project—"

"Words on a shem, dear."

"I can't even."

Naomi closed her hands around Anna's face, cool and dry. "Barnette is a golem from Hell that will never stop, Anna. Whatever drives that boy will not leave him until you and your parents suffer big time. And maybe even Timmy, too. Evil spends all its time searching our defenses for weaknesses, openings, opportunities to destroy or kill. I know this. And I don't need to step in Barnette to know dogshit. I can smell his evil from a distance.

Anna-banana, I love you. We need to work together, here and now. Put fear into him. Fear of pain is the only force that works on this species."

Anna left the conversation to disappear deep inside herself. She found it a struggle to hold onto a single strand of thought. *If I had told Bruce "no thanks" for the Coke and Seven, would all of this ever happened? I can't turn back time to find out. All I can do is try to deal with what's real. Bruce is real, and he will never stop. Look at what he's done to my family? To Timmy? God, I know You can hear me: please stop me if I'm wrong about this. Give me a sign. To protect my loved ones, I need to do something about him. I'm not asking for Your help.*

"Can't believe I'm agreeing to this. Okay, so what do we do now?"

Naomi grinned and took Anna's hand. "Lead me to a man-shaped form of organic material, then let me show you."

Anna flicked the switch, bathing the mortuary chamber in harsh bright light, causing them to squint. "This won't do, babe. Have any candles and something to light them with?"

"Well, let me think . . . okay, I do know where Mom keeps the Christmas jar candles and where Dad stashes his box of emergency taper candles. He keeps a long lighter in the junk drawer for relighting natural gas pilot lights and sometimes the outdoor propane barbeque. How many do we need?"

"All. So, this is our organic material here? Wow, big boy."

Anna's face turned pale. "You don't even want to know why he's here, trust me."

"Nope, you're right; I don't. No worries. We only need his man-shaped organic material. Want me to help you get the candles, or should I start on the shem?"

"You two get acquainted. I'll be right back."

Eyeing one of the rolling stools, Naomi walked over and seated herself at a white counter area, which appeared immaculately clean. She laid her purse down flat against the laminate countertop. Opening it wide, she pulled out a travel toothbrush case, then a small rolled-up piece of twenty-five percent rag parchment paper, and set these immediately before her. Reaching around into the back pocket of her black jeans, she set aside a folded piece of paper.

"Hey, Anna?" she yelled.

"What?" came the muted response.

"Change your clothes. Wear black. Anything you have, sweats, whatever, just make sure you have no skin showing above the ankle."

"Pain in my butt!" made its way down to the embalming chamber.

She spread open the tiny parchment mezuzah with her left hand. Using the charcoal stick sharpened to a small, dull point in her right, she carefully began wording the Hebrew, וְיֵשׁ כְלֹא מִם and below it, תמא on its own line. Beneath, for the first time in her life, she formed a combination of letters found carved into a stone tablet by an unknown rabbi more than four thousand years before tonight, carefully lettering עושי onto the mezuzah. Satisfied, she replaced the charcoal stick in the toothbrush case and closed it, then washed her hands at the sink using Mr. Dingel's chemical-smelling anti-bacterial hand washing liquid. As she tore off a clean paper towel, suddenly, a thought struck her.

"Anna, wait! Don't get dressed! I'm coming up," she yelled as she bolted from the chamber up the stairs. Anna came down from the second floor and nearly collided with her in the hallway.

"What's up?"

"Rainwater. Where can we find some around here?"

"What?"

"We've got to purify our bodies in a mikvah before performing the ritual."

Anna rolled her eyes. "I just changed my clothes. There's a koi pond out back, probably three or four feet deep. It's rainwater."

"Stagnant?"

"No, there's a pump running inside it constantly to keep it moving. Water comes from the rain barrels connected to the pump. Dad had them build a water effect, like a mini waterfall. It's clean natural water; otherwise, the fish would suffocate and die."

"Think the fish will get out of our way for sixty seconds?"

Anna shook her head. "You really are a pain in the ass."

Naomi nodded. "Go grab us a couple of beach towels, biggest you can find."

Anna returned, shaking the folds out of two brightly colored towels featuring suns, waves, and seagulls. She slapped them onto the kitchen table next to the candles and lighter.

"Anything else? Maybe some ashes and sackcloth? Some pottery shards to scrape our boils with?"

"Come on, quick: Strip all the way down and wrap up in a towel."

"In front of you?"

Naomi smirked. "Anna-banana, I'm probably the only one around these parts who has not seen you naked. And it's just me, so who cares? Come on, chop-chop."

Shooting Naomi her right middle finger, Anna complied, starting with the unwrapping of her tichel; Naomi did the same. "Okay," said Naomi. "Lead on."

It had been a hot August, and early September brought no change. Shedding towels, they stepped into the semi-private koi pond, shielded from the main road by winterberry and other shrubs. Inside the shallow pond, both felt it would be secure enough. They stepped in, gasping at the jarringly cool water. "How long do we need to be in here?"

Naomi said, "In and out. Jewish purification ritual. We're not going to splash around and shave our legs and pits in here. Just go all the way in, pinch your nose and slide under, then jump out and towel up."

After their quick dip, they stood, wrapped in towels, looking around to make sure nobody could have possibly seen them, and they retraced their steps, the asphalt of the parking lot still warm from the day, creating a delicious dichotomy against their chilled bare soles. Inside, both redressed. Naomi suggested they remain barefoot, as were her ancestors, to which Anna consented. She knew her father would never leave anything sharp or dangerous lying on the mortuary floor.

After Naomi re-wrapped and tied Anna's tichel, Anna scooped up the candles and lighter, and together they descended into the embalming chamber, hearts beating hopeful.

"Naomi, whatever happens next needs to solve my Bruce problem. If it does not, promise me that before you go home tonight, you and I will have created a viable Plan B."

Naomi nodded. "Done. But I'm excited to prove my theory and validate to the entire world that my people *are,* in fact, God's Chosen. Then, and I admit this is a little self-serving, overnight, I will become the most famous Jewish scholar of the common era—the Silver name forever overshadowing the Jacobs name. If it works. And I see no logical reason why it won't work."

"Naomi?"

"Anna-banana?"

"What if this doesn't work?"

Naomi glowered. "It won't if we go into it with any doubts whatsoever."

"Being honest. I am right now consumed with doubts."

"Trust me. I will purge them."

"How? I feel like this whole thing is a pantomime."

Naomi looked at her. "Mystical sound vibration encased in a syllable. If it is strong enough to reach the highest Spirit in all creation and transform anthropomorphic matter into a living creature, then the sound is strong enough to push out the doubts we're both feeling, I'm certain of it."

CHAPTER SEVENTEEN

Spark

"You're absolutely sure?"

"Bruce, man, I'm not blind."

"Tell me exactly what happened and when."

"It was 8:25 exactly because I had my phone on, texting. I was sitting in the bank lot under the light and close to the street so cops wouldn't hassle me."

"Was your license plate facing away from the bank?"

"Yeah. So, I look up, and across the back lot, I see both of 'em wrapped in towels, barefoot, like they're running on the beach or something. So I figure I gotta get a better look at this. When traffic let me, I crossed over, then walked around the far side of the Dingel Death Home, then looped in across the parking lot, hugging the far perimeter. I'm worried they'll see me, so I go really slow, in the shadows. And quiet. Pure stealth, man, like a ninja, picking my way across the rear of the lot, which has these thick hedges, like the kind you see carved into mazes, right? In the far corner, they drop their towels, butt naked, then step into this fishpond or some shit with a little waterfall. They were only in it a minute. Then I seen both of 'em hop out of there, naked as can be."

"How can you be sure? It was pretty dark by then."

"Full moon and those two are paler than ghosts. I saw Silver's titties and ass, only for a second. Let me tell ya, she is one hot—"

"What were they doing?"

"Skinny-dipping in Dingel's fishpond. Hot for each other, maybe. I hid until they ran back inside, then doubled back here."

"No pics?"

"Uh-uh; too dark."

Bruce exhaled. "Monday, let Sue and Tammy in on what you saw. By final bell, whether or not they are lezbos is irrelevant: Every kid in school will think they are."

Carmen sniffed. "Yeah. Cool."

"How many candles do we have, total?"

Anna's lips moved as she opened the box of emergency candles and counted them. "Twenty-two."

"No way. You're joking, right?"

"No, why?"

"The original Paleo-Hebrew alphabet is exactly twenty-two letters. Proto-Hebrew goes all the way back to the historic kingdoms of Israel and Judah. Artifacts of the Hebrew Bible in its original script use this alphabet. It's a derivative of the Egyptian hieroglyphs, the Phoenician alphabet. You'll see when I show you the shem I drew while you left me all alone here with our rigid friend."

"He was nobody's friend."

"His face looks like melted wax. I've never seen an embalmed person before." Naomi glanced about at the walls and countertops. "In this room, I'd say you should place one candle every two feet. Doesn't need to be exactly two feet; just make them even."

"Dad and Grant never finished the final phase, which is hair and makeup. So, he looks just exactly like a dead guy right now."

"What exactly did they do to him?"

While placing candles, Anna responded, "Well, first they shaved his face, cut his hair, then washed him down with anti-bacterial soap. Next, they moved him all around, flexed all his limbs to work out the rigor mortis; you know, stiffness after death. Then they pushed out all of his natural bodily fluids and refilled him with formaldehyde-based embalming fluid that preserves his flesh and gives it the realistic pinkish hue that blood normally would. And they injected fluid into organs here and there, wired his jaws shut, and inserted eye caps. My dad's intern found him that suit."

"Decent suit. Custom jobs like that aren't cheap. What about the mouth? Can it be opened?"

Anna shook her head, "Not so much. Eyes and mouth are permanently closed. Dad likes using skin glue and sometimes these plastic flesh-colored oval-shaped eye caps that sit right on the eyeballs, which secure the eyelids in place. He closes the mouth either by sewing or wires, depending on what he finds in there. If he sews the jaw shut, he threads suture string through the lower jaw below the gums, up and through the gums of the top front teeth, into the right or left nostril, through the septum, into the other nostril, and back down into the mouth. He ties the two ends of suture string together. When he wires it shut, he uses a needle injector to insert a piece of wire anchored to a needle into the upper and lower jaws. Then he twists the wires together. He'll look at photos of the living person, then wiggle and shove the jaw around until the face strikes a pose similar to what he sees. He's a real artist with this stuff, my dad. Just curious, or does it matter for what we're doing?"

"Um, so gross. Almost sorry I asked. I cannot believe you've spent your entire life immersed in this distorted alternate reality."

Anna shrugged. "It's only tissue. Remember what we Christians believe; lying on the table is an empty shell, useless in every way. Comes from dust; returns to dust. The 'program' that dwelt within it, that spark of life, is elsewhere now. If you knew what I knew about this guy, you'd know that this particular program is not destined to spend eternity in a good place. Not good at all."

"Whatever, Anna. It's gruesome and sinister. Even if you're right about souls, it's still eerie as hell, cohabitating here with the evil dead. No offense intended."

"You get used to it, believe me."

Naomi shook her head. "I could never. Yours is a far braver heart than mine, Anna-banana. So, the reason I asked about the mouth is because you will need to insert the shem under the tongue. Think you'll be able to, you know, part the lips and let me know if it's doable?"

"Sure! Soon as I'm done with the candles. Are you going to light them?"

Naomi nodded. As Anna finished placing the twenty-second candle, Naomi lit the first candle and slowly followed Anna's two-foot placements.

Snapping on a pair of latex gloves, Anna moved to the head of Marcus Midlothian. She took her first good look at him. "Everyone appears so peaceful in death," she muttered, images flashing of his victims' facial expressions, what she had imagined they had looked like during their horrifying endings.

Such macabre, unspeakably evil crimes. What did his face look like when he committed those despicable acts? Was he angry and defiant as he stared out from his death chamber at the families of his victims, when he promised to return and do the same to each one of them? She groaned in horror and shivered at these thoughts.

"What's that?"

"Oh, nothing," Anna said. She pressed her fingers down against the lips, hoping she could eventually plump them back up when they were done. Pulling down his jaw with all her strength while trying to get purchase under his front teeth, she spread the teeth apart a hair's width short of two millimeters. "Naomi," she said, holding her finger and thumb apart for her to see. "Is this wide enough for the shem?"

Naomi nodded. "Plenty! Good job! You are so brave. Balls so big the drag-marks are visible from space."

Anna laughed hard, which infected Naomi with laughter. Both had felt icicles forming deep inside, caused by fear of the answer to *What if it works?* So the moment of warm jocularity was welcome. It felt surreal, clearly the oddest, most ghoulish, and morbid moment of their lives.

After she snapped the latex gloves into a foot-pedal garbage cylinder, Anna stood, hands on hips. "Ready to shut off the lights?" Naomi nodded, and Anna flicked the switch. All at once, the scene's mood changed, affecting their states of mind almost immediately.

It was time.

Anna silently stood by the light switch, watching Naomi tightly roll her little piece of paper. From where she stood, it resembled an unlit cigarette. Shem in hand, Naomi stood at Marcus Midlothian's head, then motioned for Anna to stand to her right. Unearthly quiet. The tomblike silence, together in a necropolis, alone with a cadaver: Reality settled into them. "We really gonna do this, Naomi?"

Her right hand found Anna's left and clasped it firmly. She bowed her head and closed her eyes; Anna followed suit.

"Bless me, God, with Your healing power, protect me from all harm, shield me from pain. And when I wake, God, give me the courage and passion to fight for the sacred treasure You have granted me: my life. Amen."

"Amen."

"In the name of Adonai the God of Israel: May the angel Michael be at my right, and the angel Gabriel be at my left; and in front of me the angel Uriel, and behind me the angel Raphael.. . . . and above my head the presence of God. Amen."

"Amen."

"In the world which will be renewed, *B"al'ma d'hu 'atid l'ithaddata*, and where He will give life to the dead. Fill me with strength, God, and I will fight for my life. Our Father, our King, we have sinned before You. Our Father, our King, we have no King but You. Our Father, our King, act benevolently with us for the sake of Your Name. Our Father, our King, remove from us all harsh decrees. Our Father, our King, annul the intentions of our enemies. Our Father, our King, foil the plans of our foes. Our Father, our King, frighten away every oppressor and Adversary from against us. Our Father, our King, close the mouths of our adversaries and accusers. Amen."

"Amen."

Naomi whispered, "Ask God for what you want."

During the over nine-hundred Sunday worship services in which Anna had partaken, inside rooms filled with the faithful gathered in His name— not once had she ever physically felt God's presence in the room, though she knew He was there, as per His promise: "For where two or three gather in My name, there am I with them." Now, here, in the candlelit subterranean confines of a mortuary, in the presence of corpse, she *did* feel like God was with them, listening. The feeling of connection with the Creator of all things infused her every cell, every fiber, with excitement and also with power. Every nerve in her body tingled pleasantly.

"Our Father, our King, I do not seek revenge, for vengeance is Thine. I pray for my enemies that they may discover the clues Your Holy Spirit leaves for every one of them, that they may follow them into the loving peace that can only be realized in Your embrace. I ask only for myself that You do for me what I am powerless to do for myself. Please strike fear into the hearts of my enemies. Please make them afraid of me, Father. To every enemy who has hurt me or my family this summer, please make Your living hand real, here in this world, strong without limits, to visit deep and mortal fear into the hearts of each so that none would ever again strike against me and mine. Our Father, our King: Please protect me and my friend, Naomi Silver, our families, and our friends from harm, and may your Holy Spirit make its home inside each one of us. May Your Spirit guide our every thought and action. This, I pray in the name of Your Son, Yeshua, whom I love more than my life. Amen."

"Amen."

Naomi, glancing at Anna, whispered, "Mystical sound vibration encased in a syllable. Repeat what I say: *Aleph, Mem, Shin, Emet. Yeshua.* Like this: *Yess shoo ahh.*"

Anna soundlessly mouthed the words. Guided by Naomi's eyes, together they said the words in order, loud and clear, in perfect syncopation: "*Aleph, Mem, Shin, Emet, Yeshua.*" Naomi nodded. She pulled Anna into a clockwise motion, the first of twenty-two circles around the corpse of Marcus Midlothian. As they rounded the corner back to their original starting position at the body's head, "*Aleph, Mem, Shin, Emet, Yeshua.*" Around they went a second time. Anna *felt* the words, especially 'Yeshua,' as something more than sound produced by continuous and regular vibrations. *There is more to this than some foreign-sounding noise,* she thought. There was a mystic, almost musical quality to the words. Candle flames bowed as if on the verge of separating from their wicks. Walking and talking, flames followed behind the two celebrants as they moved. Anna's ears no longer registered the sounds of four moist bare soles slapping against tile in perfect unison. Now, all she heard, or more accurately, felt, were spectral sound vibrations encased in syllables.

Light and sound merged within them; both reeled with the sensation of their insides thrumming with every cadence. "*Aleph, Mem, Shin, Emet, Yeshua.*" Anna sensed an enchanted delirium forming deep inside, reminiscent of the cool, secluded grotto and the feelings never before experienced before Timmy. Now, she felt a similar ecstasy infusing her body and her soul, laying bare all that she knew herself to be. The critical-thinking intellectual, curious, emotive, and passionate Anna, perceived by unfamiliar peers to be quite the opposite: emotionally aloof at times, reticent, even taciturn. As from outside her body, she was shown Anna, the young woman suffused at times with anger, fear, loneliness, and melancholy. The sexual Anna, her body awakened by a boy, aching for his impassioned touch against her skin, causing her pleasure so addictively fierce that she knew a return to life before him would now be impossible. The loving Anna, who wanted more than anything to fall into the protective arms of her loving God and never leave.

During one of their rotations around the organic matter formerly known as Marcus Midlothian, Anna decided that love is the force responsible for the universe and everything in it.

All now merged into one being: Anna here, now, tethered by some fiber-optic thread to a Kingdom of love and power far beyond any corporal capacity to understand. She thought of night bugs trying to merge with false overhead lights, bright but cold. Now, suddenly, she understood those tiny simple 'programs'; she related to them perfectly. *I am but a tiny simple program, and God is the true light*, she thought.

Subliminally, her spirit ached to travel through that wormhole straight to the Kingdom of golden-white light, to a place with love so radiant, inviolable, and pervasive that it left no room for darkness or evil. A Kingdom thrumming above her, all around her. It was here, now, present in the room with her. For the very first time, she knew it existed because, now, she felt it come closer.

"*Aleph, Mem, Shin, Emet, Yeshua.*"

The sound hypnotized Anna; suddenly, she realized in horror that she had completely lost count of their revolutions. As if reading her mind, Naomi squeezed her hand, glanced at her, communicated only with her eyes: *I've got this*, said those fierce, pretty eyes.

Anna relaxed. She thought only of Yeshua and her faith—stronger than it had ever been; stronger than she ever knew possible. She watched as He raised Lazarus from four-day-old death and decomposition. She saw Yeshua, on the third day, burst the ropes and roll away the multi-ton stone that had locked Him inside His tomb; He smiled at her and held out His wrists, inviting her to touch the healed wounds. He showed her what the Kingdom of everlasting life and love looks and feels like. She felt that power now as it surged and swirled in an all-consuming, spirit-lifting tornado.

"*Yeshua! Yeshua! Yeshua!*" Anna sensed the same power working inside Naomi—felt it pass through herself into Naomi's hand. *Whatever's happening to me, some of this bright and glorious new power spilled over into my best friend. We are so in this together.*

"*Aleph, Mem, Shin, Emet, Yeshua.*"

That was when every candle flame withered, leaving only glowing wicks.

Naomi had stopped at Midlothian's head. Anna, still deeply enraptured in an otherworldly fugue state, barely registered the changed at first. She opened her eyes wide. Glowing flameless wicks rapidly cooling to black. Now in obsidian darkness, she relied on memory to find the light switch. She squinted from the flood of bright white light and watched Naomi's pupils contract. "Was that supposed to happen?" she whispered.

Naomi shrugged, then shook her head. "No," she whispered back. "Not in my research. We need to finish with the lights on, I guess."

Her left hand clutched a tightly rolled parchment. She waved it at Anna. Carefully taking the shem from Naomi, Anna bent at a forty-five-degree angle. She inserted it between the lips and teeth, angling it down until she was certain the tip plus one inch rested beneath the tongue. For added security, holding her left hand under the chin, she pushed down on the head with her right until she had closed the gap on the shem. *Locked in place. Not going anywhere,* she thought.

Standing straight, the flesh of her arms and back prickling with awe, she turned to face Naomi. She mouthed the words, "Now what?"

Naomi pointed to the mortuary door. She walked with Anna in tow. Outside of the candlelit chamber, in a starkly contrasted space filled with normal incandescent and fluorescent lighting, as well as the air conditioning Dave Dingel always kept at a chilly sixty-nine degrees Fahrenheit, both felt jarred back to full cognitive alertness, much to their chagrin.

"Did it work? I mean, how will we know if it worked? *When* will we know?"

Naomi grinned and shook her head. "I'm not an esoteric rabbi, unfortunately, in case you haven't noticed. Wish I knew if it worked; wish I knew the right expectations for how long it takes to work. I was hoping it would all happen immediately; that our golem in there would sit up, turn its head, lift a finger—something, anything. What time does your dad want me out of here?"

"Eleven-thirty, latest."

"What time is it now?"

"We stripped off everything! No watch, no phone. Hang on," Anna said, dashing up the steps two at a time, then called back down. "Eight-fifty. Come up."

Naomi joined her in the kitchen. "What's say we get ourselves a couple of iced teas or whatever you have, go back inside the chamber, and we'll hold a prayer vigil until eleven. Can't hurt; might help."

Thinking, Anna slowly nodded. "Yes, yes. 'For the power of the prayer which a righteous person prays is great.' It's from our Book of James. I've always believed it. God the Programmer reads everything in His inbox, from those who always try to obey Him."

"So if Marcus Midlothian prayed in the last minute before his death, wishing everyone around him to suffer a horrifying, painful death, where would that prayer go?"

"Spam folder."

"Ah. Do you believe God answers your prayers?"

"Believe? I know He does, always. It's a matter of how you ask. Don't pray for what you want. He already knows what you want. Pray to understand what He wants. Get it?"

"A for-instance?"

"When Jesus prayed to His Father in the Garden of Gethsemane the night of his betrayal and delivery to Roman crucifixion, knowing it was coming, because the Father had shown Him everything before it happened, He said, 'Father, if you are willing, let this cup pass from me; however, not my will, but yours be done.' So, if the golem is God's will, then something will happen. I guess what I mean is we should pray for the golem to work, but only if it pleases Him. We must never tempt God or ask only for selfish things. If God has an unfulfilled purpose, and the golem can fill it, then, well: It can work. Didn't you feel it in there?"

"Feel what, hon?"

"God's presence?"

Naomi blinked. "It definitely did not feel *ordinary*; I will say that."

Anna shook her head. "No. It was anything but ordinary. I think that, maybe, Naomi Silver, your dream of becoming the most famous Jew of the common era might just possibly come true."

"I think, Anna Dingel, that if it does, and the world as we know it changes forever because of Yeshua, then I will break from tradition and spend the rest of my life studying Him through changed eyes. But still be a devout, practicing Jew. It's who I am."

"Lots at stake here," said Anna grimly.

"Mmhmm."

"Ready to go back inside?"

Naomi nodded.

Both consciously worked to hide nervousness from the other, like some powerful current lighting up their spines.

CHAPTER EIGHTEEN

Malware

Anna knew she was dreaming, but the dream made her feel so good that her semi-conscious mind willed her dreaming mind to stay under, even if only for a little while longer. In the dream, she walked in circles, slowly at first, then faster . . . so fast that no longer could she see her milky white feet with mauve nail polish, though in the dream, mauve just seemed black. She smiled and laughed like a reveler around the maypole, a member of a human ring so bright, not entirely dissimilar to photographs of the planet Saturn, except made of pure golden light. Her dreaming mind knew that Naomi held her left hand and Timmy held her right, but neither were visible to her anymore. It was enough to know both, whom she ardently loved, were there to share this with her. The sensation was nothing like dizziness, orbiting about inside the event horizon of light; rather, it felt similar to what she had felt in the woods when Timmy pressed his face against her most private self. Any moment now, the spinning would climax into something indescribably poignant and wonderful. She had to remain asleep to find out what that magnificent zenith would be and how good it would feel.

Her phone buzzing on the nightstand ended it cold. She grabbed the angry interrupter, recognized Naomi's number, and, mouth bone dry from sleeping seven hours with it open, she answered with a croaked, "Um, hi."

"Wake you up, did I, sleeping beauty?"

"Mmhmm." She cleared her throat. "Went down fast, slept hard."

"Anna-banana, splash some cold water on your face, go downstairs, and get your cute little heinie in the mortuary to check on our experiment."

The events of last evening gripped Anna like a cold grapnel. "Okay, stay on the phone with me, let's go down together," she said, tearing away her sheet and light summer blanket. She wore only her soft cotton nightshirt as she vaulted out and down, skipping the cold face splash enroute to the mortuary. The mudroom in her periphery, she noticed something askew and stopped. The back door was open. "Did we close the back door after we returned from the koi pond mikvah?"

"Yes," said Naomi.

"Weird." She closed the door, and down she went until she arrived at the embalming room.

The door was wide open.

"Naomi, after putting away the candles, I distinctly remember going back down for one last check to see if I had overlooked anything. Then I shut the door behind us."

"Uh-huh."

"Well, the door is open . . . and the back door, which I always check to make sure is locked every night, was also open."

Silence. "Anna, you're not joking. Right?"

"I'm going inside." She reached in and flicked on the light switch.

The table was empty.

Frank Barnette's silver Ram coasted into his driveway at one-thirty Sunday morning. He found the back door unlocked. The screen door closed automatically, but the wooden inner door was open, allowing air-conditioned air that he paid dearly for to spill out uselessly into the hot, muggy night. *No doubt the unit's been cranking away nonstop, burnin' up 'lectricity,* he thought.

Cursing under his breath, he slammed the door behind himself, paying no mind to the noise it generated. He toed off his cowboy boots and walked into the living room to behold the frequent panorama of his diabetic, obese wife, Heidi, passed out on the couch, mouth open like an unlovely pink pothole. Loud and low snoring filled every corner of the untidy room. He saw the empty bottle of wine beside the prescription bottle of morphine tablets on the coffee table. *Pathetic.*

Upstairs, he hooked a left into the bathroom and brushed his teeth.

He had taken to using the spare bedroom across from Bruce's room, sparsely furnished with a twin long bed and nothing else besides Heidi's crappy Christmas wrapping stuff and exercise equipment she'd bought after watching slim young models on a televised home shopping network with not one iota of intent ever to use them.

There was a large closet across from the bed, empty, save for a few unused bedrolls from the days when Bruce wanted Frank to take him camping and a stack of old family photo albums nobody ever looked at. He did not flick on the overhead bulbs, as the full moon brought in plenty enough cornsilk-colored light, at least enough not to stub his toe on Heidi's crap and to see the outline of the bed wedged against the dark corner.

He stripped off his t-shirt, jeans, boxers, and socks and collapsed into the bed, deeply exhausted from his exertions with Jennifer, the young woman half his age whom he had gotten to know through his work and with whom he spent most of his evenings. *Showering must wait until the morning*, he thought, for it soothed him to fall asleep with her body's musky traces still clinging to him. Thinking of her made him hard again. He lay on his left side, fondling himself. He thought of Jennifer as she faced his feet and straddled his face. *God, the most perfect view in the world.* The bed squeaked as he pleasured himself. He did not care if Bruce or Heidi heard it. Thoughts of Jennifer were just so wonderfully distracting.

Those very thoughts of Jennifer had distracted Frank nearly to the point of oblivion when he suddenly realized the presence of a shadow exiting the closet, jarring him out of his fantasy and into the very real terror of the night.

———

"Naomi. We did not think this all the way through, so caught up in ancient tablets and paleo-Hebrew words. What do you think my dad will do to me when I pick him up at the airport tonight and tell him his latest project is missing?"

"Calm down. God, you sound like your head is going to explode."

"We are *way* past that. Dad's gonna kill me!"

"Stop! We'll figure this out."

"We suck at figuring things out together, Naomi. I am dead meat. What am I supposed to say? You tell me. Gee whiz, Dad, Naomi, and I invoked the original power of Creation and brought Marcus Midlothian back from the dead. Displeased with our accommodations and service level, he walked out. Think he'll buy that?"

Anna fell silent. In a tone of decided finality, Naomi said, "We will lie. I think it was Mahatma Luther Gandhi, the famous peacemaker, who said famously, 'The truth shall set you free. But when it does not—lie. But lie well.'"

Through the pain, Anna laughed. "Yes, that guy. You know that you truly are crazy, don't you?"

"Crazy problems call for crazy solutions. Also, the bigger and weirder the lie, the more believable it becomes. First, you must convince yourself of it before you can expect others to believe and buy in. You kicked me out at eleven-thirty. Bank security cams across the street will confirm this. Someone came in the back door—probably one of the Barnette rocks-and-paint squad—and stole the body while you slept. Cams wouldn't confirm or deny that. They came in through the backyard and back door. If Carmen, Earl, and Bruce don't have iron-clad alibis for last night, they'll be the ones questioned. Your dad will see you as the lucky survivor of yet another near-miss tragedy happening to you and your family. Instead of blaming you, he will love you all the more, not only for surviving but for keeping a cool head through it all. You will hang up and report the theft to the police."

Anna remained silent. "Maybe. But police won't find any evidence of forced entry."

"No maybes! That is exactly what happened. To police—to the entire world—someone got in somehow and snatched the body. Nobody would think otherwise, and nobody would blame you. Not kidding; call them right after we hang up to report a crime. They'll file a report. They can't speak with your father today because he's not here, so just respond to their questions honestly and succinctly. What time I came over, when I left, how we talked for hours, how you locked the back door before going to bed. How you noticed the door was open. You must report the body missing in order for this to work. Your father won't be home until tonight. You can't bother him; he's away at his best friend's funeral. They'll be gentle and view you as a crime victim. They'll dust around doors for fingerprints, take your statement, and leave. Then, you're covered. I mean *we*, bestie, are covered."

"I locked the door. I really did."

"Yes, you really did! Your dad knows your routines. See? You're all worked up for nothing. And missing what's really important here."

"My heart is about to pound out of my chest, Naomi. The last person to raise the dead was Yeshua. Oh. My. *God!*"

After a pause, "I believe that now. All of it. Sorry I ever doubted it."

"What do you think's going to happen now that it's . . . out there?"

———

Sunday evening, Earl swung by Carmen's parents' house to pick up his friend. "Some place the cops won't look twice at us," Earl said.

"The spot. Varnum's Redoubt."

Earl nodded. "Good idea." He wound out the first gear of his careworn Toyota Corolla. Stunned from the day's events, Earl said, "Holy *crap*, man! What just happened?"

Carmen shook his head. "Cops interrogated me for almost two hours. Where was I at precisely this time last night. 'Where was Earl, where was Bruce?' 'Dude, I was passed out asleep at one-thirty in the morning like I always am—what the hell do you even want with me?'"

Earl nodded. "Same here. Exact times, where, and who with. I had to remember every minute. Like living my life twice."

"I still haven't heard from Bruce. Have you?"

"No, Carm, for the eleventh time: No."

"Can't believe his old man's dead. Who do you think did it?"

"Who hates us, Carm? Had to be the Dingelberries."

"Come on, man. Those Bible-bangers ain't into murder. No way."

"Well, who then?"

Carmen shook his head and returned to his comfortable, reflective silence. The gas station came into view up ahead. "Rumor has it that his ass got split open like a ripe melon. Had his guts ripped out. I don't think we know anybody capable of something like that. Not even those animals in County."

Silently they walked, hugging the tree line, using the hiking trail as much as possible. They avoided Route 23 driver sight lines to the extent possible. Mosquitoes plagued Earl, but not so much Carmen. "They love me, what can I say? My blood is sweet, like me."

Carmen hissed. "Yeah. Sweet as piss. I still can't believe it. Bruce must be a mess. I mean, I know he and his old man were on the outs ever since the arrest. But still, it's his dad, man. Imagine if your dad got done like that?"

"Yeah, I'd find out who did it for sure. He'd spend a good hour roasting over a slow fire, impaled from ass-to-mouth on a metal spit while I turned and basted him."

"Same. My dad's a dick sometimes, but he never beat me for nothin' I didn't earn."

"Carm, we know these people. Did Mr. Barnette have any enemies? Was he into some illegal shit or something?"

He shook his head. "No way. Not Frankie B. He was a cop way back when till he got shot in the line of duty. Was a prison guard, too, fairly recently. Maybe it was an ex-con who got let out; had a beef with him. He was no lawbreaker. You can't get jobs like that, with all the background checks and investigating they do on you if you're hooked up somewhere with criminal types. Uh-uh, no way, not a chance. The only time he was ever charged with anything was when he popped Daddy Dingelberry in the eye. Bruce said so, too."

"So maybe his murderer is somehow tied to Dingel. Maybe some mob hit man who owed Dingel a favor, like in that mafia movie about godfathers. Remember the undertaker owed a favor?"

Considering it, insofar as his limited critical thinking capacity allowed, Carmen nodded. "I'll buy that. Could be Dingel."

Earl's mouth drew into a tight line. "I will fuck that guy up. Keep Bruce out of it. You can help if you want. I can trust you to keep your mouth shut, take it to the grave, can't I??

Carmen nodded. "Damned straight I'll help."

Having arrived at 'the spot' finally, the two bounded up the rear of Varnum's Redoubt. Inside the grassy bowl, they sat cross-legged, shielded from park rangers along Route 23. The whole of the grass-covered indent was bright enough to see clearly underneath the crystalline delight of a few trillion stars and a moon so full and clear that it seemed within arm's reach.

Digging into his back pocket, Earl withdrew a flattened pack of cigarettes and a disposable lighter. He shook one out and offered it to Carmen, who accepted, and then he took one for himself. Carmen grabbed the lighter and lit Earl's first, then his own. He inhaled deeply, held it for a five count, then blew it to his left side, as he always did.

At a quick glance, the shadow on the ground at the far-left side of the redoubt struck Earl's frontal cortex as possibly a log or thick tangle of weeds, thrown by shadow in strange relief under the bright full moon; he'd never seen anything like it there before.

Yet, something deeper inside his lizard brain, not dissimilar to a large invisible hand, now turned his head left for him, forcing him to take a longer second look.

"Psst. Carm," he said, pointing to the shape. Following Earl's finger to the source, Carmen stopped drawing on the cigarette and stared.

"What is that?" he asked, normal volume.

"Shh! Hell if I know," Earl whispered. He didn't think he wanted to know what that something might be, although the word 'payback' whirled far back in his mind. Earl knew he could summon that idea if he wanted to, but he didn't. *Something creepy is going on here, something* extremely *creepy.* He found he could not escape the idea that it *did* have something to do with their persecution of the Dingels. The drone of male crickets scraping out their desperate fall mating music suddenly moved from pleasant background noise to a major annoyance as he strained his ears in the direction of the shape that did not belong.

"Animal in the weeds? A deer, maybe? They're protected here. Have full run of the place, and so they multiply like rabbits. See 'em dead all the time on Pawlings and Route 23," Earl muttered.

"Earl," said Carmen and searched for his eyes. Finding them in the darkness, he said, "Ain't no deer, man."

Suddenly overcome with a feeling of stifling, directionless panic, Carmen watched as a darkness, in the shape of a Goliath, arose robotically, slowly, stiffly. He thought of a Frankenstein monster waking from its two-hundred-four-year nap. Except that this wasn't fiction, and the thing was dressed like some acromegaly diseased banker. Not a single sound belied its movements. It sat fully upright now. "Doesn't move right," he whispered. He watched the head turn, an unnatural movement, toward them. It had seemed mechanical, like a painted fiberglass-resin spook figure in a Jersey Shore haunted house.

"Hey! You there!" Earl shouted. He unfolded his unsteady legs to stand. Carmen followed Earl's example.

The still night air now reeked of nervous sweat. Two hearts thrummed along at unusually high rates. Mankind's most primordial survival instinct—fight or flight—demanded a quick decision. Carmen felt the sudden urge to take a burning wet shit. Decision made. "I'm outta here," he said. In the time it took to blink, Earl's hand shot out and grabbed his friend's wrist. Carmen, immobilized and restrained as much by emotion as by Earl's hand, stopped.

"Hey. Asshole. Yeah, I'm talkin' to you," Earl said loudly. He flicked his lit cigarette at the outsized man figure, which now stood, unmoving. Both watched a trail of sparks follow, then explode a little as the cigarette found its mark somewhere near the waistline.

"Is he smokin' a cig? What's that in his mouth?"

"He's about to be smoking in Hell," Earl growled.

The thing took its first step toward them: crunch, scrape, crunch. It appeared to step forward—more like lurch—with its left leg, then it dragged its impossibly long right leg up from behind, even with the left. These were the steps of a giant, the biggest they had ever seen. Now four feet closer, they both saw the cigarillo canting down from the mouth.

"Let go of me, man!" Carmen said. "I'm out!"

"Carm. Two of us; one of him. We're taking this pervert out." Then, louder, "You got no business lurking in parks after dark trolling for boys. Time for you to die."

Carmen whispered, "You really mean to take him out?"

Earl nodded. "Good practice for David Dingelberry. Stand your ground. Make him come to us. When I say go, rush him. I'll hit him high; you take out his knees. Then I'll stand on his neck until the flopping stops."

Carmen desperately needed a toilet. "You're nuts, Earl! Let's go! C'mon, now!"

The thing that had risen from the ground like Hell's version of resurrection took another crunch–scrape step. It closed the gap now to only eight feet. Carmen recognized the preternaturalness of these movements. Now, under pale moonlight, he could make out facial features. Eyes that were closed tightly made no sense to him whatsoever. It didn't walk; it *shambled.* Just then, it took another giant metronomic step, crunching and scraping. Eight feet away had become five. Neither saw the rise and fall of a breathing chest nor heard any sounds that would indicate respiration. No twitches of neck or arm muscles as would happen with any adrenalized combatant. Wooden fingers extended, unmoving, from arms that hung rigid like stalactites.

Bruce always said Carmen had a nose like a bloodhound. Claimed he could tell whenever a girl was on her period simply by standing within five feet. Even made him prove it to him on several occasions. Tonight, Carmen's acute olfactory senses detected, along with the boys' own stink, a chemical smell unfamiliar to him. And something else—something awful. *Spoiling pork, perhaps?* The malodorous tang grew stronger with the next step.

The head beveled slightly, waxen, glued-shut eyes angled down as if looking Earl squarely in the face, perhaps to size him up. Then it rotated slightly, closed eyes aimed down directly at Carmen, who screamed, horrid, harsh, and piercing, once again triggered that most ancient of all animal instincts within him—but to no avail. Earl was intent on dragging him into this fight.

"Now!" Earl screeched as he sprang forward and upward, head down. He connected his right shoulder with the neck of the figure in the suit. As if tackling a building, Earl bounded backward, pinwheeling to keep from falling onto his back. That was when the stalactite right arm shot out quicker than an arrow. Impossibly large cigar-like fingers gripped Earl's hair. Arm straight out, from the shoulder, it lifted Earl off the ground as he kicked and squealed out some inhuman sound, rage commingled with the deepest possible fear: pain, and grief, in a way—for Earl now feared he might be experiencing his last moments on earth.

Carmen, stunned temporarily from the sudden change in predicament, screamed in terror; screamed relentlessly, fueled by the hot debate transpiring within him: to abandon one of his only two real friends, or to stay and try to help against . . . against something that defied the known universe which, in Carmen's case, was quite even, predictable, and small. Stay to attempt a full-frontal attack that his larger, meaner friend had just failed at miserably, defeated in the blink of an eye. He screamed nonstop through it all, his brain wholly unprepared for and incapable of processing this moment.

Finally, his reptile brain commanded him to cut his losses and run.

As if sensing imminent escape, a giant left arm cannon-fired a viselike hand around Carmen's neck. From the vocal cord compression on two sides, Carmen's screams transposed two octaves upward while his feet now kicked the air above the grass. A sudden memory flashed of watching a Chinese lantern fly struggling inside a large spider's web. The harder it clawed and moved, the more entangled it became.

His feet touched ground, and then he was kneeling. He used all of his strength to work his sweat-slicked but strong fingers against the cold vice-grips that had completely immobilized his neck—to no avail. It felt like an iron collar. Earl, he saw, was pinned to the ground now as one giant knee bore down against his lower lumbar. For a freakish moment, Carmen wondered why; but then he saw. The kneel freed up the giant right hand. He now watched it shred Earl's jeans as effortlessly as a normal man might tear through wrapping paper. Carmen could not look away from his friend's widely exposed buttocks, as sallow and achromatic as the moon that illuminated it. Carmen tried, though he could not turn his head even one millimeter in either direction.

He detected something malignantly joyful in the monster's movements. The kneeling giant with the formaldehyde cologne had unzipped himself. Carmen saw the hideous black, maggoty, reeking log no longer constrained. The only action he could take was to scream, though it sounded no louder than the chirp of one of the park's millions of crickets.

CHAPTER NINETEEN

Blue Monday

With the embarrassing court scene behind him, Taylor's regular days consisted of sitting around his apartment, wallowing in guilt and shame, replaying the judge's condemning words in his mind.. The harsh condemnation no longer suited the once-favored former intern. *I'm not a bad person. I'm a good person. It isn't rape if she's dead, Your Honor.*

Fucking Dingel. Why didn't you just stay upstairs with that piece of ass daughter of yours like you'd promised?

His attorney had petitioned the court, citing an otherwise clean record, and succeeded in winning a reduced sentence of twelve months' probation. However, living entirely off his meager savings and State unemployment checks, along with weekly visits to the probation office, had severely handicapped Taylor's lifestyle.

He had emailed his resume to prospective employers outside the funeral industry. Not one met with any interest or even rated the courtesy of a reply. But this morning, he had awakened to crystal clear images of himself fishing—an activity that used to calm him, and the thought of free food appealed to him. *A sign*, he thought, when he woke from his dream. Trout season ended in less than a week. Right now, he could think of nothing else.

He loaded his rod, tackle box, and a lightweight folding chair into his van. He drove to the local park. A creek for which the region was named—a Native American name if he'd ever heard one—flowed through the green area. Taylor parked under a warm mid-afternoon sun and walked to his usual, if oft-forgotten, spot. The ideal time to hook rainbow trout was early morning, just after a rain. The timing and conditions were not ideal today. But there had been filtered sunlight in last night's dreams, too.

A second sign.

He had fished here once or twice in the distant past, usually with little success, but today felt different, somehow. Neptune or some other god had caused him to dream of fishing all night long; of this, he felt certain—although atheism was his standard understanding of things.

The familiar path down to the creek's bank reminded him of simpler times. Though he tried, in those gray, still moments just before sleep and upon waking, he could not purge the memory of her dead bacteria scent; the image of her pretty face, the taste and feel of her blue lips, and the cool, buttered silk glove gripping him as he thrust himself over the edge. *No living woman could ever compare.*

Was she worth losing a career over? Maybe. Yes. I think that maybe, she was.

He baited the tiny hook with an acrid-smelling ball from a jar; a delicacy trout purportedly find irresistibly tasty. He eyed a dark, placid-looking section of creek directly underneath the large, exposed roots of a black walnut tree. He wound back and cast across. *Bam! Still got it.* He watched the baited hook hit the dark pool dead center. The red and white plastic bobber remained close to the center of the darker, deeper depression where trout might be hiding.

May I possibly entice you into the mood for a tasty little midday snack, little fishies?

He sat watching the bobber float undisturbed. He inhaled the comforting and familiar earthy aromas of the creek; that distinctive muddy, stale, sulphury smell of dimethyl sulfide, not dissimilar to his obsession's beautiful blue pussy. He surveyed his surroundings, attuned to sights and sounds. *Quiet, peaceful.* The creek moved silently, no rocks jutting up to interrupt the water's flow. He heard the chirping of birds but failed to spot any. He thought of Dave Dingel. *What a high and mighty, self-righteous tool.* He pushed away the thought. Instead, he thought of his skinny strawberry-headed blue-eyed daughter lying there dead on the table, so young and silky, cool to the touch, fresh enough to smell alive, still—a little, just enough—in all the right places. Blue lips and tongue. He felt the swelling in his underwear.

"Screw that guy."

He mused over what new career path he could take to support himself now that *the tool* had blackballed him from the industry. *Well, I'm pretty good at handling dead meat. Butcher, maybe? Taylor's Butcher Shop. Has a nice ring to it. Do they still even have those anymore? Seems like everyone now just relies on supermarkets. Who wants to work as a deli manager in a supermarket?*

Becoming a mortician would have satisfied his lifelong fascination with death. But, he knew other verticals in the industry were not influenced by Dave Dingel's far-reaching network. Grave markers, for instance. Buying real estate and selling grave plots. He remembered reading about mobile crematoriums active in China and now sat wondering if such an enterprise could ever grow legs here in the States. It appealed to him. *Maybe down South—some depressing place where they can't afford standard funeral fees? I'd still have direct access to bodies and have them completely to myself. If there were ever a natural disaster or pandemic, oh,* man, *would that ever be a sweet gig. They sure grow them pretty down there, too.*

Green leaves on tree branches were still a month and a half away from turning into vibrant fall colors, but last year's fallen leaves clung on here like stubborn ghosts in places along the path and the entire forest floor. Seasons of snow and rain, of heat and dry, along with nature's natural decomposition processes, had left the entire area with a crisp, crackly brown carpet underfoot.

Crunch . . . scrape . . . crunch. At a distance, Taylor heard the sound, rhythmical, measured in cadence. He thought about the sound, eager to distract himself from all the many and macabre problems of his own creation. His was generally curious in nature. He wondered if perhaps a small tributary feeding into the larger creek could be the source.

Crunch . . . scrape . . . crunch. The noise was becoming a moving barricade of grinding, splintered sounds. Part of it would seem to come into focus but then drop back again just before Taylor could identify it.

Crunch . . . scrape . . . crunch.

Definitely louder now. Which means it's moving closer. Not flowing water or wind, he decided. Slightly alarmed now, he shifted in his chair. A cloud overhead blotted out the beating sun, and Taylor craned his neck to glance toward the sky.

"Whoa!" he gasped when he realized he was now at eye level with two black pinstriped kneecaps. He jumped and recoiled as far as the little beach chair permitted.

Taylor worked to calm his pounding heart. His eyes appreciated the fine summer wool of the man's suit, but the height bewildered him, for as he raised his sights up, he still did not see a face. All the way up, he saw a shadow shaped like a head with the sun behind it—*a cigarillo protruding from the mouth*? "Whoa, dude! You startled me. You lost or something?"

He tried again to see the face eclipsing the sun, a face nearly seven feet above ground. He saw painted lips frozen in a waxen downward sneer, from which protruded a roll of paper like an unlit cigarette rolled too loosely. *Not like any rolling paper I ever saw.* Where the eyes should have been, there were only eyelids. *His eyes are closed,* Taylor realized. *Judge thought I was a weirdo, a creep? He oughta get a load of this superfreak!*

"Oh my God," Taylor said, as it suddenly dawned on him that the eyes were glued shut—he had put in more than enough mortician's apprentice hours to recognize exactly who, or more accurately *what*, stood before him. Taylor struggled from his low-slung angle, but he stood to face the giant corpse. Panic chased all thoughts from his mind. His solitary instinct, childish and primitive, was to squeeze his eyes shut and pray to a God in whom he never believed to please make this unwanted visitor go away. He opened them. "It's you. Midlothian! It really is you."

He actually felt himself shrinking before the undead Goliath. Terror sat on his chest like an ape. He tried to scream but managed no more than a breathless squeak.

Hot panic surged in Taylor's head like the roar of the ocean in a storm. His bowels turned to water.

Taylor coiled his legs like a frog about to jump, his most primitive survival instincts now fully the boss of him. Precisely then, the zombie freak's hand launched at lightning speed around his neck, like a giant steel lobster claw fired from a harpoon gun.

The last sound Taylor Rydell heard was a zipper closing, a sound he himself had generated thousands of times while standing before toilets.

His last view of the corporeal world, lying on his left side, was of a pool of his own intestines now liberated from his belly like so many blue and purple snakes making their escape. Dirt and leaf residue clung to purply-pink ropes in places. The Midlothian-thing still stood; the monster Taylor's rational mind had been unable to explain. It cast its shadow over his eviscerated belly. Even still, he could feel blood leaking from his ravaged rectum. Lights began to dim from blood loss and mortal shock, tunnel vision tightening. It had begun slowly, from the outside of his eyes, then narrowed inward.

God forgive me.

———

"Just got in from school," Naomi typed into her chat window. "Haven't even peed. So much to tell you. First, how was your dad last night?"

"O-M-G. So mad."

"At you?"

"No. I told him I had the police over. He said, 'My smart girl.' Though I'm pretty sure he wants Bruce, Carmen, and Earl to take Marcus Midlothian's place on his slab."

"Timmy call?"

"Mmhmm."

"Well?"

"Did you see him in school today?"

"Yes. But only in passing. He didn't look up. He knows you and I are besties, so, if he'd seen me, I'm sure he would've told me himself."

"How did he look?"

A pause. "Anxious. Rattled."

"Geez. Maybe because Gordon asked him to fly back next Thursday night, skip school Friday and Monday, and spend four full days in 'extended audition,' what he called it, along with three other guys around his age."

"Huh. I guess that's, like, amazingly good. Right?"

"It means Gordon has narrowed it down to the final four. No others are being asked to audition. Now he wants to make sure they have 'synergy' and 'X factor,' whatever the heck that means."

Thirteen-second pause. "Oh my God! Seriously?"

"Yeppers. 'Timmy C' is only maybe one step away from the big time. Whether he gets an offer or not, I couldn't be prouder of him for going this far, this fast."

"My little Anna-banana. Wife of a pop star. Oh my God. This is so unbelievable."

"I know, right? My Naomi-baloney, this future with Timmy . . . it's like all my dreams are about to come true."

"Oof. I almost don't have the heart to lay a ton of bad news on you."

"Oh geez. For just a moment there, I was free of this world of crap. Lord, give me strength. Okay, lay it on me."

"Well, there's so much . . . not sure where to begin."

"At the beginning. What happened this morning when you got to school?"

"Straight off, I was hit by a rumor. That you and I were seen getting it on in your dad's koi pond."

"What?!"

"Yep. One of Brucie's bastards was spying Saturday night. Sue and Tammy activated their mean-girl mill. Word got to Abe, who is the most charming, socially manipulative guy I know when he turns it on, clever in ways I'll never be; like a political campaign manager, maybe. Immediately he launches this counter-rumor that no, it wasn't us in a backyard fishpond; rather, it was Sue and Tammy in her dad's pool."

More typing. "And I guess it worked, sort of like one bullshit rumor canceled out an equally bullshit rumor. People hate those jerks since the Anna-Timmy sex pic email. So they'd rather believe what they choose to believe about those two, figuring they created the rumor about us to throw everyone off their scent. Abe read the room and realized people are stereotypical—Tammy looks like a linebacker—so that, plus the two of them being inseparable . . . it wasn't hard to manipulate the perception of Tammy and Sue's relationship."

"Close call. Please give Abe a sloppy wet kiss from me."

"Haha. Will do. Now, for the really, really, REALLY bad news."

"God. It gets worse?"

"Afraid so. Because of what we did, people are dying."

"*What? Who?*"

Bruce's father, early Sunday morning. Someone broke into his house and murdered him, alone in bed."

"Wait, what? No way!"

"Carmen and Earl were found early this morning by dog walkers in Valley Forge Park, murdered the same way."

Anna felt dizzy. Her face suddenly burned hot as her stomach gurgled. "Oh my God." She looked down to see that she had crossed her arms and dug in her fingernails.

"Your father's intern, Taylor: The news about him hasn't broken yet, heard it from my dad, who's tight with the district attorney. He was just found murdered in Evansburg State Park."

Vasovagal syncope rapidly overtook Anna as her blood pressure suddenly plummeted. She flopped the tablet onto the bed, then lay down beside it. She closed her eyes, inhaled deeply through her mouth, and exhaled slowly. Her face and body were now greasy with sweat. She fought hard against her brain's insistence on shutting her body down into unconsciousness. Aware she'd left Naomi hanging, her mind continually hammered out one question.

Anna glanced at her tablet: Eight minutes had passed. She left Naomi's dozens of questions and question marks unread as she slid to the edge of her bed. Finally able to stand, she ran from her room, held her mouth under the faucet, swallowed the tepid, metallic-tasting tap water, then splashed her face ten times. She sat on the toilet and gave hot, burning relief to the cramps in her bowels. She flushed, then sat there for a long time. She wept piteously.

She returned to her room, closed and locked the door, then climbed back into bed.

She grabbed the tablet. Into a chat window, she typed, "Sorry. Hard to take. I'm okay now. How did police find them?"

No response. Then, just over fifteen minutes later, Naomi responded. "Sorry too. But I wanted to make sure I gave you a vetted response. Dad is the most legally and politically connected guy I know, so I asked him in a way that sounded like I'm interested only because I know two of the victims, and I promised not to spread it around if he told me."

"Well?"

"Yeah. And it's awful. Each was found with a completely destroyed anal canal, rectum, and sigmoid colon. Not prolapsed: We are talking ripped up, shredded, like someone had done them with a dry baseball bat. Bellies sliced open, guts hanging out, all while alive."

"I need you to pick me up. I'm in no condition to drive right now. We can't type anymore. Not secure. Your words."

A minute later, "Leaving now, see you in a few."

———

"I can't believe it! This can't be happening! Bruce's dad; Carmen and Earl. Everyone in school thinks you and I are a *thing* . . . how could all of this just . . . happen," Sue Nastro said with a sharp finger-snap, "like that? My life gets unraveled—no fault of mine . . . everything is just over in a day?" Sue shouted from the driver's seat of her Mustang. She parked in the farthest spot from the high school entrance in the auxiliary student parking lot. With the convertible top rolled back, she knew sound carried, as did the skunky marijuana smoke from her mini aqua-pipe. She glanced up at late afternoon clouds, orange and red, wandering lazily across the sky, fraying at the edges, but they managed to hold their shapes. One reminded her of an owl. She loved owls.

She unbuckled her seat belt and glared at Tammy, who shrugged. "Dunno. Seriously: No clue. Pass that, please." Tammy tried opening her door. Finding it locked, she inhaled through her nose, faced the passenger window, and hocked forward the last hour's post-nasal drip. She watched her viscous projectile as it sailed over the door frame and hit the black asphalt with an audible slap. "Can you *puuleeze* figure out how to work that stupid child-lock button, Suebedoo? Pretty girls are so inept."

Sue appraised herself, looking down at her cleavage, blue flowery dress, and gold strappy sandals. "Well, I guess if you were ever hot for girls, I'd be the best place to start."

"Pfft. I see how you look at me."

Despite enduring the most intense anxiety attack of her life, Tammy's remark commingled with THC hitting Sue's brain hard, she laughed. It felt good. "Look at *what*, exactly?"

Maintaining a straight face, Tammy said, "The only girl you know who can squat, bench press, deadlift, and military press your narrow, bony ass.

Guys like a fighter in bed. Not a stick-figure pushover lying there painting her nails while he eats her out like some prima-donna princess."

Both lost it completely; the intensely dark emotions of the day that had wound them up like tightly coiled springs all at once unwound. "Pass it back, Jones-er," said Sue, and Tammy did. She tuned the radio to an EDM channel. Sue looked displeased, but she silently agreed that the pop station she liked no longer felt appropriate for the new mood in the car.

After another hit and hand-back, Tammy returned to her contemplative state. "Riddle me this, genius: What does Mr. Barnette have in common with the convicted necrophiliac and Carmen and Earl?"

No hesitation. "Dingel."

Tammy nodded. "Could it be Daddy Dingel who is killing our friends?"

Sue took the question seriously. She maximized her dot-connecting abilities, forced her brain through various scenarios, and quantified all that she knew of David Dingel. "No, not him. He's a dweeb. Too weaselly for violence."

"Could he have maybe hired someone with balls?"

Sue Nastro's eyes opened, half wide and dry from the smoke's effects. "Hell yeah. Tamster, you do have your moments. Maybe some lowlife who couldn't afford his services. Or a crime syndicate who owes him one."

"Then consider: Frankie Barnette punched Dingel in the face. Carmen and Earl trashed his residence and business. That intern banged one of the smelly old corpses—"

"Um, eww?"

"Right. So who does that leave on the list of those who recently pissed off David Dingel? And who pissed him off the most?"

Sue leveled her gaze at Tammy. "Oh. My. *God.*"

Tammy nodded. She swatted at a mosquito. "Damn, I hate bugs. Out already, and it's not even dark yet."

Sue glanced up. "We're near the woods, that's why. Hang on," she started the car and put the windows and top up. "We'll just run the AC."

"I'd say that what you did to Anna easily rivals what Bruce and gang did to her. What he did doesn't go away. I'm a little fucked up in the head from my mom's creepy boyfriends trying to touch me. He finger-blasted her in a parking lot. For the rest of her life, she'll never forget the first boy to penetrate her—"

"It was only his finger!"

"It's still a violation," Tammy said. "Rape by finger. But then what you did—"

"What *we* did."

Tammy shook her head. "I came along for the ride like always. You cooked this up. You snapped the pics. You sent the email. It forced her out of school, Sue. And those pics will follow her around for *life*. You could go to jail for what you did. Honestly? I think you'd be safer behind bars than living free. Dingel's hitman can get to you a whole lot easier out here than in there."

"Stop! You really think I'm in danger?"

Tammy nodded. "I don't believe in coincidences. Dingel's enemies are all getting killed by the same killer. I think the anal destruction thing is meant to send a clear message."

"What message?"

"Put something in my daughter, and I'll have something put into you."

Sue shivered. "God, please tell me this isn't really happening. Tell me this all only just a really super-bad dream, and soon I'll wake up."

Sue believed that Tammy was looking at her. Then she noticed the faraway look in her eyes. "Take me home, Sue. It's not worth it anymore, hanging out with you."

Sue's jaw dropped. "You're serious? You want to dump me as a friend?"

Tammy still stared out at the empty lot. "I just don't think—"

"Shh! Wait. Hear that?"

"Hear what?"

"That clunk, from the engine or wherever. Shh," she said again in an abrupt, inarguable sibilant. "Something's wrong."

Tammy shook her head. "I don't hear anything. If you heard it just now while you're in Park, we can rule out the transmission, drive shafts, angle gear, propeller shaft, final drive, and brakes. If you hear it while driving and the engine RPM is steady when it clunks, we can probably rule out the engine, which is good because cha-ching! Big bucks. So what's left? When was the last time somebody checked the PS steering fluid level? When did you last have the AC serviced? Why doesn't your so-called boyfriend, Bruce-the-auto-mechanic, take care of your car? Oh wait, that's right. Because he is not now, nor was he ever, your boyfriend. He doesn't give a shit about you."

Sue appeared dumbfounded. "How the heck would you know *any* of that, Tamster?"

"Ha. You've always been the beauty; I've always been the brains. Now, take me home."

"Shh. Heard it again. Did you feel the car move?"

Tammy nodded; eyebrows raised. "What? It's not the car, so . . . What is it?" Tammy shrieked.

Sue could not mistake the deep concern etched on Tammy's face. Her fear was infectious.

"What—*tell me*! Forget it. Just hit the gas. We are *done here*," said Tammy.

Instead, Sue cut the engine. "Listen. Just listen. The doors are all locked."

Like two dry-mouthed meerkats, the girls' heads bobbed over the dash looking in every direction. They forced their ears and eyes to work double-time as they watched the orange-red sun descend like a bloody eye socket until it sunk below the highest point of the brick high school. Inside the car, panic rose like a storm.

The air inside was already hot and stale. Sue's stomach gurgled audibly, followed by a wet fart.

"Oof. Fucking pig! Okay, start the car, blast the AC, I'm rolling down the window; we're outta here. Otherwise, I'm getting out and walking home. I am *so* not even kidding—" Tammy shrieked, a shrill, panicked scream to end her sentence, followed by a stream of disjointed profanity. Sue watched her weed-dried eyes suddenly moistened by fear as she covered her mouth. Her entire body shook. She jumped in place so hard that she hit her head on the soft black cloth convertible roof. She folded both legs under her and maintained her wide-eyed stare at something outside, past Sue.

Sue Nastro turned in time to face the crotch area of a nice suit in dire need of cleaning. Not entirely unused to older male stalkers, she tried to smile at Tammy and thumbed her left hand at her window. "My fans. They are dedicated. Gotta give 'em that."

Her confidence crashed with the window; shatterproof glass, she now discovered, was only used on windshields. Sparkling crystals, sharp as knives, baptized the left side of her face, head, and neck and rained down onto her lap like a hailstorm of clear razorblades.

Vaguely aware of cuts beginning to bleed, it was the sheer high-decibel noise assault on her eardrums from Tammy's screams, like sitting beside a freight train horn, that frightened and pained her even more. A hand, so impossibly large that it seemed inhuman, reached through the opening where seconds ago, there had been a window. Jagged chunks of glass stubbornly clung in places along the window frame like shark teeth. Fingers the size of sausages reached down and pulled her thin legs up toward the window with the strength and ease of a crane winch. Two-inch stalagmites of glass cut deep into the backs of her thighs. As her lower half emerged into the warm September evening, red-hot pain blossomed like the blood quickly saturating her dress. Her shoes came off and fell down to the footwell.

She felt her toes touch the warm blacktop. A sudden and sober thought: *Run.* She saw it perfectly: She galloped like the wind, her long legs loped across the asphalt to the tree line separating her from the road—where there were people. *People are basically good. Drivers will stop and protect me, then drive me to the emergency room.*

The daydream evaporated like steam from a knife wound on a windy winter day. She felt her torso being turned. In slow motion, five or six peaks of glass, differing in height, sharper than any razor, sliced through her lower abdominal epidermis, separated muscle, and shredded sensitive nerve endings. Pain receptors overloaded, the apathetic glass continued to travel, rudderless and indifferent, past fatty layers. Some shards went deeper still and opened blood vessels.

Tammy's voluminous cries sounded far away to her now, like white noise. Sue's hands rested flat against her seat, still warm from recent occupation, while hydraulic hands slipped beneath the waistband of her white underwear and ripped them off, the jerky motion massaging her gored insides deeper against the sharp glass. More nerves and vessels ripped with every movement. Unimaginable pain jig-jagged through her entire middle.

Sue Nastro cried like a child, hard and with no self-consciousness. She raised her head and saw Tammy's uncomprehending eyes glassine with shock, quite sure her own looked the same. "I want mommy."

Effects from the recent smoking session had now completely worn off, replaced in Tammy's brain with the chemistry of mortal fear. She had a sudden rational thought: *Call 9-1-1.* Reaching into her seat for her purse, she looked up and stopped at the expression on Sue's face.

Tammy had never before witnessed another person in this much physical agony—an entirely novel experience. Giant ham-hands gripped Sue's waist for balance as giant thighs thrust forward, forcing Sue's abdominal muscles and nerves to ride the impossibly sharp glass. Blood dripped in red torrents down the door's inner plastic in obscene, iron-smelling rivulets.

Piteous crying, punctuated only by bright agonized yelps. Unfocused eyes told Tammy a story that she did want to read. A story of anguish, lonesome misery, and most of all, fear: Fear of that last great change owed to the world by each and every guest upon it. Tammy never believed anything bad would happen to her; she considered herself a strong person and, essentially, a good person. Now, the bedtime story told by the prettiest eyes she had ever seen convinced Tammy that she had been wrong about her invincibility—and also that the boogeyman, the hungry monster in her closet and under her bed, is real.

I'm next flashed across her brain like a red neon Vacancy sign at a cheap motel.

She spun right and pulled against the door handle, then remembered the child locks. She watched as one of the hands released Sue and disappeared from view. Then it reappeared, clutching a small surgical knife. When the blade pushed slowly upward into Sue's stomach just beneath her ribcage, screams intensified to ear-splitting levels. Tammy watched as the hand slowly dragged the blade down her abdomen in a perfectly straight line. When pubic bone prevented further movement, Tammy saw human intestines for the first time. She caught whiffs of severed bowel. The large and small intestines uncoiled onto Sue's seat like a nest of pink-purple snakes.

Sue's screaming tapered down in volume. Breaths came now in great watery swoops. Tammy saw that those beautiful eyes were now dead to the world, the brain behind them short-circuited from pain, blood loss, and shock. Finally, Sue's eyes closed, and her head hung down, blissfully unconscious now, Tammy hoped. Then, those awful giant hands unceremoniously grabbed Sue's thin hips and pulled her limp form fully outside. Some entrails got tangled in the bloody window glass, like giant red teeth eating uncooked sausage. Tammy heard Sue's body hit the asphalt and then muted crying.

God. She can still feel.

A man's head then filled the entire viscera-garnished window opening. It appeared to be looking in at her. *But its eyes*, Tammy observed. She saw sculpted lines where upped lids met lower that seemed never designed to be real or functional. An absurd doobie of some kind hung down from between waxen lips. *This cannot be happening. I must be dreaming because none of this can possibly be real. Wake up, Tammy! Wake the fuck* up, *girl!*

She closed her eyes in the hope that the universe would blot out the hellish vision. Atheism had left her feeling completely and utterly alone in her time of greatest need. Her bladder released, her pants and nostrils flooded. She began to cry. She saw herself next to a little pink bicycle, age six, training wheels off, right after taking a hard fall onto the sidewalk that had sanded the skin from her knee. There was Daddy to pick her up, hug her, make everything all better every single time. Daddy was the name of God on her lips for so long. *But he's long gone.*

Hands reached across the grisly driver's seat.

Fingers, like hooks, sought purchase.

And found it.

CHAPTER TWENTY

Full Moon

"What did your parents say? How did you manage to slip out? I thought it was house arrest until they ship you to the Southern Gulag," Naomi said. Anna sat down in the Mercedes and buckled up.

"My mother was screaming something, who knows. I've tuned them out for now. Had to. Can we go for ice cream?" Anna found Naomi's puzzled expression, a silent demand for more explanation, mildly irritating. "Please, can we just get out of here? I'll explain on the way."

Engaging Drive, Naomi pulled away smoothly. "You've never blown off your parents in your *life*, girl." Anna nodded and started crying.

"Oh Anna-banana, I'm sorry, I didn't mean to—"

Shooting up her hand in protest, shaking her head, Anna reached into her purse for tissues. Finding only a fast-food napkin, she wiped her eyes and blew her nose. Eyes, red and swollen, looked at Naomi. "We messed up big time. I mean . . . *I* messed up. Not putting any of this on you."

Naomi drove in silence. Then, "Tell me what you're thinking, okay, hun? Spill it."

"I asked if we should use earth. You said any organic material. Remember?" Naomi nodded. "The spark of life we would have invoked into a golem made of earth would have come from God."

"Well, from where else could it have possibly come, for our golem?"

Anna shook her head. "Not from God, this I can tell you."

"How can you be so sure? You seem to leave no room for any alternative theory."

"You believe in Satan, right?"

Naomi sighed. "Judaism does. Ask two Jews; you'll get three different opinions. Satan, yes, for sure. The word means 'Adversary' of God. Heaven, yes, sort of. A new Garden of Eden, which in concept is probably close. As to Hell, well, some Jews believe in Sheol, which is like Hell; others in Gehinom, which I think Catholics call Purgatory. I believe the truly evil souls are either eternally damned to Gehinom, or the energy completely dispersed, maybe repurposed, kind of like bleaching a hard drive but not tossing it into the cosmic junk heap."

Anna blinked. "If a Jew were to sodomize seven boys and girls, and men and women, slicing them open during the act because their death throes increase his sensations down there, and then promised to return and do it some more, *and then* he died unrepentant, tell me: What are the chances of him spending eternity in the Garden of Eden?"

"Zero. God. Where did you ever come up with such a sick example—"

"Satan would be his keeper."

Naomi nodded. "Or, like I say, his spark of life, his soul, memories, character, would be melted down, obliterated, like recycled soda cans, that spark used for making a new, completely different soul."

"Naomi, Marcus Midlothian was executed by the State of Texas for doing exactly what I just said, to seven people, exactly as I said it."

Naomi drove distractedly for a moment, snapping out of it at the sound of more than one horn honking. Turning into the ice cream store lot just in time, Naomi parked off-center, straddling the white lines, an imprecision she had never allowed herself in the two years she had been driving. Putting the Benz in Park, she stared hard at Anna. "You're saying that somehow . . . instead of praying for and receiving from God a simple *program* for our golem, like that of a German Shepherd, loyal and obedient, which obeys only simple commands, we somehow restored the damned soul of Midlothian back into its original shell? I think that's what you're saying, Anna."

Her volume increased, tone angry and shrill. "*Is that what you are saying?*"

Anna nodded. "Something got messed up, somehow. Wires got crossed. Only God has the power to restore souls to bodies. Many Christians believe that in the three days Jesus spent in the tomb, His soul went down into Hell to forgive souls, release them, pardon them, whatever you like, you get the idea. But this . . . this *abomination*. This *thing* we've empowered has *nothing* to do with Yeshua. Understand?"

Naomi blinked. "But how do you *know?*"

Tears dripped from both eyes. "Because the only way to enter the Kingdom of God and to be with Yeshua is to forgive our enemies. Vengeance is God's purview and His alone. This monster is killing people, Naomi! Never did I want this . . . it's not what I asked for, not what I prayed for. God knows! He knows my heart! I only wanted them to leave me and my family alone, that's all." Tears flowed freely; Anna's thin ribcage heaved, and her shoulders hitched.

Gingerly, Naomi reached over and lightly stroked Anna's hair. They sat in silence, car running, minutes passing, as Naomi patiently waited for the storm in Anna's heart to pass. After Anna blew her nose, Naomi said, "We have to stop it."

"How?" Anna asked, voice cracking and weak.

"Well, good question. The golem appears to catch your enemies by surprise. Funny how nobody has seen a thing by now, isn't it? Seems like he must be invisible to police or security cameras, or we'd surely have heard *something* by now, right? It's otherworldly; like, maybe it's Midlothian's pestilential essence inside, yet it's guided, controlled by something like a satellite signal from somewhere, telling it exactly where to be at all times in order to fulfill our prayer."

"*Not* from God, *not* from Yeshua. *Not* from Heaven."

Naomi nodded. "You're right. Logically, you must be. The golem belongs to Satan now. We tapped God's power and Yeshua's restorative power, but we know that only God can create new and real life. Satan cannot. But, he's really good at messing things up here on Earth."

Anna nodded. "The devil intercepted; interceded. Marcus Midlothian will come for Bruce, Sue, and Tammy next. Whether God or Satan—or both—saw inside my heart Saturday night as I prayed for the golem to save me from enemies, whom I did not specifically name . . . somehow, my enemies are known to it. And there's only three left."

"We can't follow them around twenty-four seven. Bruce hasn't been in school. I hear his mother flipped out, had to be adjudicated into rehab. Nobody that Abe and I know have seen him in days."

"I feel responsible, Naomi. God's going to damn my soul to Hell for what I did."

"Banana-butt, listen. *You* did not kill. Nor did you pray for your enemies to get killed. And you surely did not resurrect Marcus Midlothian, the murderer. Nor did our loving God. His power we tapped, but then another power must have interrupted a blessed moment. As it often does. It's what he does, the Adversary. God is not about to condemn a sweetheart like you."

Anna stared at the burl wood interior trim above the glove compartment, unblinking. "The candles!" Naomi nodded. Shaking her head, Anna said, "I started this. It has to be me who stops it."

"I don't see how. You could go to the police, who will put out an APB for a walking giant, an executed prisoner in a custom suit with a giant blood-soaked schwanz and rolled-up parchment in its mouth?"

Naomi watched Anna's eyes move rapidly. "My mother smacked me twice over the sex photos. I hated her, only for a few minutes. But I did. Lord forgive me; I truly hated her in that moment. And when Timmy asked me if I blamed him for the photos and for the risky public situation he led me into, I told him no. But Naomi, a big part of me *does* blame him. For only a moment, anger toward Timmy flashed through me. I had to reason it away. And *you*, Naomi: This whole mess was all your idea. Before you picked me up, I was thinking about all of this, and I felt pangs of real anger towards you for architecting this whole golem thing."

Naomi nodded. "Understandable."

Anna grabbed Naomi's wrist. "*Don't you see?* If whatever dark spirit in control of that abomination can read my heart like an open book . . ."

Naomi's eyes opened wide. "*God.*"

Anna nodded. "Yeah. I mean, obviously not *Him*, but yes, you're correct. I have forgiven all of you in my heart. I've prayed God to forgive *me* for feeling angry at those I love most in this world. And I know He hears my prayers. But you just sat here and logically committed to the fact that He's not directing this . . . undead obscenity."

"We have to stop it!"

"Right. But how?"

It was Naomi's turn to analyze all data. After a few minutes, she said, "Bait. Somehow, we have to get it to come to us. We know how to stop it. That part's easy."

"I don't think Sue is going to go for it."

Naomi laughed humorlessly at Anna's deadpan effort to introduce a small measure of levity into their cloud of all-consuming fear and bone-deep panic. Their eyes locked. "Me. Has to be. I got you into this."

Anna shook her head. "No. No way. What if I'm not there and it over-powers you? It must be me who removes the shem, remember?"

Deep inhale, then exhale. "I will pray for our God, our King, to forgive me, too."

Suddenly aware of her parched, burning throat, Anna said, "I need something cold. Let's run in really quick. Shall we?"

Naomi nodded with enthusiasm. "I'm burning up, too."

"You forgot to turn off the car."

"Leave it running, I'd rather keep it cool inside. Nobody'll steal it; GPS tracker, and we can keep an eye on it from inside. No worries. Let's go."

Though the parking lot was three-quarters full, which eased their security concerns a little, anyone watching would have seen two teen girls rubbernecking in all directions as they returned to the car, hands filled with sweating waxed paper cups with long red plastic spoons jutting up from within. Sitting down inside at the same time, then syncopated closing of doors, Anna said, "Eat here? You sure? I don't want to be responsible for one drip onto this leather."

Naomi nodded as she stared down at her cup. "I generally take care of my things, but in the end, they're only things. Eat up, Banana. But if you spill one drop on my upholstery, you're riding home in the trunk."

"Do exactly what I say when I say, or you'll *both* be riding in the trunk in twelve pieces," said Bruce Barnette, voice dark, deep, placid as a Scottish loch. Surprised screeches accompanied the splat of thirty-two ounces of ice cream now decorating Naomi's entire dash console, portions of the windshield, and both leather seats. Too shocked to move, hands in the air, they froze. "I don't want anybody to get hurt, but . . ." He pushed a

Colt thirty-eight Detective Special snub-nose revolver between them so that they could see it in peripheral vision. In the fetal position on the floor, he slid himself across the back seat but lay low.

"Drive. Right out of the lot. Keep driving till I tell you to turn."

Naomi's hands shook as she followed Bruce's instructions. *Fling open the door and run. Or spin back and try to disarm him with a throat chop, like in Krav Maga class.* As Naomi calculated the odds of success for every possible move, Bruce Barnette studied her eyes in the rearview mirror.

"Open the door and run, go ahead. You'll hear me put three holes into Dingel right before I put three into you. I'm an excellent shot. Or, you can just drive."

He had left her without another choice. She saw no pedestrians in the rear and side mirrors. She engaged Reverse, then Drive, and headed to the exit. She made a right into traffic. Neither Anna nor Naomi dared look anywhere but straight ahead. "You guys smell sweet," he said, then chuckled at his own joke.

Naomi's sense of self returned. She tried to sound authoritative but only managed unease. "Where are we taking you, Bruce?"

He did not answer at first. Eventually, he said, "We're close. Make a right on Evansburg Road."

She knew then that he meant to harm them in the State Park—out of the way, closed at night, seldom patrolled by police. This now understood, her mind whirled through their advantages. *Two unarmed combatants against an armed aggressor. We're calm; he isn't. He can't cover both of us efficiently. Anna has to separate, put distance between us. Give me time to bend down, pick up a handful of dirt and rock. I only need one second to blind and disorient him. Stomp-kick his knee, hard chop to the throat. I don't care how big he is; he'll go down.*

"Left into the lot, park in the left corner farthest from the road. Turn off your headlights." She briefly considered laying on the horn as she coasted into the rear of the lot. Occupants of nearby homes would definitely look out their windows, and maybe call 9-1-1 as no cars were permitted here at night. As she pressed the center of her steering wheel, she blared the horn for a fraction of a second before he whipped his gun hand, butt forward, and connected with her skull. Naomi screamed as her hands flew to her bleeding head. "Brake, bitch!" he yelled, now seated directly behind her. "See that path leading into the trees barely wide enough for a car?" He pointed. "Drive straight through it till you come to a clearing."

Naomi complied, right hand on the wheel, left held to the knot already formed on her scalp. The purple sky skated quickly into full black. Here, along this footpath, she struggled to see her left-right boundaries of green leafy overgrowth, which scratched through the paint's clearcoat. The car bounced and scraped bottom for forty yards until they emerged in a wide clearing covered in tall grass. *Park visitors use this trail into the woods, but they avoid this open tall grass area, sure to be loaded with Lyme disease ticks. It's undisturbed. If we scream or make noise, we are now outside earshot of any local residents. They'd hear a gunshot, but that's about it.*

"Okay, I think we're close to the middle. Roll down your window, Jew, then park it here and shut it off." Naomi felt she had no other choice. She complied, then watched in the mirror as he opened the driver's side rear door. Before he got out, calmly, he said, "You might be tempted by these woods to try and lose me here. But that would be very bad because, you see, my six little friends here would find your hamstrings before you even got to the tree line. You'd have to slither like the filthy snakes you are. Now, get out. Yell all you want; nobody will hear you." He got out, shut his door, and stood in front of it.

Naomi went first. She opened her door and got out. "Shut it. Now, Dingelberry, get out and stand in front of the car where I can see you. Don't make a move." Trembling, Anna got out, walked to the front, and stood there in the tall grass.

It was full dark now. Stars gleamed like sequins on an evening gown. Like a great pumpkin, the Harvest Moon rose low, fat, and orange-red just over the cloudless eastern horizon. Anna and Naomi scanned the area. Though they could see perfectly well under Heaven's surreal witch light, neither could grasp one viable escape opportunity. Anna stood separated from Bruce by ten feet; she watched in horror as he reached into his right rear jeans pocket, from which he pulled a set of steel handcuffs. He walked to Naomi. "Turn around and put your hands on the roof." Reluctantly, she complied. From behind, he dangled the cuffs triumphantly before Naomi's eyes. "Picked these up at the gun show. Always wanted to try 'em out," he said, then pushed his full weight against her until her torso mashed against the door. Terror filled her mind, muscles, nerves—even her bones—in a gigantic, coruscating fire flash.

"Reach in, grab the steering wheel like you were making a turn." She saw no other choice but to comply. He reached around her arms and snap-closed the cuffs onto her wrists. Chained to the leather-wrapped steel steering wheel, bent over the window opening, she realized what was about to happen. She screamed as she watched him drop the handcuff keys on the seat.

"No, Bruce! No! When Abe finds out, he will kill you. Jews don't play. He will kill you dead with a rock-solid alibi that he was hundreds of miles away on Harvard campus at the time of death."

Bruce snickered. "If you can figure out how to unlock them using your mouth, you can get away."

She strained her neck but knew it was impossible. *Just another sick tease*, she concluded.

He hiked up her dress and pulled a spring-assist knife from his front pocket. In two smooth cuts, her underwear fell to the grass. "*No!*" she yelled, voice muffled and strained. "Bruce, you don't want to do this. They'll lock you up for twelve years."

Anna moved closer.

"Stop right there, Dingelberry. That's far enough. Now, let me explain the rules to you two. Whatever happens here tonight stays here. You will not tell anyone. This will remain our little secret. Because if you ever do, understand that I made all kinds of hard-case friends in County who will get released, some this year, some next year. Even if I were to end up back inside—which ain't happenin'—one of them will take out your families one by one and save you two for last. So, just relax; consider what's about to happen the most fun you two nasty little cunts will ever have."

CHAPTER TWENTY-ONE

Golem

Bruce kicked Naomi's legs wide apart and knelt between them. "Never tasted Jew before. This is a first." With that, head between her thighs, face tilted up, he indulged his curiosity. Naomi screamed.

He licked his fingers and lips. "Mm. Not bad. Gonna enjoy gaping that little ass and pussy."

Somehow, she managed to make herself less turbid, more focused, and rational. *He's trying to objectify me in his mind.* She thought fast. "Bruce. It's me, Naomi Silver, from class. I never did anything to hurt you. Please don't do something you will regret for your entire life."

Bruce laughed heartily. "For that to happen, Five-O would need to find your bodies. That ain't gonna happen."

"Oh my God! Bruce, you're not a murderer!"

"I am today."

Timmy's exact words when I asked if he was vegan, too, Anna thought, as he leveled the gun at her then used it to make a 'come here' gesture. She did not move. On her in three strides, he flattened her onto her back, a sharp groan as the wind got knocked out of her. He grabbed her wrists and dragged her to a point twenty feet behind Naomi. With his right forearm, he pinned both wrists over her head. Her breathing returned, and she screamed and kicked her legs underneath him. He reached into his left rear pocket and withdrew a second set of handcuffs; he snapped them onto her wrists.

Looking down at her, resting a moment, he smiled. "I saw your pics, Dingelberry. You surely are one hot little piece of ass, you know that?"

"Bruce," she said and started to cry, "The prettiest girl in the county is in love with you. Isn't that enough? Who am I? I'm a nobody. I never did *anything* to you!"

He slapped her. "What do you call getting me sent to prison for the summer, huh, cunt?" There was no confusion in Bruce Barnette's eyes. But there was no mercy in them either. In the heat of the evening, Anna shivered. "Who had my dad and my friends killed? You actually think that I'm stupid enough to believe you and your fucked-up ghoul family had nothing to do with that?"

"You tried to rape me in the parking lot!" She cried openly now. "I never called the police on you!"

He pressed his lips to her ear. "Know what they did to me in there?"

Crying, she shook her head.

"They punched my ass. Two guys took turns holding me down while one of them stuck his hard dick in my ass, dry. Any idea how that feels, Dingelberry?" She cried louder, realizing now her immediate fate. She did not respond. He answered for her. "It hurts a lot, and it's more humiliation than one person can stand. I can never get it out of my head. Worst thing that's ever happened to me. I am fucked up for life because of *you*. The whole time they were doing me, all I could think of was getting out and doing this to you. Been saving it all up for ya. Got the biggest, hottest load boiling inside, and now I'm gonna pump it so deep inside you'll be puking it up a half hour from now. I'm gonna take my time, make it last, hold it back till I can't anymore. I really want you to *feel* this, Dingelberry. Then you can watch me do your Jew whore over there."

All three of them froze at the sudden arrival of a new sound.

Crunch . . . scrape . . . crunch. It sounded faint and faraway. He unbuttoned Anna's blue jeans and flipped her over, face down. *Whatever it is, he doesn't think it's a threat,* Naomi thought as she helplessly watched Bruce pull off Anna's shoes and socks, then yank off her tight jeans. The underwear he sliced off. Anna was now entirely nude from the waist down. He stood over her, and shifted his weight onto his right leg as he raised his left to remove his boot, then switched legs to pull off his right. He dropped his jeans, stepped out of them, and then straddled Anna's bare legs, dressed only in his olive-green tee shirt and white boxer briefs.

Naomi thrashed and threatened. Suddenly she fell completely still when she spotted in the distance the figure of a man at the edge of a copse of cedar trees, partially obscured by the car, slowly advancing one long step at a time.

Crunch . . . scrape . . . crunch.

Bruce knelt, grasped Anna's ankles, and jerked her legs apart, using knees and hands to keep them separated. He pressed his face down against her. She felt his weight mash her bare belly against the rough grassy ground; skin scraped and itched terribly from biting insects and tiny barbed claws at the bottoms of their tarsi. Beetles and fire ants crawled across her tender flesh with impunity. Pain from fire ant bites felt like stabs from an ice pick dipped in hot acid. "Let me up, it burns!" she croaked as insects worked along her perineum.

Crunch . . . scrape . . . crunch.

A scream, hot as magma, erupted deep within Anna's soul. Anger, fear, frustration, guilt, and shame—horrified by the self-awareness that after this, she would never look at Timmy the same way again. Grief, for what would amount to the slow, inevitable death of an innocent and perfect love that would soon dry up and wither away like a baby left alone in this field. The best part of her was about to die in tears, unloved, discarded. If she survived the ordeal, which Bruce had made clear, she would not.

Crunch . . . scrape . . . crunch.

The cacophony of two women screaming and sobbing only fueled Bruce's lust; a musical aphrodisiac. Still, the rational portion of Bruce Barnette's brain vaguely registered that something was out of place. His overconfident bully narcissist swagger had raised him far out of touch with his most primal survival mechanisms.

Crunch . . . scrape . . . crunch.

The ominous sound grew loud enough to make Naomi quiet her terrified storm and really listen. Rhythmic, consistent, entirely out of place in a State Park clearing. Another factor that escaped his notice was the unearthly absence of animal sounds, of robins settling in for another night in their nests; of night birds shaking off the sleepy heat of the day, calling out their songs of anticipation to one another. Naomi noticed it all.

Crunch . . . scrape . . . crunch.

The primary, secondary, and tertiary auditory cortexes in Bruce's brain screamed for his attention; instead, he chose to ease down the front of his underwear and free the urgency straining for release therein. He flopped it against Anna's cleft and whipped her skin with it. He ground his sensitive organ provocatively between her nether cheeks, his idea of foreplay, as he enjoyed the dichotomy of textures he experienced there: Thick skin, but then patches that felt delightfully smooth, silken, and warm.

The moment had come at last. So completely elusive, limited until now only to masturbatory fantasies. With his right hand, he positioned himself, aimed his weapon, and tensed for the singular thrust that would send Anna Dingel into a whole new world of humiliation and pain, with the same indifference and sadism as the convicts had done to him. He laughed. "Caperila wouldn't have anything do to with you if he ever learned about this. Hey Dingel: ya think maybe he'll be the one to find your body? Wouldn't that be somethin'."

He anticipated her physical reaction, the delicious high-pitched screams, the fruitless attempts to squirm away. Thoughts of inflicting sexual pain fueled a monstrous animal part of him that had waited over seventeen years, patiently, like the Kraken beneath the ocean's deepest trenches, to be unleashed at long last by Hades.

Crunch . . . scrape . . . crunch.

No longer able to dismiss the alarms in his head, Bruce turned to look over his right shoulder; from behind, what felt like two giant-sized vise grips closed around his neck like a steel garrote. So tight was the noose that it stifled his choke reflex. His eyes bulged in panic when he felt his body hoisted by the neck until his socked feet hovered above the earth. Fruitless kicks and air bicycling achieved no change in his status. He saw Anna Dingel turn over and witness the shock and horror on his face as the moonlight began to dim around the edges of his oxygen-deprived eyes.

In another moment, he was lowered and pushed flat against the ground. He felt the unmistakable heel of an oversized shoe digging into the small of his back. It felt like the weight of a car had rolled a tire onto his spine and shifted into Park. *I can't believe it . . . I'm really going to die.* Coughing, gulping air into his bruised throat, he managed to scream.

Anna stopped crying. She looked up at their creature's head as an entomologist studied an insect specimen pinned alive to a stretching board. *Almost like it's alive, except for those eyes glued shut,* she thought. She had seen the face before but never like this, and it frightened her in a way she had never imagined. One thought dominated her brain: *Get away from it. It's an abomination in the eyes of the Lord and an unclean spirit.*

With great difficulty, as her hands were chained together, Anna rolled over again, pushed herself to her knees, and from there, she stood and wobbled. Awkwardly, she worked to brush insects from her skin, though her eyes never left the golem and its victim. The sight of it mesmerized her and pushed out all other thoughts.

As cortisol and norepinephrine levels slowly normalized in her bloodstream and organs, Anna felt the return of her rational self. She walked backward a few steps toward the car. With Herculean effort, she tore her eyes off the golem, turned, and ran up behind Naomi. She grabbed the cuff keys, which she used to free Naomi, who immediately grabbed the keys from Anna and unlocked both of her cuffs. *We're free! Thank God,* Anna thought, and she saw the identical emotion pass across her friend's face. Together they watched the thing's hands unzip its pants, further sickened by what flopped out.

The girls hugged tightly and squeezed wet eyes closed to choke back further tears. Together, they fought within themselves to stay present. "What do we do now?" Anna asked.

"Grab your pants, and let's go."

Naomi opened the driver's door and sat down. She started the car and switched on the lights, which brightly illuminated the entire clearing. Now, she could see more clearly, with horror, the 'Angel Lust' Anna had described Saturday night; rigid, waxen, coated in blood, gore, and maggots. She thought of Carmen and Earl, whom she knew from school, getting raped by it. She raised her left hand to her mouth, suddenly overcome with a powerful wave of nausea. She threw up the partially digested three bites of ice cream she'd gotten to eat before Bruce had surprised them and gulped down the rest of her bile.

She watched Anna struggle for balance as she first pulled on her underwear, then her jeans, socks, and shoes. Naomi motioned with her hand for Anna to hurry.

Instead, Anna froze. The thing that had once walked the earth as Marcus Midlothian, now an embalmed corpse, bent itself at a perfect ninety-degree angle. It shredded Bruce's underwear with a single pull; she watched them fall, a formless white pile beside him in stark contrast to the dark, flattened grass. She watched as the monster hydraulic-pressed its impossibly large hands against Bruce's middle back. Legs astraddle in a squat, she saw the awful maggoty appendage descend until the tip made contact with Bruce's rear exit.

You made me know exactly how you feel right now, Bruce, she thought. In a single smooth movement, which struck her as mechanical and unnatural, too powerful and unachievable to be considered human in any way, it thrusted. She heard Naomi gasp from the car. Bruce's upper body convulsed. He squealed, an inhuman sound, followed by a screech like a firehouse siren. Anna cringed. She watched the damage happening close up—she heard the subtle but audible splitting and tearing of tender flesh—and thought mostly of her own narrow avoidance when lying face down in the pit of Hell.

"Help me! Help me, Anna, God, please, *please help me!*" Bruce's mind had become a vast chambered hive as pain raved and roared through every irregular room and crooked corridor. Pain blared through his bowel like trumpets. Clouds of murder hornets, furious and stinging as though themselves made of molten lava, flew from Hell's trombone as it blew a welcoming paeon to the soon-to-be-deceased Bruce Barnette.

In her periphery, Anna saw Naomi's furious hand-motion urgently beckon her to retreat to the safety of the car, where the gift of freedom, wholly unexpected and unearned, awaited like a cool blessing.

But then she remembered: There could be no freedom, *ever*, not in this world or the next, if she did not atone for her grievous sin. She felt her mind tumble helplessly. Immobilized, she thought that she had never in her life been, up until this moment, the focus of such ferocious, concentrated intensity of larger spirits. The convergence of powers unimaginable, with and inside her right here and now: *Acknowledged and accepted*, she thought.

But what went wrong? Somehow we channeled and invoked the life-giving powers of the realm of God. We tapped this positive force in the name of His Son, the eternal Lamb. Please answer.

At that moment, she realized the precise nature of her mistake.

In the greatest single act of bravery and love, Jesus—Yeshua—had sacrificed everything to point the way to God the Father, toward the difficult, narrow path leading to the Kingdom of love and peace . . . a ransom to save losers like me. In those agonizing final hours, His body broken and flayed, dying the slowest, worst, most ignominious death possible, He begged His Heavenly Father to forgive His own killers. The Lamb of God sacrificed Himself even for evildoers like them!

"Because it is possible for anyone to be saved," she said. "Even you, Bruce."

She watched Bruce Barnette experience his final miseries. She knew, and he knew, that what would happen next—disembowelment—would happen any second now.

Who am I? she thought. *Who do I want to be? I have tried to keep some reasonable account of myself, and suddenly now all my books are in the red. This is my chance to balance them, and I mean to take it.*

As she witnessed this vile act of retribution unfolding before her, another thought entered her mind: *If I fail to sever the link between the Midlothian thing and whatever force powered it, eventually, it will come for Timmy, Naomi, and Mom next.*

Fear, loathing, and trepidation consumed her as she walked to where Bruce's head was turned to the right. *I know you are with me, Heavenly Father.* Summoning great courage, she knelt, hands on knees, and lowered her face to within inches of his. A ghastly feeling hit hard—that this thing might turn on her. *For it most definitely is not of God. Not by any stretch of the imagination.* Her insides felt inverted; fear stabbed at her all over like electrified pinpricks. All she wanted to do was to run and keep running. Bravely, she swallowed her fear.

"Bruce, Bruce. Can you hear me?"

Through his agonized, dolorous crying, he managed to nod his head once.

"I *will* save you. And, I want you to know that I forgive you. In the name of Jesus Christ, of Yeshua, I forgive you."

She reached, grasped the shem, and pulled it up, down, left, right. The wired-shut jaw would not give it up. She placed her left hand flat against its forehead for leverage and pulled with her right, using all her strength.

The shem came out.

It was like watching someone get shot through the heart. There was no dramatic ending as with Hollywood movie deaths. When a man dies from sudden trauma, he collapses, like clean-cutting all of a marionette's strings at once, the spark of life gone in one instant. A living person crumples like so much meat dropped through the butcher's hands onto wax paper. So it was when the golem froze in place on top of Bruce, still deeply embedded inside his bleeding sigmoid colon. It dawned on her that now she and Naomi were thrown back into real danger. *If he wriggles out from underneath the weighty corpse of Marcus Midlothian—we are done for.* Anna turned to spring back to the car—but then, she felt a message, loud and clear, like a voice from within, which sounded a lot like her own voice.

The voice said, *Zip him up.*

The same old question, *how do I come by this knowledge*, remained unanswered—indeed, the most interesting question in her life— though she had learned long ago to trust her inner voice. Again she stood behind the inert golem. Making a face, she pulled the giant tube out of Bruce, shoved it back inside the pants, and zipped them closed. Hastily, she wiped her hands using the only material available—Bruce's torn underwear—choking back a wave of nausea. *Like picking up a dead anaconda covered in reeking slimy gore and maggots.* She turned and sprinted back to the car as though her feet had sprouted wings.

Safely inside, seat belt fastened, Naomi smoothly executed a perfect three-point turn and accelerated back to the break in the woods directly behind her. In taillight splashes, they watched the golem fall to its right side like a toppled statue as Bruce freed himself. They saw his genitals flip-flopping. His fists pounded the air at them awkwardly; due to his injuries, he stumbled forward in chase of the car.

Taking no chances, Naomi locked the doors, looked straight ahead, and drove forward as fast as the thought the car could handle. She covered the bumpy yards of the trail at a reckless speed, beating the low-clearance bottom of her Benz; she gave no thought to expensive mechanical consequences.

Anna glued her eyes to the right mirror outside her window. When front wheels connected with black asphalt, she saw Bruce naked from the waist down. Red taillights exposed rivulets of blood drying down his thighs. His face showed only fevered anger, flavored with criminal insanity. The Benz bounced violently along heavily ridged earth not meant for high-speed vehicular travel, which slowed them down enough for him to close the gap. She heard his hands smack down onto the lid above the hollow trunk. In a moment, his hands would reach the rear passenger side door handle. The car emerged from raw ground back onto smooth parking area blacktop.

"Gun it!" screamed Anna, Naomi complying without question.

Having cleared the park by several miles, Anna said, "Pull over."

"Great minds," she squeaked, heart still racing, also sensing that a pause and regroup was needed. Naomi coasted into the empty parking lot of a donut and coffee franchise and parked, though she left the engine running.

Under the pinkish parking lot lights, Naomi surveyed her interior for the first time since the appearance of Bruce in the backseat. Her heart sank. Dried ice cream on her dress and Anna's jeans, as well as the expensive leather interior; she shook her head. "You have grass and schmutz in your hair. Need to borrow my brush?"

Anna shook her head. "What I need before that are antibacterial wipes. Got any?"

"As a matter of fact, yes, I do," she said and opened the center console. She grabbed a narrow plastic cylinder, pulled out several wipes in quick succession, and handed them over.

Anna felt that the act of cleaning her hands with these microbe-killing cloths was one of the most relieving moments of her life; the muscle memory of that grotesque dead thing in her hands was finally beginning to recede. Reaching into her bag, Anna fished out her hairbrush and went to work on making herself look halfway presentable, blood pressure and respiration beginning to normalize. The adrenaline come-down felt something like her first and only hangover. Her muscles felt languid. She thought that if she closed her eyes, she'd fall asleep. She wanted to talk to her best friend about everything that happened, to confess feelings of guilt and culpability in the murders. Try and figure out where things went wrong. Should they go to the police with their story? Would anyone possibly believe them? *I'm just too tired.*

"We need to make ourselves presentable and go home. Your dad takes one look at this interior—he is *not* going to be happy."

Naomi nodded. "Right. So much to talk about, but okay . . . okay."

"Okay, what?"

"Anna, we need to protect ourselves until we figure out where to go from here. I hate to tell lies for many reasons, both moral and practical. They're damned hard to keep track of. But for now, we need to sync up. Here is exactly what happened. Paying attention?"

"Yes, I'm listening."

"We tell our parents we went for ice cream. We decided to drive to your house with it but started eating it along the way. We had every intention of parking in front of your place so that your parents could see you because we know they are worried sick about your security. Somewhere along the way, a deer ran out in front of us. I slammed on the brakes, but it was in the middle of a curve. I ran off the road and into the woods a little to avoid hitting the deer. Ice cream flew everywhere. I got out, inspected the car, and saw no body damage apart from paint scratches from branches. I waited until traffic was clear, backed into the road, drove you straight home, and dropped you off."

Anna sat in silence, eyes moving rapidly. She nodded. "Yep, plausible. What about Bruce? What's his story going to be?"

Naomi shrugged. "I know what that rapist's story almost was, and now won't be, unless I decide to tell Abe what he did to me, at which point Barnette would be a dead man walking. By the way, what did you say to him?"

Anna blushed. "I forgave him."

"You did *what*? Come again?"

"Didn't think you'd understand.."

"Try me. Why, though?"

Anna inhaled, exhaling slowly. "Because I sinned. Sins are forgiven in the next world, for the Elect, those whom God has chosen to hear the voice of His Son and to love Him. But sins are always punished in this world. Some refer to it as karma if that helps make it relatable. What I did, sex before marriage, is a sin; but then this fiendish golem thing resulted in people *dying*, Naomi. Sin sets up chain reactions—sin snowballs. No, I didn't kill them, not directly. But my actions led to their deaths. My sin was in disobeying God, then tempting Him. I misused His unconditional love. Used the name of His Son for my own selfish purposes."

A single tear rolled down her cheek, and her whole body shivered. "I know what you're going to say, Naomi. That it wasn't me who murdered them. But still, the word for what I did almost came into focus, then slipped away. Just another shadow among shadows in my insane life . . . but one with shiny feral eyes glued shut. Ah, here's the word: complicit."

Naomi shook her head. "Nope. I was paying close attention. You asked God to strike fear into the hearts of your enemies. Anna-banana, how in your mind does 'striking fear into the hearts' become murder? What happened here has nothing—and I mean absolutely *nothing*—to do with you."

"Wrong, sorry. If you ever sit and read the Gospels and New Testament as I have, literally hundreds of times—I practically have them memorized—and some teacher required you to summarize them all in one short sentence, you would say: Love God more than all; also love and forgive yourself, and others. We *must* forgive our enemies. There is no forgiveness for us if we do not forgive others who hate us."

"Pshaw, yeah. Lot of good it did. Even after you saved his life and forgave him, Barnette still tried to hurt us."

"That's an HP, not an MP."

"What?"

"His problem, not my problem. My account with the Lord is clean, I hope."

"What do you think will happen now? Barnette's more dangerous to us now than ever."

Anna nodded. "They're sending me away because they're afraid of what he'll do to me. You'll still be here. You need to grow eyes in the back of your head."

Naomi smiled. "I was born with those."

Anna nodded. "Take me home. Time to face the music."

CHAPTER TWENTY-TWO

Salvation

"Anna! Come down here!" In an uncharacteristically insistent tone, this shouting from her father, far less polite than his usual, woke Anna at six minutes past eight Friday morning.

"Be right down!" she answered, then leaped out of bed, yanked jeans off a hanger, knocking the hanger to the carpeted closet floor, which she uncharacteristically ignored in her mad scramble. After a quick swish of strong minty mouthwash, barefoot, she bounded down the steps. In the front foyer, her father stood facing two men in blazers and slacks. Law enforcement badges hung from lanyards over neckties. She felt a guilty pit in her stomach, noticing them eyeing her dispassionately as she joined her father. "Morning, Dad. What's up?" She made eye contact with the two men and offered them a smile and a single sweeping left-to-right arc wave.

"Good morning, Miss Dingel," said the gray-haired one of the two. "I'm Detective Winston; this is Detective Reardon. We're here to ask you a few questions."

"Me?"

They nodded. The guilt pang cramped her stomach. *Be cool*; she heard Naomi's voice. *Coffee. That's the ticket.*

Dad? Shouldn't we all move to the kitchen, sit down, and have coffee like civilized people? Sorry, Officers, we should be used to this by now."

Dave Dingel stroked his chin. "Yes, yes, where are my manners? Yes, please, detectives, follow us to the kitchen, won't you?"

A glance between them; in silent assent, they followed the Dingels, then sat. *Rigid as golems*, Anna thought. She poured coffee from the old-timey silver percolator into four cups set on saucers, grabbed four spoons, set them down at the table, then fetched napkins, opened the fridge door to grab a plastic container of creamer, and finally, the porcelain sugar bowl. The table thus arranged, she sat. "Where's Mom, by the way?" she asked.

"Needed at church. Said she'll be back by nine to fix breakfast," Dave answered.

"Miss Dingel, we—" said Winston.

"Please. You make me feel like one of my kindergarten teachers. Anna."

The younger detective, Reardon, grinned at this, and Winston continued. "Anna, you filed a report two Sundays back about a property theft."

She nodded. "Mmhmm, yes, sir."

"Well, I am here to report good news: We found your missing property."

Anna's eyes flew open. Dave's jaw fell, incredulity etched into his face. He answered for Anna. "My God! Gents, that is absolutely fantastic news!" His eyebrows raised provisionally. "What kind of shape is it in?"

"Sir, I am happy to describe the . . . missing property is in fair shape. We noticed no visible damage apart from the hands, which appear to have been stabbed multiple times. We did not disrobe it seeking evidence that might lead us to its origins since we know it came from here.

"The damaged hands are enough to convict on 'abuse of a corpse.'"

Detective Winston leaned forward and said in a conspiratorial tone, "You'll need to do some serious work on the hands. And get the suit dry cleaned; it's muddied up, got wet, then dried. Kids probably kept it outside somewhere near the field where we found it."

"Detective Winston, you said kids did this. And you mentioned getting a conviction. Does this mean you have a suspect?" Anna said, trying to mute the whirling cacophony of anxiety on the rise. "And if kids did this, will they be tried as adults?"

Winston fixed his cold, even gaze on her face. "Anna, how well do you know Susan Nastro and Tamara Goldsworth?"

Anna's expressions ran the gamut, and she felt the detectives' experienced eyes studying every change. "Not well," she said, glancing at her father. "They don't like me."

"You don't like them either, we'd gather. We learned about what they did to you and Timothy Caperila, with regard to certain photographs."

Anna blushed, fully sanguine from scalp to soles. She shook her head, lowered it, snorted, then looked at the detectives again with wet eyes. "I have prayed to the Lord for forgiveness for my transgression. I can do no more besides using better judgment from here on out."

"When was the last time you saw them?"

"I passed them once in the hallway before Dad pulled me out of school. That was the last time. I haven't seen anyone outside this house except for my friend Naomi when she took me for ice cream on Monday and then dropped me back here."

"And Bruce Barnette? When did you last see him?"

Anna recalled with vivid clarity the post-park incident conversation four nights prior, knowing these two may have already asked Naomi the same question—and if not, they would soon. "The night I watched him get pushed into the back of a police car in the tavern parking lot."

Both detectives' eyes softened, apparently receiving the response they needed. "Those were our only questions, Miss—Anna. Thank you," said Winston.

Dave Dingel's eyebrows furrowed. "I don't feel my daughter is safe with Bruce Barnette free to roam. I've arranged for her to leave Pennsylvania because of him. I'm now paying for a private boarding school far from here. All because of that boy. My wife and I are inconsolably upset about losing our daughter. Not having her with us, all because of that . . . *boy*."

Reardon gave Winston an answering, imperceptible nod. "I'm not permitted to discuss active cases outside of the department," said Winston. "However, given the trauma this actor has put you and your family through, I would like to offer you an opinion, based on thirty-two years in the business. The opinion is mine and mine alone. Although I must insist that in return, you both are to keep this strictly and utterly confidential. Meaning you may discuss it with no one else, including your own family. May I?"

Dave and Anna exchanged glances, intrigued. "Please, Detective. You have our full confidentiality," Dave responded.

"I believe Bruce Barnette will trouble you folks no further. A squad car picked him up Monday night along the road outside Evansburg Park.

Brought him to the station, ran him, pulled up his conviction for his crime against your daughter, locked him up for the night. He had no lawyer to call. Our department has been working overtime on several recent local murder cases with zero leads. We were about ready to ask the FBI for assistance. Here we had this Barnette kid, son of one of the murder victims, so we ran him through the Palantir software. Turns out he is also first-person connected to all but one of the other recent murder victims. Next to your missing corpse, we found Barnette's clothing. Later, we sent it to the crime lab. DNA evidence, blood, and other bodily matter found in his underwear, and more we discovered during a body cavity examination directly connects him to the murder victims. Francis Barnette, Taylor Rydell, Carmen DeSalvo, Earl Gallo." He glanced at the younger officer. "Because of this DNA evidence, several additional suspected murder victims got added to his list this week."

"Oh my God. Who?"

"Susan Nastro and Tamara Goldsworth."

Anna shrieked, high and shrill. She jumped in her seat; hands covered her face, eyes wide as tea saucers. News of all these deaths, each the downstream consequence of her actions, unintended though they were, nevertheless rolled a stone against her heart.

"Given this evidence, defensive wounds, connections to victims, including his DNA and prints found on some of the victims, also a complete lack of alibis placing him elsewhere during the times of death established by the coroner, and decades of professional experience across multiple DAs: I can all but tell you that Bruce Barnette is facing six murder indictments likely leading to convictions. Our current District Attorney has a ninety-eight percent conviction rate. A magician with juries, he is. I have never seen anyone like him. We already have Barnette on a probation violation and abuse of a corpse, if nothing else. We picked him up not far from the location of your deceased customer. But the DNA evidence makes this almost a no-brainer."

A thought needled Anna. Searching . . . searching . . . yes, she remembered now. The voice, Monday night in the clearing. *Zip it up.* Had she not done so, Bruce's underwear and body cavity would not be the only places victim DNA would've been discovered. Finding it on Midlothian's penis would open up an entire new world of intrigue, which could siphon some of the focus off Bruce.

Anna felt her blood pressure elevate. "Has he confessed?"

Winston shook his head. "Again, confidential: But he claims your corpse is responsible."

"What's that?" Dave asked.

He nodded. "Yes, sir, Mr. Dingel. During skilled interrogation, Barnette is not budging on this crazy story that your stolen corpse walked around killing his father and friends, then tried to kill him. He also claims your daughter and her girlfriend are directly responsible. He claims they are eyewitnesses to your deceased customer's attack on him Monday night."

Dave Dingel fumed. "So that's why you asked Anna about her whereabouts Monday night."

Reardon nodded. "Checking boxes. You understand. Procedural requirements."

Winston added, "But, when questioned separately, the girls' story checks out. Plus, the damage to the Silver girl's car fits her description of what happened with the deer."

Dave stood, face red, fists balled. He stood so fast his chair skidded noisily backward. "I want that young man executed. He has forfeited his right to membership in the human race. Execute him, then bring him to me after for embalming. I'll give him back to his mother-of-the-year who raised him. Maybe now those two can spend some quality time together at a cemetery, probably more time than she spent parenting this animal. Utter failures as parents, raising a psychopath and trying to pass him off as a normal student. The whole family should be arrested." Anna grabbed his hand and squeezed it firmly, urging him to sit back down.

The detectives exchanged glances. Winston spoke. "I certainly can appreciate your feelings about Mr. Barnette, sir. But, the good news," he said, then paused to drain his coffee cup in two very hot, very black swallows, "is that he will trouble you no further. Bet my pension on it. Can't say more. Wish I could, but this is an active murder investigation, so I cannot. Please understand."

"What about my property?"

"They sent the meat wag—County sent out a vehicle to impound it. Since it is not part of any evidence exhibit, I expect that after I call the ADA, she'll release the subject to you. Knowing her—she's good people—she might even have the sheriff's department drive it over and drop it off. Spare you the fuel and hassle."

Dave nodded. "Well, gentlemen, this is a great deal of information my family must now process. Thank you for your service, and please let the DA and ADA know that we—Anna, Margie, and I—would be willing to testify under oath against this monster, Barnette. Just putting that out there."

Winston nodded, then extended his hand. "Good day to you both," he said. Reardon followed him out. Anna watched them drive away. She turned to her father. "They just saved you a boatload of money."

"How do you figure?"

"Because now you don't need to send me away. I'll be just as safe here."

"How can you be sure, honey?"

Anna closed her eyes. "Because everyone who hurt us is now either dead or in jail." Guilty feelings made her face feel hot.

Dave rubbed his head. "I don't know."

Anna's face alone told him everything. "Dad? What exactly don't you know? I'm not going."

"Your mother is concerned about your relationship with Timmy."

"*Concerned*? About what exactly?"

"That it's serious. Plus all the usual: STDs, teen pregnancy, falling in with the wrong crowd. She is very pleased with St. Anne's-Belfield, having watched a video of their weekly non-denominational chapel services, although clearly, it's a secular school, very much unlike your last. She feels very strongly that you should spend your senior year focusing on academics, not on the boy."

"Dad, that *boy* is going to marry me. I'm eighteen. There's nothing that she or anybody else can do to stop that from happening. She can either be a part of our life together or not. I hope she chooses wisely. What do you think?"

His hands on her shoulders, he smiled into her eyes. "I'm not happy with Timmy. Taking you into the woods, throwing caution to the wind like that was highly irresponsible. But like I told your mother before the photograph debacle, overall, I like Timmy. Good kid from a good family. Mostly because I watched his music video, the one inspired by you."

Anna flushed. "Oh my God, Dad. You *did*?"

He nodded. "Which is why I trust him. His feelings for you, well. Let's just say that I can relate them to myself. I would never hurt the one who has my whole heart, which is you, Anna. Neither would he, and you have his whole heart, too. The signs are plain to see if you know what to look for. As a very old dog with very sharp eyes, I can see the signs in him."

"So, you're not sending me away still, are you?"

"Let's discuss it as a family over breakfast. Your mother should be here any minute now."

———

"Crush? Did he think this up?" The video chat feature allowed her to see Timmy's facial expressions clearly enough not to question whether or not he was joking.

He laughed. "Yeah, he has already named the band. Listen, this guy has earned more money than some countries have in their treasuries, all from discovering, commingling, training, then blowing up talent. Gordon Shomacher is known in the biz as a marketing genius, a true mogul, Anna."

"Well, okay then. So. The big question: Did he make you an offer to be in Crush?"

Her heart pounded as she watched his eyes leave the camera to search down and to the right. She saw his shoulder move. Then, he held up a piece of paper. He tried to hold it close and steady for her to read, but his shaking hands made it impossible. All she saw clearly was the title: Band Agreement.

He watched her face. To him, she looked like someone had doused her with ice water. Serious and somber, her eyes stared back at him, unblinking. Then, "Oh. My. God."

He nodded, smiling. "Yes."

"When?"

"Immediately. I'm only coming home to get stuff I need, wrap things up, say my goodbyes. Shouldn't take a week to end my old life there, then it's off to new horizons."

Anna appeared on the verge of tears. Then, tears did flow. She had no words. She managed to collect herself but for a moment. She managed to put on a smile. "Congratulations, Timmy. I knew you were too big for this town. Mom and Dad are sending me to Virginia to finish high school. Guess I'm too big for this town, too."

"Hey, Anna. About what I'd said . . . you know. About us getting married, you coming with me, getting tutored, graduating high school, together weekends, and on tour."

Sniffling back grief, she said, "I know. Heat of the moment stuff. Don't worry, not holding you to it. No hard feelings. I loved what we had together. It was like a fairytale. But we know fairytales are make-believe, and they always end." He watched her battling back a major emotional meltdown.

"What? Anna?" He reached for something again.

This time, instead of holding up paper, he held up a small dark box. He opened it. "Cost me just about every penny I had saved for college. I called Naomi. Together we figured out your size. She thinks you're a four. Well, what do ya think? Isn't she a beauty?" A classic round solitaire diamond set in a simple white gold setting. Even through the poor camera lens, the incredible stone burned and sparkled.

"It's the most beautiful thing I've ever seen," she said through tears of joy, laughter, and deep relief. For a moment, he disappeared. She watched his chair wheel aside. His head reappeared, holding the open box. "Anna Dingel, this is me down on my knees. I would stay there for you, if you asked. Live a simple life, just another working schlub like our fathers and their fathers before them. But I'd rather take this thing as far and as high as God allows, with you by my side all the way. Anna, won't you please marry me?"

Smiling, nodding, crying, she squeaked out, "Yes!"

He beamed. "Well then, it's settled! You've just made me the happiest man who ever lived, all the way back to Adam. That's right. I am going to love you with a love that is more than love. What about you?"

Wiping her eyes on her sleeve, she sounded nasal. "Timmy, shut up. Just get your cute butt back here this instant! We need a marriage license, a church that'll take us on short notice. You Catholics have that Pre-Cana stuff that takes weeks, right? A small ceremony, immediate family only.

I need a dress; you need a tux. Then there's the whole reception and honeymoon—"

"Anna Caperila. Listen to me. We don't have time for *any* of that. Crush will take off without me if I stay long enough to make all that happen."

Anna nodded. "So what we do?"

He smiled. "Pack a bag. It's all arranged. We're flying to Vegas. I spoke with my priest and explained the situation. I emailed him my video, along with a copy of the offer letter as proof of my story. He promised to get me a dispensation on the Pre-Cana requirement. You'll—" he struggled to choose the right way to present the condition carefully. "Anna, you'll have to sign a bunch of papers binding you to raise Catholic children."

She laughed.

"What?" he said.

She laughed hard, and it felt so incredibly good. "Told you before, that's fine. It's just that I'm picturing my mother's face when she finds out."

Timmy smiled. "Be ready. I'll come get you. We fly Saturday. Okay?"

She nodded. "I have so much to tell you."

His grin widened. "We'll have a lifetime together for you to tell me everything. I want to know everything you know; feel everything you feel. God, Anna, thank you. You don't know how happy you have just made me."

She shook her head. "Yes, Timmy, I do know. Because we are one heart now."

"Together forever."

She nodded. "Forever."

"Anna-banana, oh my God! I am *so* jealous! Yes, of course, I'll be your witness. Who's Timmy bringing?" said Naomi.

"His older brother."

"How's Marge? Scraping her flesh with pottery shards, sitting in ashes and sackcloth?"

Raucous laughter into the phone. "Pretty much, yes! Wish you could've seen her face when I told her. Seriously, Naomi-baloney. Clearly, this was a day of days."

Chuckling. "Oh, I'll bet. So, so, *so* incredibly happy for you both. And super-happy to learn about Bruce Barnette. I mean, *wow*."

"Don't tell a soul, Naomi. My dad and I swore our absolute confidentiality on this one."

"Mum's the word. Squad car, purely."

"Squad car?"

"Don't you watch police reality TV shows? Whatever gets said in the squad car stays in the squad car. Never ever leaves the squad car."

"Hm. No, I don't watch TV, ever, but okay then. Squad car."

Naomi remained quiet for a bit. Then, "I know what you're going to ask me. And the answer is . . . no."

Anna considered the meaning of her words. "You had made two promises to yourself, Naomi. One was that you were going to publish a paper about the stone tablets bearing Yeshua's name, the Sefer Yetzirah, about why Kabbalists have never succeeded in making a golem. The other was that you were going to study Jesus Christ."

"Good memory, AB. Nix to the first. No, I plan on publishing a paper about the direct linkage from Abraham's time to Yeshua's time, validating the existing written record of the history of my people, that it is all accurate and that nothing was lost. And not only merely study Jesus Christ: My parents don't yet know it, but I have joined a Messianic Jewish community a few miles west of here. They—we—believe Yeshua is the Jewish messiah and Son of God and that the Tanakh and New Testament are the authoritative scriptures. But we still say all the same Jewish prayers and do all the same stuff, celebrate the same traditions exactly as I was raised. We still identify as Jewish, which is something I would never give up."

"Wow! Really? Oh Naomi. Welcome to the Kingdom."

"I feel welcome. What did you call us: God's Elect? I'm really feeling that now. Born-again: I never understood that, but now I totally get it, seeing everything in the world, also above and below it, through new, wiser eyes. Abe knows, and he's not just pretending to be interested; I think he's actually starting to get it. The Messianic Jewish community is filled with people as intensely smart as he is, and they're arguing with him. He's running out of counterarguments. He'll come around. But, Anna-banana, your powerful, unwavering faith in Yeshua enabled us to summon life for the first time in two thousand years."

"It's almost like a dream. Like maybe it never happened."

"Oh, it happened all right. But it must remain between me, you, and God. That's it. Not even Timmy and Abe can ever know. Not that they would tell anyone because the story sounds so batshit crazy that, like, who would ever believe it? But say that it did get out: Any kind of power like that will be abused by some people. When someone else connects the same dots as I did, that's a TP, not an MP. Their problem, not mine. I feel guilty too, about the murders. So, we need to bury this. I need to. Like, imagine if ISIS ever connected the same dots as I have. Armies of the undead would descend upon us all.

"Oh geez."

"Right? Though I doubt that haters like that could ever do it; could reach the highest power. Because it was your unique faith and love for Yeshua, Anna, that made the magic work. The words we spoke, the moves we made; had I done this with Abe or anyone else, it would not have worked due to our lack of faith, pretty sure, and my theory would remain unproven. Remember what you'd said to me back there, that 'if God has an unfulfilled purpose, and the golem can fill it, then, well. It can work?' Maybe I am that purpose. God wants me to keep hidden from the world what I have learned and also wants to save my immortal soul, for His reasons, to keep me for Himself.

"But more important even than that is *your* faith and *your* love that saved my life and my soul. I'm most grateful to *you*, always, in this world and beyond. You are my angel."

ABOUT THE AUTHOR

John James Minster was born in Norristown, Pennsylvania. He has been publishing short horror stories in major magazines and horror anthologies since 1990 and has been operating a successful international business career in the technology sector since the 1980s. In July 2018, his debut middle-grade horror novel, *Dreamjacker*, was born of nightmares.

As a child, John walked in his sleep. His parents found him at the top of the stairs about to leap down, dreaming that he could fly. He still talks and punches walls in his sleep during nightmares, which he describes as "Nightly mini horror movies—so, no writer's block on the horizon; no chance that I'll run out of stories." Learn more at JohnJamesMinster.com.

Made in the USA
Middletown, DE
27 October 2022

13572699R00137